AMBER ROYER

# *70% DARK INTENTIONS*

**GOLDEN TIP
PRESS**

GOLDEN TIP PRESS

A Golden Tip Press paperback original 2021

Copyright © Amber Royer 2021

Cover by Jon Bravo

Distributed in the United States by Ingram, Tennessee

ISBN 978-0-9914083-4-4

Ebook ISBN 978-0-9914083-5-1

Printed in the United States of America

To my mom, who is one of my biggest cheerleaders. She encouraged me to pursue my writing as a kid, and still tells all her friends on Facebook to go read my books.

Mom, you are THE BEST!

# Chapter One
## *Monday*

I hand the last customer of the day a small bag with my shop's logo on it, and a receipt. "Thanks for visiting Greetings and Felicitations, Mrs. Guidry. Enjoy your chocolate."

She's one of my regulars. She pats my hand. "You just keep making it, sha."

*Sha* is the Cajun way of saying *chéri*, or *dear* in French. You can use it to address just about anyone.

I hand her a wrapped mini-square one of my newest chocolates, made with beans from a collective in Peru. It's a 70% bar, which means that it's made up of 70% cacao, and 30% sugar. "Try this. It's a little lagniappe for you."

Lagniappe, as in a little something extra thrown in for free.

She smiles at me for using the word of Cajun French. Though half my family's Cajun (while the other side is Italian), I don't speak much of it – not many people do anymore, to be honest – but it doesn't take much to make Mrs. Guidry happy. She's in her sixties, and she's one of the people who came into the shop for the first time about a month ago, after everything that happened when my shop assistant, Emma, was murdered. Mrs. Guidry seems to like hearing the stories – but she isn't morbid about it. Not like some people, who come in here to gawk at the Jane Austen Murder Books, because of how the books had held a vital clue. The volumes had helped me, a bean to bar chocolate maker with no experience as a detective, solve a murder. The gawkers tend to forget that part.

Mrs. Guidry studies the label before she pops the square of chocolate in her mouth. "Peru, eh? You actually went there, right? You'll have to tell me all about it."

"Later," I tell her. "I promise." I mean it, too. I love talking about my travels. "But I have to get things closed up here. Girls' night out and all." I flip my long brown hair back away from my face, trying to look glamorous. I'm wearing foundation that makes me look less pale and more sunkissed, paired with thick pink lip-gloss – which is a bit of an upgrade from my usual work makeup. I intended to leave here early, but there had been a series of emergencies at the shop. Even if I head out now, I'm still going to be late.

Mrs. Guidry gives me a knowing smile. Then without another word, she turns and leaves my shop to go back to hers – a brand new café that specializes in gumbo and jambalaya. Her restaurant is across the street.

A voice near my ear says, "I wonder what she meant by all about it. Did something happen to you in Peru?"

I jump. "Mateo." He's my new shop assistant. Emma's replacement – and thinking about how quick I had to replace her makes me a little emotional. But seriously. "You have got to stop sneaking up on people."

"I wasn't sneaking. I was bringing you this." He gestures with the bowl in his hands in a way that is meant to be cool – but seems gawky given the 26-year-old's stick-thin arm. He's got spiky light brown hair, and pale skin, and just the trace of an accent. "You have to learn to walk softly in the rainforest."

I'm not sure he's right about that. I'd been in the rainforest recently, and I hadn't come back any stealthier. Then again, I'd mainly been photographing cacao trees, and pods and beans in the early stages of being turned into chocolate. Mateo, on the other hand, had been part of a privately funded group mapping the types of cacao growing throughout different regions in South America. He'd been down there for three years, and had shown me spectacular photographs of the local wildlife. Personally, I wouldn't have had the nerve to sneak up on a jaguar just to take a picture, but Mateo is a bit of an odd guy. Likeable, and unintentionally funny, but odd.

He's here on Galveston Island as part of a project with an international group of marine botany and biology researchers, and he took a part-time job with me while he is here. He wants to learn how chocolate is processed, so he can offer tips to the farmers when he returns to South America. Which is beyond flattering, really. After all, my little chocolate factory just had its grand opening a few weeks ago. But Mateo's a smart guy, and a conscientious worker, so I'm grateful to have him.

Only, he's looking a little nervous right now.

I take the bowl, which is full of deep red sauce with Spanish chorizo and green olives and chicken floating in it. It looks amazing. "Why does this feel like a bribe?"

Mateo's wearing skinny jeans and an expensive-looking white Henley. Which makes him look perfectly European. He fidgets with the buttons on his shirt as he says, "Felicity, can I ask you a favor?" His accent makes it, *Felitithy*.

"Sure, but then I've got to go," I say, trying to sound calm. But his nervousness is catching. "What kind of favor?"

I don't know him well enough to anticipate what it might be.

Mateo pulls a set of keys out of his jacket pocket. "I'm going out of town next weekend. Remember, I asked for the days off?"

"I remember." I eye the keys.

"I need somebody to feed my pet octopus. I asked Carmen, but she doesn't have time. Somebody has to go by my apartment every day."

"Is that all?" I take the proffered keychain. There's three keys and a fob shaped like a poison dart frog. I hesitate. "Wait. What does an octopus eat?"

"Live fish and live shrimp. You grab them from the tank in the study and drop them into Clive's tank in the living room. But don't let him see the live food tank, or he'll sneak out of his tank for sure and feast on shrimp tartare."

How would the octopus be able to see a tank in another room? And how am I supposed to catch a live shrimp? I blink, trying to sort the questions. But what I ask is, "Your octopus's name is Clive?"

Mateo shrugs, gesturing with upturned palms. "It suits him."

Mateo is originally from Spain, and talks with his hands – a lot.

"So you want me to stop by once a day and give Clive some shrimp." I pocket the keys. "Sounds easy enough."

"You think so?" Carmen asks, coming out of the kitchen. Her long dark hair is swept back into a ponytail, her Mexican features emphasized by dark eyeliner and blush that brings out her high cheekbones. She dresses athletically – she's into surfing and running – with a long-sleeve tee and yoga pants – but she has a frilly polka dotted apron over the outfit. She just turned thirty, and with Mateo in his mid-twenties, I'm the oldest person in the room at 32. I don't mind. I feel like it gives me more of a sense of authority in my shop, since my employees are both smart, accomplished people.

Carmen's holding two napkins, each with three tiny chocolate cookies stacked on top. It's a new recipe she developed today.

I take a napkin, inhaling the heady scent of cacao blended with orange and chili. I snap a few pictures of the cookies before I try one. I can Instagram them later, on the shop's account. "Am I missing something octopus-wise?"

"You have to handle the octopus every time you go over there, to keep it from going nuts from boredom. And if you startle it while you're holding it, it will ink. Which means you have to clean the tank." Carmen scrunches up her nose. I get the feeling she's speaking from experience. "I took care of Clive one time, and he stole my lipstick right out of my purse to decorate his tank."

"To be fair, you did leave your purse on the floor," Mateo insists. "That's easy access when he gets out."

Carmen starts to say something back, but I interrupt.

"I thought octopuses were venomous." I can't imagine holding one.

"They are," Mateo says. "But only certain species are dangerous to humans. There are a number of pet species you can hold in your hand. Clive is an Abdopus aculeatusis. Sometimes called the walking octopus."

Carmen rolls her eyes. But it's more playful than sarcastic. "If you travel so much, you should get a pet that requires less maintenance."

Mateo shrugs again and gestures in the vague direction of Pelican Island, where his research group is located. "When I leave here, I'll donate Clive to one of the local universities. But an octopus usually only lives a couple of years, so I'm trying to give him a good life as long as I can."

Carmen looks a little hurt, like maybe she forgot Mateo isn't here long-term. I don't think it's a romantic interest thing – Carmen seems to have worked things out with her current boyfriend, Paul. But more that it would be nice to have a consistent set of co-workers. She works well with Mateo – unlike the relationship she'd had with Emma, who had fought with her right up until the day Emma died. I'd actually believed for a while that Carmen might have murdered Emma. I'm still trying to make things right between us about that. My first step had been giving her the official title of pastry chef, and a raise.

"I've got people waiting for me over at Chalupa's," I tell Carmen and Mateo, as we all head through the kitchen towards the back door. "So I need to head out. Mateo, write me a list of how to take care of an octopus. You're not taking off until Thursday, so we have plenty of time to talk about it."

Or for me to find someone else to octopus sit, if it is really as complicated as Carmen says.

"Sounds great," Mateo says. He opens the back door, and steps backwards through it. "I'll just-"

He breaks off his words with a squeak as he trips over some guy who's standing there, about to knock on the door. Mateo lands on his butt. The other guy stumbles backwards, leaning heavily against a giant crate on a pallet jack. The crate is about as tall as the guy. I've ordered a piece of equipment for the shop that could have showed up in a crate that big – but it isn't supposed to be here until next week. Unless they made a mistake on the date.

That must be it. A thread of excitement bubbles through me. I gesture at the crate. "Is this what I think it is?"

"Optical sorter," the guy announces. "Free setup is included with the order. Where do you want it?"

I eye the crate, greedy to see the machine inside. "I thought you were delivering it next week."

The guy squints at me. He's a tall white guy, built like a refrigerator and bald as a cue ball. "You want me to take it back and come back next week?"

"No!" I say, more loudly than I intended. "Please. I need it set up in the bean room."

He nods and gestures to the doors for cargo deliveries, which are usually kept firmly locked. They lead directly into the bean processing area. "Let's do this."

I'm conflicted. I love tinkering with machines. It's one of the things that drew me into the whole chocolate making business. That, and the fact that my late husband and I had wanted to do something amazing together. I want to stay and try out the sorter.

But my best friend Autumn said she has good news to announce. And she's waiting at Chalupa's to tell me and the rest of our friends. I hope she's going to say that she's started writing again. Maybe even that she has a new book contract.

"I can stay, and help get this where you'll want it," Mateo volunteers.

"What is this thing?" Carmen asks.

The geek in me is excited to tell her, "You know how I have to sort through all the beans to get rid of rocks and plant material and such before I can start roasting them to make chocolate?"

"Yeah. It's like the least fun part of watching you work." Carmen gestures back inside, towards the kitchen. "That's why I prefer baking."

"This machine does all of that automatically." I step over and pat the crate. I'd like to at least *see* the sorter before I leave, but it doesn't look like that's going to happen. "I know it's a bit of a splurge for an operation our size, but business has been good despite all the negative publicity."

"*Because* of the negative publicity," Carmen says.

I nod. "That's fair." I'm still not happy about Greetings and Felicitations being the chocolate shop that all the murder geeks stop at, like my factory is a tourist attraction. But they seem to be a group with a lot of pocket money. So I have no choice but to humor them.

"I'll stay with Mateo," Carmen says. "I'd like to see how this thing works."

Mateo looks at me. "I don't know if we should run it. Felicity, don't you want to be the first one to use the machine? I know I'd want to if it was mine."

I do want to be the first to play with the shop's new toy. But I also want Carmen to know I trust her. I tell them, "Y'all feel free to try it out." I point at Mateo. "But don't use that bag of beans you brought me from that farm you stayed at. I'm still trying to figure out what to do with it."

The beans are Criollo Porcelana, which many consider the finest variety of cacao in the world. They grow in smooth, ivory to pale green pods, and the beans are famous for being low in astringency while being deeply nutty. The particular ones I've got are from a single cacao plantation in Venezuela. I need to do something special with such rare beans.

I slide into the booth at Chalupa's. There are a bunch of empty glasses on the table. I am definitely late. And Autumn has already shared her news. It's obvious from the way the others are all giggly and glowing.

There are five people waiting for me at the table. Autumn is dressed up, a glittery hairband pushing her afro into shape, matching the sparkly sheen of her blouse. She has a curvy build and a round face, and a there's glitter in her dark plum lipstick too. I feel even more terrible about being late, since this is obviously special to her.

Maybe she really did get a new book deal.

Sonya and Sandra are sitting on one side of her. The twins, who are equally tall and thin, with identically distinct Romanian noses, are even harder to tell apart because they've both dyed their naturally brown hair bright red. Sonya is wearing a flowy pink and purple dress that looks as if it was made of a series of napkins. For once in her life, she doesn't have a yarn project in progress in front of her. In contrast, Sandra has on a plain, blue blouse and a heart-shaped necklace. She's a lab technician, and the most practical of all my friends.

Tiff is sitting on the other side. Her relaxed hair has a little upturn at the bottom that goes with the professional feel of the black business suit she's wearing. Even when she's not working, her look still screams real estate agent. She's a people person through and through, which makes her a great friend, because she always notices when something's wrong.

My aunt Naomi is sitting next to her. Naomi looks like a slightly older version of me, with similar long dark hair, brown eyes and lightly freckled cheeks. Naomi has her hair pulled up in a loose bun, and she's wearing a blouse with geometric printing on it, which my Uncle Greg bought her before he went back offshore. I'm a little surprised to see her here, since she only occasionally hangs out with my friend group – usually when I've invited everyone over to the house I share with her. Autumn's news must be really important.

Sonya nudges Autumn's shoulder and says, "Go ahead. Show her."

Autumn puts her left hand on the table, showing off a very significant ring on a very significant finger. My mouth drops open in shock. It's a nice diamond, teardrop shaped and surrounded by smaller chips. All the other girls let out little squeals as Autumn says, "I got engaged!"

"Wow!" I try to put some enthusiasm into my voice. But really. "To a guy you've known for all of a month."

Autumn shifts her hand closer, though she can't really reach me that far down the table. "Sometimes, when something's right you just know."

I bite my lip, holding back what I really want to say. Sure, Autumn's Librarian Guy seems nice enough. But this feels a bit rushed. Right? I take a deep breath. Maybe I'm missing something. Because everybody else at the table looks ecstatic. But she's my oldest friend in the world, and I don't want to see her get hurt. "As long as you're really sure you're sure."

Autumn's grin has decreased in wattage. "Are you saying you don't want to be my maid of honor?"

"Matron of honor," Tiff reminds her. Because I'm a widow. Even if I'm currently single, there's no going back to being a maid. The weight of a shared life no longer shared follows you around forever. I dance around the pain in my heart, which is a little less these days. It's only been just over a year. I still feel a measure of guilt around that sense of letting go.

Because even through Kevin's gone, things are moving forward. Changing. I manage a bittersweet smile as I make eye contact with Autumn. "Of course I'll be your matron of honor. It'll give me a chance to get to know Drake a little better. Make sure he actually deserves you."

She smiles, and everything's all right between us. Because that's how best friends are.

We spend a couple of hours at the restaurant, letting Autumn tell funny stories about her and Drake. Autumn's a writer, which makes her a born storyteller, so we all wind up laughing uncontrollably. Which feels really good.

When we're finally leaving, Sandra pulls me aside. She pulls nervously at her red hair. "Promise me you're not going to let your feelings about love ruin this for Autumn."

"My feelings about love?" I didn't realize I had any troubling feelings about love.

"That idea in your head that there's only one right person for everyone. That you found yours with Kevin and now nobody else can be good enough. That's why you want her to wait longer to be sure. Right?"

I look out at the street, busy with traffic along the seawall. "I used to think that. But I don't know." A specific male face flashes in my mind, an intense pair of green eyes. "I'm more open to possibilities these days."

Sandra splutters her lips. "Yeah, right. That's why you haven't spoken to Logan since he stopped being your bodyguard."

Heat flushes my face. It *had* been Logan I'd been thinking of when I'd mentioned possibilities. But I'd made it clear to him while he had been my bodyguard that I'm not ready to date again, and there's no really coming back from that. "I've talked to him. A couple of times. We even had coffee once."

But it's not like he's been at my shop every day or anything. Even though I secretly hope it's going to be him every time the chime over the door rings. But then I feel guilty all over again, about even thinking of moving on from a man who had so truly loved me. Kevin really had been the one.

Which I guess is what Sandra's been getting at.

A sense of panic rising in me, I look Sandra in the eyes. "I'm a horrible choice for matron of honor. We have to convince Autumn to choose you instead."

Sandra is the most logical and responsible of all of us, after all.

Sandra takes my hands in hers. "No, Felicity. You can do this." She squeezes my hands. "It might change you, but you can do this. And we'll be there to help you."

The thought of change terrifies me. Still, I swallow back the fear. "Well, I can't disappoint my best friend, now, can I?"

It's early July, so it's humid-hot, and the mosquitos are coming out, but the five of us cross the street at the light – you'd be taking your life in your hands trying to cross Seawall Boulevard against traffic – and go to take a group selfie of ourselves with Pleasure Pier and the sunset in the background.

Then we all go our separate ways. I'm still happy living with my aunt in the flip house – which is finished now, and just went up for sale. But I'm not ready to go home. Not with my new sorter there at the shop, tempting me to go try it out.

I get in my catering van for the short drive back to the Strand. I park where I usually do, in a parking lot farther down and a block over, so that I can leave the close spaces on the street for customers. I walk past the front of the shops, instead of down the alley to my back door. Sometimes it is fun just to look in other peoples' windows and see what is for sale, especially in some of the kitschier tourist shops. Out on the street, there are benches and signs and public sculptures – including ones bringing attention to the plight of the endangered Kemp's ridley sea turtle. Which always makes me think about Logan. The logo for his puddle jumping business is a Kemp's ridley. And I'm not sure I've been fair to Logan. Which means the sculptures themselves make me feel vaguely guilty.

I pass the last turtle sculpture, and there's nothing left to obstruct my view of my shop. I spot someone sitting there on the sidewalk. The guy is leaned back against the wall, right outside my front door. Startled, I hesitate, consider going around the block to the back after all. But that feels like over-reacting. It's not like I'm about to be attacked. It's probably some homeless guy, who fell asleep trying to get cash from the tourists. He has a rough flannel on over a tee-shirt, and his head is turned away from me.

I walk a wide arc around him, definitely not making eye contact, but staying aware enough of where he is that I will notice if he moves. I still feel intimidated. And then once I'm past the guy, I feel stupid for being so nervous. This is still a relatively busy street, because a few businesses are open until 8 or even later, so it's not like we're alone out here. And he's asleep.

I go into Greetings and Felicitations, and I feel bad for wanting the guy to just disappear when he obviously has nowhere to go. So I turn on the espresso machine and make him a latte. And I put some of Carmen's test cookies – which she's stored in the fridge in a sealed container – into our smallest bag.

I don't know exactly what my plan was. If I intended to wake him up, or just leave the coffee near him on the sidewalk and hope for the best. But when I get in close to the guy, I freeze. From this angle, I can see that his gray tee-shirt is bright with blood. And his face – there's no way this guy's sleeping. He's dead.

For a split second, I think maybe it's a prank, because of the whole murder book thing. But he's not breathing.

The paper coffee cup slips from my hand and hits the pavement, splattering the leg of my pants and my shoes. There's been another murder, at my shop. Any hope I had of eventually losing the morbid gawker trade just disappeared.

Embarrassment flames through me. That is not the first reaction of a normal, empathetic person. I should try to offer aid.

I'm pretty sure the guy's gone, but I still kneel down next to him and check for a pulse. There's nothing. Of course.

A cursory examination tells me that the injury is a gunshot wound, and it happened fairly recently. The body is still warm.

I make sure not to touch him anywhere else. The last time I'd been this close to a dead body, I'd wound up the primary suspect in a murder investigation. But that doesn't mean I can't take a good look at him. He doesn't really look homeless. He looks like a college student, with perfectly styled hair combed up and back, and the rough shirt chosen for contrast against the fine-fabric tee. There are four beaded and cloth bracelets around one of his bloodlessly pale wrists.

I have no idea who this kid is, or how he wound up dead on my doorstep. But I'd better call Arlo and report this, before someone reports me leaning over a dead guy.

Arlo is a detective on the local police force. And if Logan is the mysterious stranger in my life, Arlo's the one who got away. We'd had a spark, during his investigation of Emma's death. Only -- he's seeing someone else. So much of love comes down to timing, and we missed ours – twice. I've been trying to let him live his life with his new girl.

I take out my phone, and call Arlo's cell. It's a small island. I'm going to run into him from time to time. I might as well get used to it.

"Lis?" Arlo sounds surprised. "Everything okay?"

I don't blame him for assuming something has to be wrong for me to call him.

My voice sounds high and squeaky as I say, "No."

"Felicity?" Now he sounds alarmed. "What happened?"

I try to keep my voice more under control. "I just found a body on the sidewalk outside my shop."

This is met with stunned silence from the other end of the phone connection. Finally he says, "Are you sure it's not another prank? Like the kid who left you the bloody phone book? That turned out to be corn syrup and food dye."

I hadn't realized Arlo had known about that. The police department had sent an officer to deal with it, and the culprit had turned out to be a fifteen-year-old kid trying to impress his girlfriend. I think the officer had scared the teen more than the teen had scared me. There hadn't been a follow-up incident.

"Oh no, this is real." I look down at the poor guy cooling in the evening air. "I checked for a pulse."

There's the sound of a door slamming, and then of a car door closing from Arlo's end of the line. He must have been getting himself together to come to my rescue, taking me seriously, despite his attempt to lighten the mood.

"You touched the body?" He sounds like he disapproves.

"Just to see if there was anything I could do. I do have medical training."

I was a physical therapist, before Kevin's accident, when I'd left Seattle and my practice. A lot of people didn't understand the career change, but I had followed a passion – and a need to come home and regroup.

There's the noise of Arlo fumbling the phone, and he says, "Don't touch anything else. Go inside and wait. And stay away from the window, just in case. Do you feel safe enough for me to let you go? I need to call this in."

"Yeah. I understand." Though I really don't want him to hang up. I hadn't even considered the possibility the killer might still be in the area. After the click of Arlo disconnecting, I feel the hairs prickling at the back of my neck. Which is probably just the power of suggestion, and not someone watching me. Right?

I go back inside my shop and lock the door. Part of me feels like I should guard the body, make sure no one makes off with it, like would happen in the movies. But Arlo had said to stay away from the window. I go to the bathroom to wash my hands – twice. Then I try to sponge some of the coffee off my pants. I'm wearing my cute white flats and the coffee has soaked completely through the fabric. They're ruined, which is a stupid thing for me to be worried about. I can get new shoes. That guy out there – he just lost his life. Somebody – a mother, a girlfriend, maybe even just a workmate – has to be worried about him. Somebody's life will be devastated when he doesn't come home. I know what it's like to lose a loved one suddenly. My breath comes in tinged with remembered grief and helplessness. Mixing with the fear that whoever did this horrible thing might still be nearby, it's a sickening mix of emotions. I splash a little water on my face, and I leave the bathroom.

I look around the shop. I've had someone break in before. But everything looks just as I left it. The optical sorter – which looks a bit like an oversized printer – is set up and there's a bucket of sorted beans off to the side. At least I know it works.

And I realize – it's possible that Carmen and Mateo were still sorting beans when – well whatever happened outside happened. I shudder, thinking about my two employees being in here while someone was killed outside. Should I call and check on them? Or would Arlo get mad at me for releasing information on his case?

I hear sirens in the distance. Which fills me with relief. Arlo will tell me what I should and shouldn't do, so I can avoid being a suspect this time. And it sounds like he's almost here.

I go into the kitchen and take the container of cookies out of the fridge. I snag one for myself, enjoying the fact that Carmen got just the right amount of heat into the batter. Then I move the open container to the counter near the drip coffee urns, so the police can help themselves, when, inevitably, they wind up inside the shop. And I get the coffee brewing. I'm not sure if this is how most people would prepare to meet the cops after a brutal crime, but I need to have a sense of order and control and to be doing something instead of just sitting here alone.

It's weird. I have no connection to this young man, except that he happened to die outside my place of business. And yet, I feel possessive of him, like whatever happened somehow relates to me. I realize the paper cups are low, so I turn to go get more from the stock in the back. As I'm walking behind the counter, I notice a piece of paper sitting on it, with instructions on how to take care of Clive detailed out in Mateo's neat handwriting. It's extensive – the details take up half a page of extremely small hand printing – but it breaks off in the middle of a sentence. Which seems very unlike Mateo, who is always fastidious about everything.

There's a pen on the floor, near where he must have been writing, which is also unusual. Cold unease fills my stomach.

Could Mateo have seen what was going on outside and tried to stop it? That doesn't make sense. He would have called the police to report the death. Unless something had happened to him, too. I can't help myself. I call his number to check on him. It just rings and rings, and I start to lose myself in the certainty that he's out there somewhere too, just as dead as the flannel guy.

Which is why I jump when Arlo knocks on the door. Arlo's Cuban, with warm brown skin and thick dark hair, but not a trace of an accent. He doesn't even speak Spanish. He fills out his well-tailored suit extremely well. He's standing there alone, though two other cop cars are just turning onto the street. I move over and unlock the door.

Arlo gestures at my phone. "Calling Logan?"

Heat flames in my face. "Now why would I do that?"

Arlo gives me a look that means, *I'm not dumb, you know*.

I shake my head. Whatever connection Arlo had thought he'd seen between me and Logan hadn't turned into anything. It hadn't even occurred to me to call the rugged pilot.

"I was calling Mateo. I can't seem to get ahold of him, and I'm worried. He was one of the last people here." I tell Arlo about Mateo's schedule, his habits at work, and about how he asked for the weekend off.

Arlo says, "Maybe he just decided to leave a few days early. It could be a coincidence."

"I guess that's possible. But it feels a little odd. He left me this half-finished note-"

"Oh?" Arlo suddenly looks interested. He holds out his hand for the paper.

I hand it over. "I'm going to need that back."

Arlo raises a skeptical eyebrow. "Because?"

"Because I promised to feed that octopus." And then I feel stupid. Surely nothing has actually happened to Mateo. He just got distracted mid-way through writing or Carmen said it was time to go. I'll see him tomorrow, and he will finish the instructions list.

And yet, Arlo shifts the note towards me. "Take a picture. Just in case."

Alarm spikes through me. But I snap the shot. "You really think Mateo might be in trouble? Maybe we should go look for him. He could be bleeding, somewhere on the street."

The Crime Scene guy, Fisk, comes in the door. He's wearing his windbreaker with CSI printed across the back, his sandy-blonde hair just as messy as I remember. I can see someone outside putting up crime scene tape across the pillars in front of my shop. I just hope they'll be done out there by morning, so that I can open on time. So that people won't think I'm a suspect – again.

I gesture Fisk towards the coffee. He gives me a grateful nod, then moves over to fix himself a cup.

"We'll have people looking for him, all right." Arlo gives me a sympathetic look. "I think Mateo's probably our suspect."

I shake my head. "You don't know him. Mateo is timid. He's a little odd, but he's a good guy."

Arlo's expression shifts towards skeptical. "Odd how?"

Word seems to have gotten out about the coffee supply, and one at a time, three other cops come in to grab a cup. One of them is the officer who had comforted me after the break-in at my aunt's house. Only now, she's dressed in a gray skirt suit. She must have been promoted to detective since I last saw her. I'm glad. She deserves it.

She brings her coffee over and stands next to Arlo. Detective Meryl Beckman has gobs of curly dark hair, which she has constrained into a low ponytail at the base of her neck.

He repeats, "Odd how?"

I shrug. I don't want to get Mateo in trouble. "He's quiet. And a little awkward. But that doesn't make him a bad guy."

Arlo makes a noncommittal noise.

"Don't go all Columbo on me again," I tell him.

After all, real life isn't like a detective show. The first person a cop suspects isn't necessarily going to be the culprit.

Detective Beckman says, "Does Mateo own a gun?"

"No." I blink. "At least I don't think so." It's not on the list of interview questions for a job selling chocolate and sweeping floors. "But even if he did, I know he wouldn't have brought it to work."

She nods. "Reasonable. Still, we'll send a couple of officers by his place to talk to him."

"You think he's home if he's not answering his phone?" I ask.

"We won't find out until you give us his address," Arlo says.

I pull up Mateo's contact on my phone and share it. They're right. There are any number of reasons why Mateo might not be answering his phone. He could be in the shower. Or his phone battery might have died. Or he just might not have his phone on him at all times, like the rest of us.

Arlo asks, "Who else was in the shop after you left?"

I suck in a breath. I am not excited at the thought of implicating Carmen again. But I have to be honest. "Carmen was here. She wanted to stay and help Mateo and the delivery guy set up the new machine." I tell them about how the delivery came early, which is odd.

Detective Beckman asks me to give a specific description of the delivery guy. Then she tells me to go home and get some sleep.

Arlo says, "It's possible that this has nothing to do with Greetings and Felicitations or with any of your employees. Please, just let us figure it out this time. You promised you weren't going to get involved in anything like this again."

I nod. It's true. I had promised. And I'm too in shock to be nosy anyway.

## Chapter Three
### *Still Monday*

So I go home to tell my aunt what happened, and to check on my bunny, Knightley. He's hiding burrowed inside a blanket I'd left on the floor by the big chair. Which means he's caught wind of some kind of tension in the house.

I move over to the side table and coax him out with one of his treats, which I keep in a sealed container on the coffee table, next to Aunt Naomi's tablet.

Aunt Naomi comes into the room. She looks worried. "Are you okay?"

I start petting Knightley, who seems to have decided that all is right with his world, now that I'm here. No matter what state Naomi might be in. After what had nearly happened to me last time I'd been adjacent to a murder – I can understand her worry.

"I'm fine," I assure her. "I just found the guy -- after. The whole thing was over by the time I got there."

Naomi looks at me like I'm missing the point. "So you didn't get my text message?"

I take out my phone. There, indeed, is a missed text. Which says, *That blogger is already at it again.*

My stomach sinks. I know exactly who she's talking about. Ash Diaz. I had thought Ash would leave me alone, after he'd been coerced into writing a positive article about me – after he'd slandered me by insinuating on his blog that I might have killed one of my own employees. But I guess I overestimated him. I groan. "What did he do this time?"

Naomi picks her tablet up off the coffee table and hands it to me. I feel a weird sense of déjà vu. Because we have done this before. The tab is already up for *Gulf Coast Happenings*, Ash's so-called "news" blog.

The headline that greets me is, *Death and Chocolate and a Seaside Town.*

Ash has formatted his story like the beginning of a noir novel, with me cast as a gritty detective-turned-chocolate-maker, discovering a body on her own front door. *Felicity will never be able to ignore the siren call of another case, any more than the salty ocean can refuse to crash upon the shore. Is it her shop that is a magnet for murder? Or Felicity herself? It doesn't matter. No matter how much the police tell her to stay out of it, we know our nosy Nancy will be there, chocolate in one hand and a magnifying glass in the other.*

He's got a picture of me, proudly holding up one of my 70% Peru bars. It's a flattering photo. I blink at it for a moment. Is it possible that Ash thinks this is a positive story? That he's doing me a favor?

Unable to manage a coherent response, I say, "I was a physical therapist before I became a chocolate maker. I never wanted to be a detective."

Aunt Naomi says, "I know, honey."

I sigh. "I'm not a murder magnet. That's not even a thing."

Aunt Naomi pulls me into a hug. "That's right, honey. Two murders is a coincidence. Not a pattern."

Two *honey's* in a row. This must be worse than I thought. She only calls me that when she's feeling bad for me.

I pull out of the hug. "How did he even know about this so fast?"

Naomi blinks at me. "It's all over the news. When it's a company as big as FloboCon, the CEO's son's death is going to be a big deal."

I feel my eyes widen. I hadn't even thought to ask Arlo who the murder victim was. "Whose son?"

"FloboCon International. It's that big media conglomerate with the clean water charity." She's staring at me, obviously puzzled by why I don't know this yet. "Nobody seems to know what Fabin Obodozie was even doing on this island. He was supposed to be at school, in New Hampshire."

I feel like the air has gone out of my lungs – though not in the same way as an asthma attack. This is going to be a big deal. I sit down in the big chair. Knightley hops back over to the blanket, and huddles into it. I guess all is not right again with his world after all. It's certainly not right with mine.

I heat up the bowl of Spanish chicken stew that Mateo gave me. I need something warm and comforting right now. The chorizo packs a punch of umami flavor, and the olives lend a salty element. And the thick, slightly greasy, tomatoey broth is somehow perfect for my mood.

My phone rings. I hope it is Mateo calling me back. It's not. It's Autumn. Without preamble, she says, "How are you going to go discover a dead body and not call me? What kind of best friends are we?"

"I haven't called anybody," I protest. "Besides, it doesn't seem right to throw that much cold water on your good news. Happy engagement. I should have said that earlier."

"So you're coming around to the idea?" Autumn sounds happy. "Good."

"Maybe we can have a little engagement party for you and Drake at the shop. I have this mold for chocolate doves I've been wanting to try out. We could do it on Thursday night, after the shop closes. Just something quick, with family and a couple of friends."

"I'd like that." Autumn hesitates. "Have you called Logan yet?"

"Why does everyone think I need to call Logan?" I protest. "I promised Arlo I wasn't going to get involved in investigating this crime. I don't think I'm going to need someone protecting me, just because it happened outside my shop."

"Felicity, really," Autumn says. "I meant you're going to need a date to the wedding."

"Oh." And then it hits me. "Oh!" I scramble to get myself together mentally. It hadn't even occurred to me that I'd need a plus one. And Logan and I certainly aren't at a place where I can just ask him out. "Have y'all already set a date? How long do I have to find someone?"

Not necessarily Logan. Just someone that I'm comfortable with. Otherwise, I'm going to risk having Autumn try to set me up with one of the groomsmen.

"The big day is six months out," Autumn says. "But make sure you invite Logan to this engagement party. It doesn't have to be as a date. Just as a favor to the bride."

I force myself not to growl in her ear. Instead, I look down at Knightley, his white fur and lop ears a comforting constant in my life. "I thought you promised me you were never going to get into matchmaking."

Autumn laughs. "I just don't want to have my mama trying to set you up with one of her friends' sons. She believes that couples ought to have couple friends."

I feel someone staring at me intently. I glance up, and Aunt Naomi gestures at the phone. Naomi, on the other hand, loves playing matchmaker. I may need to hire Logan to protect me after all – from her and from Autumn's mom.

Desperate to change the subject, I say, "Can we just talk about the murder?"

I get to the shop early the next morning. The police tape is gone, as is any sign that Fabin had been there. I guess it doesn't take long to process a crime scene that is outside. Out on the sidewalk -- instead of a chalk outline – we have a line of customers waiting to get in the door.

Which is giving me another hit of déjà vu. I walk quickly down the back alley and enter the shop by my back door.

My shop is meant to be inviting, with the décor all pink and gray and shabby chic. There's a section on one wall, with books I've picked up on my travels, and quite a few additional volumes from estate sales I've attended with my aunt. None of the books I've found lately have been quite as troublesome as the vintage volumes of *Emma*, which I have on display – but not for sale. After all, those volumes mean something to me now, something about self-confidence and peace, after I'd solved such a horrific crime.

I also have display shelves stocked with bars of my chocolates, with little sample containers in front of each variety, alongside gift sets involving multiple bars. All of my bars have an open space on the back where there's no printing on the wrapper, so the customer can write a message, because the bars are meant to double as all-purpose greeting cards. Hence the playful name, Greetings and Felicitations. Most of the bars have my lop-eared bunny Knightley printed on the front, as part of the official logo. But a few of them are part of my select Sympathy and Condolences line, with somber wrappers and images of Carmen's German Shephard Bruce.

And in a long case, there are truffles that I make with my chocolate, which serve as a decent gateway for people who are hesitant to try single origin chocolate. Most potential customers can be won over with the flavors of traditional desserts, which I've incorporated into the ganache. Behind the counter, there's a station for making lattes and other coffee drinks, while in front and to the left of it, there's the plain coffee station where customers can pour their own refills.

I put a lot of work into designing the image of this place. Which is why, despite the added business, it's distressing for people to come because it's darkly fascinating, instead of warmly inviting.

Carmen is already in the kitchen. She clears her throat meaningfully as I come in the door.

"Hey," I say. "I guess you heard what happened here last night."

"Yeah," she responds. "I did. I caught it on the news, and then a ton of people called my house."

"Me too," I tell her. Ash had just been the first of the media pointing out that I've now found myself at the center of two murders. There had been concerned calls from friends and acquaintances – and offers for interviews.

"You want to tell me what happened to all the cookies from yesterday?" Carmen points at the container, which is sitting half-empty on the counter.

"I gave them to the cops." I force a super-bright smile. "For what it's worth, they really liked them. I think the recipe is a hit."

That at least gets me a smile in return. "Well, I hope you don't mind manning the espresso machine." Which is usually Carmen's job. "I'm baking as fast as I can, so we can try to capitalize on this early-morning rush."

"I guess you haven't heard from Mateo either," I say, already moving to grab milk and soy milk from the fridge to start prepping the expresso station. I'll come back for the pitcher of horchata when I need it.

"Not since last night," Carmen says. "You know it seemed like Mateo knew the delivery guy? They had a little fight before the guy left. He said it was because the guy wanted too big of a tip for unloading the sorter, but I think it was about something else."

I pause, holding the two containers out front of me. "Oh? Did you tell that to the police?"

Carmen shakes her head. "No one asked me about it yet. I assume Arlo will be by today, right?"

I say, "Probably. He asked me who was here last night. Did you leave when Mateo did?"

Carmen's cheeks go crimson. "I left just a bit after you did. I'm sorry. I got a call from Paul. He has his son this week, and he wanted to take him to get ice cream last night. So I waited until the delivery guy left, and then Paul showed up. Mateo was still playing with the sorter."

"Paul came here?" I breathe a sigh of relief. This time, Carmen has a rock-solid alibi. Even if Paul is an ex-car thief. "That means he came in through the front door. I take it he would have noticed a body on the sidewalk."

Which means that the murder had to have taken place after Carmen left.

Carmen says, "Everything was fine. We didn't even hear about it until we on our way home. Paul's ex-wife called, because she'd heard on the news. She already doesn't like it that he's dating someone who works at Death by Chocolate, as she likes to call it. But there's not really anything she can do about it."

I cringe. I hate that my shop's bad publicity affects more than just me. "You need to tell all that to the cops. It could help them pinpoint the time of death." I gesture with the soy milk. "And mention the fight between Mateo and the delivery guy. It might be important."

Carmen looks startled. "You think Mateo had something to do with this?"

I shrug. "He never returned my calls last night. So I have no idea."

I make my way over to the coffee station. There are three people standing at the window, their hands cupped around their faces, staring in. The coffee station is in view of the main seating area, so they have to see me moving around inside the building, but I pretend not to notice them, even if they are smudging up my glass with handprints. I'm beginning to regret putting in the big window when we remodeled this place.

I get everything set up. It's about time for Mateo to come in, but there's no sign of him. I take my phone back into the kitchen and try calling him again. There's still no answer. It feels like there is definitely something wrong.

I still have my phone in my hands when it rings again, and I jump, startled. It's Logan.

My pulse races a little as I answer it. I'm not sure exactly why. We've talked before, recently in fact. "Logan, hi!" I try to keep my tone casual, though I'm not sure why he's calling me. Surely Autumn didn't tell him about the wedding date thing. Or did she?

"I'm on turtle patrol today," Logan says. "But you can meet me out on the beach this afternoon. I turned on Find a Friend, so you can figure out where I am."

"Why?" I ask, truly confused.

He hesitates. "I assumed we were working on this murder, before the media spin around Felicitations gets out of control again. Are we not?"

Now I hesitate. "I promised Arlo I wouldn't get involved."

"Since when has that stopped you?" Logan scoffs. "I've already pulled a background check on this Fabin kid. There's some interesting stuff in here."

Now that's intriguing. And I would love an excuse to spend time with Logan again. But it would definitely get me in trouble with Arlo – potentially in his official capacity. "I'll think about it." I sigh. "I do need to talk to you, though. There's this party for Autumn on Thursday. She'd like you to be there."

"Why?" Logan asks. "I barely know Autumn."

"It's – complicated. Does that mean you can't come?"

"Oh, I'll be there," Logan says. "If nothing else, just to find out why she invited me."

We talk for a few more minutes, and when I hang up the phone, Carmen is staring at me.

"Party?" Carmen asks.

"You're invited too," I say.

"At the last minute?" Carmen looks skeptical. "You're just saying that because I happened to be standing here."

I shake my head. "No. This whole party is last minute. She just told me yesterday she got engaged."

Carmen lets out a squeal, and says something in rapid-fire Spanish. The only part I make out is, "Me encantan las bodas." *I love weddings.* So she's in.

I also happen to know she likes planning parties. Which is going to come in handy.

"I thought you were too cool for that kind of thing," I tease. "With the whole surfer vibe and all."

"That doesn't mean I can't also love a good love story. Tell me how Autumn's librarian popped the question."

"I don't exactly know." I'd missed that part when Autumn had told it to the girls at the restaurant yesterday. "I am seriously the worst matron of honor ever."

"What are her colors? If we order party decorations now, they'll be here by Thursday. I have Amazon Prime."

I feel my cheeks go hot. "I don't know." I wave a hand helplessly, "I was thinking this party would be a bit lower key. Like without decorations."

Carmen rolls her eyes at me. "You're right. You are the worst maid of honor ever."

"Matron," I correct. "Let's deal with the crowd and then we can call her together. I'm going to text Miles real quick, to see if he can come in and help, since we're so shorthanded."

"Good idea," Carmen says. "I still don't see why you didn't hire him instead of Mateo in the first place. Miles is a born barista."

Miles is a college kid, and a friend of my nephew. He also risked his life recently to try and save me. I tell Carmen, "I offered him the job. He didn't take it. He said the thought of coming in every day to the place where Emma died would make him too sad. But he'll be okay for today, I'm sure."

I text Miles, and he texts back that he is on his way. It will be good for him to be here, to at least start to process his feelings. He's been closed off since Emma's murderer had tied him to a chair and threatened him with death. I think that's the real reason he turned down the job. No one wants to be reminded that they are that vulnerable, especially not a young man.

I go out to unlock the door. The line of people starts moving into the shop. With this many people here, I really could use Mateo here to keep an eye out for shoplifters. Almost as if she's reading my mind, Carmen leaves the kitchen and fills the empty section of the case with baked goods. Then she starts moving through the crowd, keeping an eye on things, while I take the first coffee order and start custom boxing truffles.

A woman comes up to the counter with a stack of books from the section over behind the door. "Would you autograph these for me?"

"I didn't write any of those," I protest.

"I know," she says. "I don't care what you write in them. I just want a souvenir."

A souvenir. Of Fabin Obodozie's murder. I start to protest that that's a bit twisted, but Carmen clears her throat.

It still feels weird writing in someone else's book, so in each one I write, *Purchased at Greetings and Felicitation's Chocolate. Sold by Felicity Koerber.*

Which is at least honest. And represents a significant amount of cash going into my register.

Arlo's girlfriend, Patsy walks in. She's looking elegant in a red blouse and black skirt. Patsy knows Arlo and I have a history. And she and I have made our peace over that.

"Hey!" Patsy says, making her way directly to the counter. "What are you doing tonight?"

Is she spying for Arlo, to make sure I'm not getting involved in the case? I try to sound nonchalant. "Uh, not much. Probably just starting a batch of chocolate."

"Cancel that. You're going on a double date with Arlo and me. My brother Wallace is in town, and I promised to introduce him to someone nice."

Why are all the people in my life wanting to set me up all of a sudden? "I'm not sure that's a good idea."

"I'm not taking no for an answer." Patsy picks up a couple of the impulse-buy bars from the square basket on the counter. As I ring her up, she says, "Be at The Steak House tonight at 7."

"Mmm." I don't actually tell her I'm not going. Though I obviously have no intention of showing up. Dinner with my ex and his new girlfriend's brother – in what universe does that turn out well?

When the crowd thins, Carmen goes to check on a batch of brownies. We're selling out of her treats and pastries faster than she can make them.

About half an hour later, Arlo and Detective Beckman come in to take Carmen's statement about the night before, so I gesture the two cops to the kitchen. As focused as she is right now, I'm sure Carmen will make them talk to her while she's working.

They aren't back there long. Which makes sense – Carmen told me she left before anything bad started happening.

As the two cops are heading back out, I ask Arlo, "What's up with this dinner?"

Arlo gives me a sheepish grin. He always was cute when he's embarrassed. "Patsy's brother came into town a week early, and she feels like she has to keep him entertained. I know you're not a big fan of setups. I don't blame you if you told her no."

"I didn't tell her anything."

"That's probably for the best." He straightens his tie, another sign that he's embarrassed. And then he and Detective Beckman leave.

I glance around to see if any of the other customers noticed the exchange.

There's this brunette white girl who's been in here since we opened this morning. She's sitting at one of the tables in the corner, looking lost. I finally get free enough to walk over there and ask her, "You doing okay?"

She responds by bursting into tears.

I move to the drip coffee station and pour her a tall paper cup. I go back over to the girl and put it in front of her, along with a thick stack of napkins. "On the house."

She picks up a napkin and blows her nose. She's starting to get herself back together. "Sorry. I just wanted to find out – I mean, Fabin never said anything about Texas."

"You knew him?" I ask, sitting in the seat opposite her.

She nods. "He was my cousin. My parents died when I was young, so Fabin and I grew up together. He was like my much younger brother. Without him, I don't think I could have gotten over the loss."

"When was the last time you saw him?"

"It's been a couple of weeks. He only came home from school when it was time to do laundry. I've been waiting here for a chance to talk to you about it."

I put a hand on the table, leaning towards her. "I wish I could tell you what happened. But I never even got to meet your cousin."

She nods. "I'm sorry to waste your time."

I ask her, "Fabin never mentioned having a friend from Spain, did he?"

The girl looks at me quizzically. "Spain? Why?"

I notice someone watching us, a Latino guy in his mid-twenties, who's wearing a plaid hat. When I said Spain, coffee practically shot out of his nose. And then he started coughing uncontrollably. Now, he's trying to pretend that nothing happened, that he's scrolling on his phone. But I swear, he just took a picture.

So maybe Fabin didn't know Mateo. It had been a long shot.

The girl hands me a card. According to the printing, her name is Leslie Franks. "I just checked into the Bergamot Hotel. I'm staying in town for a while, trying to figure out what happened. If you think of anything else, let me know." There's grief in her eyes, but also determination.

"Be careful," I tell her. "There's a killer involved here. You don't want to wind up getting hurt." I make a point not to look over at the guy in the hat. He could have something to do with all of this. He could *be* the killer for all we know.

Or he could just be a murder aficionado, or another annoying blogger. With this crowd, it's impossible to tell.

He's looking back behind his chair now, like maybe he dropped something. What is he looking for?

"Nobody else cares enough to find out what happened." Leslie shakes her head. "I asked Uncle to hire a private detective, but he said to just let the police handle it."

My first instinct is to tell her I'll look into it. But I'm not actually a detective.

"You *should* just let the police handle it," I tell her. I sound just like Arlo. "Please." Arlo and Detective Beckman were just in here. I wish we'd had this conversation before they'd gone.

Carmen comes over to the table and hands me the office phone. "There's a woman from a spa in Seattle. She's talking about a large order. I think you should confirm the details."

"I'll be right back," I tell Leslie. "Don't go anywhere, please. There's something I need to tell you." I haven't had a chance to let her know about the guy who's watching her, and he's still sitting a table away. But she should be safe as long as she stays here.

I go into the bean room. There's my brand-new optical sorter, ready for another batch of beans. And I still haven't gotten to play with it. I'll have time tonight, though, because I'm ditching Patsy's invitation.

I answer the phone, and flinch back at the shrill voice that meets my ear. Then I realize that I'm on hold, and there's Celtic chanting serving as hold music.

I really don't have time to wait. But since I am stuck – I turn on the optical sorter and run half a bucket of beans through it, listening to the noise the machine makes as it drops the impurities into one bucket, and my cacao beans into the other. The sound is an interesting juxtaposition to the chanting. The beans are still running through when the hold music abruptly stops, and a hesitant voice says, "Hello?"

"This is Felicity," I say.

"Yes, I'm Serena, from Spa Ultima." Of course she is. I can practically smell eucalyptus and lavender wafting through the phone connection. "What is that racket?" She sounds disappointed in me.

"This is a working factory." The sounds of the beans being sorted tapers off, and I shut off the machine. "We craft our chocolate bean to bar."

"I am aware. Your assistant told me she couldn't verify whether you could handle an order as large as we require." She sounds even more disappointed. "But you were recommended by one of our therapy partners."

"That's flattering." I guess one of the therapists I used to work with, or maybe a referring doctor back in Seattle, has been following my new career. I'm not sure how to feel about that. Nobody had specifically said they wanted to stay in touch when

I'd left the medical community, and I haven't talked to anyone since I left. I'd cut the ties more cleanly than I'd realized, not even following my former colleagues with my new social media accounts.

Serena outlines what she needs: Two thousand gift baskets with an assortment of chocolate bars, hot chocolate bombs and truffles to go out to some of the spa's best clients – with the caveat that the baskets be delivered over the weekend.

My breath catches. I'm shorthanded. I promised to throw Autumn a party. I've never made a hot chocolate bomb. And I'm about to leave to go check on Mateo and his octopus. But I'm not about to say no to the biggest order my company has ever had. I just won't sleep this week. I'm off the meds that had me severely restricting my coffee intake, but I'm still careful not to drink too much – just in case. In the next few days, I may have to make an exception.

"Send over the contract, and we'll get started." I sound excited yet professional, if I do say so myself. We finish the arrangements, and I head back to check on Leslie. Only, she's gone. But the guy in the hat is still there. I guess he wasn't following Leslie after all.

## Chapter Five
### *Still Tuesday*

Miles walks in. He still looks nervous about being here, which is heartbreaking, considering the amount of confidence this kid had only a few short months ago. He's got everything going for him: football scholarship to the local A&M, good grades, and classic good looks, his black skin framed by a stylish amount of facial hair.

"Did you see a girl just now?" I ask him. "Brunette, very pretty, mid-twenties? Maybe leaving in a hurry?"

"Mrs. Koerber," Miles protests. "I really don't need you to fix me up."

"Oh?" I raise an eyebrow. "Is there somebody new in your life?"

"Maybe." He flashes me a wide grin. "Probably."

Miles and Emma had never even had an actual date, but he'd taken her death hard. I'm glad it hadn't affected him deeply enough to keep him from moving on.

The guy with the hat pushes past us, on his way out, a determined frown on his face.

Miles says, "Hey, Enrique!"

"Hey!" Enrique responds, but he doesn't stop walking. He could still be following Leslie – giving her a lead so she doesn't get suspicious. Or he could just be nosy, and bored now that Leslie isn't there to eavesdrop on.

"You know that guy?" I ask Miles.

"Sort of. He's on my college football team." Miles looks confused. "Is he in trouble."

"I don't know." Impulsively, I head out the front door, onto the Strand. I see Enrique's hat easily, despite the thin crowd of tourists. I follow him, as discreetly as I can. Leslie is nowhere in sight, but something about the way Enrique keeps glancing around him makes him seem suspicious.

He's heading towards the end of the Strand that dead ends into the street that leads to the cruise ship terminal. He takes a right, and in a few blocks, he'll be at the terminal.

But the cruise ships aren't in today, so as soon as I turn the corner the street is pretty much abandoned. It doesn't take long for Enrique to realize I'm following him. He takes off running. Dang. That's one thing I'm not prepared for. My health still doesn't allow for me to sprint.

Unfortunately for him, he's paying more attention to me than to where he's going, and the sidewalk is both narrow and uneven. He trips and goes down hard, crying out in pain.

My need to help instantly overpowers my need to get information. I walk quickly over to where Enrique is sitting on the pavement holding his ankle.

"Let me see," I tell him.

He shakes his head and tries to get up, but the ankle won't hold him.

"I'm a physical therapist," I tell him.

He blinks at me. "I thought you were a chocolate maker."

"Before. I used to be a physical therapist, and then I became a chocolate maker."

"Why?" He looks flummoxed.

I half-babble, flustered for a moment. Then I say, "Look. This isn't about me. If you want to keep playing football, you're going to want to let me check out that ankle." The expression of desperation that crosses his face makes me add, "Let me guess. You're on scholarship."

He nods miserably, and stretches out his leg so I can examine the injury.

"Good news," I tell him after I test the flexibility of the joint. "It's probably sprained, not broken. Get it iced soon and stay off it for a couple of days, and it will be fine."

He gestures helplessly around. "How am I supposed to do that? From here?"

"Wait here. I'll take you home." I pull out my keys. "And we can talk on the way."

"Great," Enrique says sarcastically. "I can't wait."

I get my catering truck and pull back around, and there's Enrique, still sitting where I left him. Some lady with a serious sunburn is trying to give him some cash, without much looking at him. He takes it. I can't help but laugh. I wait until she's walked away, and then I pull my giant truck up to the curb. I help Enrique into the passenger seat. He's able to put a little bit of weight on his ankle, further confirmation that it's not broken. Once he tells me where we're going, I ask, "How do you know Fabin Obodozie?"

"Psht. What makes you think I have any connection with some rich dude?" Enrique isn't a good liar. He won't make eye contact.

I return my gaze to the road. "I saw you watching Leslie at the shop. And then you tried to run from me. It doesn't take a genius to figure it out."

"I don't know why I ran. I didn't actually do anything wrong. But I've never had anybody following me before."

I feel my face flush. He was glancing around nervously because he'd spotted *me*. I probably owe him an apology.

Am I completely on the wrong track here? "Sorry about that. But you were eavesdropping on Leslie. I wasn't imagining it."

Enrique hesitates. Finally he says, "Fabin and his girlfriend have been staying with me. I wanted to find out if Leslie knew. She'd already been asking questions of a friend of mine who gave me a heads up that she was headed to your place."

"Why didn't you tell that to the cops?" I ask. "They're trying to figure out why Fabin is in town."

"I mind my own business. Like everybody."

I tell him, "Not everybody has a houseguest wind up murdered."

"I still can't believe he's dead. He left my place last night acting like he was on top of the world. And a couple of hours later." Enrique makes a cutting motion across his throat.

I don't let that derail the conversation. "I saw you checking the floor on the inside of the shop. It felt like you must have been looking for something specific."

"Yeah. Fabin took my aviator glasses. They're Cartier, and if someone traced the serial number, it would come back on me. I wanted to see if they were in your shop."

I almost laugh. "Cartier sunglasses? Seriously?"

Fabin hadn't had any kind of sunglasses on him when I'd found him.

Enrique takes a pair of silver-frame aviator glasses out of his shirt pocket. "I retrieved them from your lost and found."

"So maybe you do fit in with Fabin." After a second it hits me. For those glasses to have wound up in the lost and found, it's likely that Fabin was inside my shop before being killed out front. A chill runs down my spine. But I ignore it, focus on what Enrique can tell me. "But how do you know him? And why are you so leery about the cops?"

I'm expecting him to say something about theft or drugs. But he sighs and says, "I'm a chef."

"I thought you were a college student," I tell him.

"I'm both. I grew up with my dad in Miami, basically inside his Michelin starred restaurant. I don't like the grind of an actual restaurant, so I do these super-exclusive pop-up events, here, in Dallas, even as far as New Orleans. Fabin contacted me to put on a special one. I don't have permits, so they're not exactly legal. How am I supposed to explain him staying with me for the past week, without winding up in jail for being talented with food?"

I'm pretty sure that if Enrique goes to jail, even for a short time, he'll lose his scholarship. "Just tell them Fabin hired you as his caterer or personal chef. That's not exactly a lie, right?"

"I don't suppose you could convince his girlfriend to say the same thing?" Enrique asks. "She's inside, waiting for me to come back."

What exactly have I gotten myself into here? "I don't know that that would be appropriate. I don't want to compromise the investigation. I'll get you back to your front door. You take it from there."

I park in the driveway at Enrique's house, next to a cherry red Porsche. I start helping him hobble up the sidewalk, but before we get halfway there, the door flies open and a girl in a tee-shirt with a metallic tiger's head printed on it runs out. She's got flawlessly creamy pale skin, and she looks to be in her early twenties, but with the obvious plastic surgery on her face, who knows? I'm guessing mid-thirties, at least. Her hair has been bleached and adorned with silver streaks, making her head oddly devoid of color.

"I was so worried," she says, pulling Enrique away from me and wrapping him in a hug. She gives me a dirty look, like I was trying to steal her man. "After what you did for me. So impetuous, and mad with love. I was sure you would get arrested."

Enrique extracts himself from her embrace. "Kimmy, please. I told you that kiss between you and me was a mistake. I didn't kill Fabin. I wasn't trying to take you away from him."

She looks at me and then winks exaggeratedly at Enrique. "Okay, Mr. Latin Hottie. Whatever you have to say while we've got company."

"Well, I really do have to go," I say.

Enrique looks at me like he's drowning, and I just said I'm taking my life preserver and going home. I really don't think he's a murderer, and I feel bad, because his busted ankle is partially my fault. He won't be able to run away from this potentially unstable girl, even if he tries.

So I ask Kimmy, "Don't you think it would look better if the cops do come to check out Enrique's story if you were staying somewhere else?"

She squints at me. "Why would the cops come here?"

I shrug. "They keep coming by my shop and asking questions. And I'm not going to lie if they ask where Fabin was staying. There's no reason I should, right? Since you didn't do anything wrong?"

There's something in her eyes that is so cold at that moment that I wonder if maybe *she* killed Fabin. But I doubt I'm going to get a confession. She's obviously not as dumb as she likes to pretend. Kimmy says, "I'm not going anywhere. Why would I do anything to hurt my Boo? He told me he was bringing me to Galveston for the best dinner of my life – and that he had a huge surprise present for me. I have witnesses to that conversation."

I have no doubt that if Enrique really is the killer, Kimmy would have no problem throwing him under the bus. But murdering someone to steal his girlfriend seems a bit unlikely. Enrique could have just asked Kimmy to break up with Fabin.

None of this is adding up. Why is Fabin's car here, if he'd gone out last night? Why hadn't his girlfriend gone with him? Why on Earth would he have borrowed sunglasses to wear after dark? And what could have happened in my shop between him and Mateo – who had been the only one left at work after all – that would have led to him getting killed?

Or had Mateo not been alone? Carmen had said he'd seemed to know the delivery guy who brought the sorter. That hardly seems like a coincidence. I pull up the contact for the company I'd ordered the sorter from. I call their office number.

A polite receptionist answers, and when I explain my confusion about the sorter arriving so early, she puts me on hold. When she comes back, she tells me, "The delivery to your address was cancelled at your request, Mrs. Koerber. Our records show that you sent a Mr. John Smith to pick the machine up from our facility. Are you saying the machine never arrived?"

"No. It arrived all right. Thank you." I hang up, more confused than ever.

How did this fake delivery guy know I had ordered an optical sorter? And how would he have had the required information to pick the item up? Was he eavesdropping on my e-mails or something?

And why would he go through so much trouble?

There are so many questions, all demanding answers. I format a text, to send along everything I've uncovered to Arlo. But I can't help trying to piece the puzzle together myself.

Arlo texts back, *What part of staying out of this don't you understand? Driving a murder suspect home and interrogating him is dangerous. Stop now before you get hurt.*

He's got a point. But I still keep thinking about how the edges of these puzzle pieces don't quite fit, even as I swing back by the shop to pick up the coffee and snacks I'd promised to bring to Aunt Naomi, who is working out at the new flip property. I've got a lot on my plate today, but I can spare her a few minutes.

I drive over towards the old hotel, which represents most of the money previously in my bank account. I'd fronted Aunt Naomi the cash to buy the place, even though the house we're living in hasn't sold yet. I don't mind. She's been kind enough to let me stay with her since I'd moved back to Galveston, rent free. She keeps saying she likes having me around, what with Uncle Greg working offshore and her son Wyatt away to school. She gets lonely sometimes. I do too. We're good for each other.

Naomi is already inside the hotel, and the noises of construction are audible, even outside. I'm used to her projects being both noisy and in the middle of everything. But this is a bigger undertaking than any of her other flips, and she's hired a couple of people to help with the initial phase. This building is dilapidated, but gorgeous, with a view of Galveston Bay from the back windows. It was built in the 1920s, with plenty of Art Deco charm, and when Aunt Naomi is done with it, it's going to be a showpiece destination on the island. Two guys are carrying out a cracked piece of marble that until recently was the topper for the front desk. I don't recognize them. I let them go past me, and then I step inside the building. Aunt Naomi is sanding the wood floor. It takes a few minutes before she notices me and turns off the machine.

"Who were those guys?" I ask. "Did you hire marble workers?"

"Have you ever heard of Craigslist?" Naomi asks.

"Yes," I say slowly. "It's for listing garage sales and stuff, right?"

"It also has a section where you can list freebies. Like big pieces of ruined marble and stacks of cracked water pipes. Those two are artists, who want to cut down the marble to make train sculptures to sell at the Railroad Museum. And that guy-" Naomi jerks a thumb in the direction of a man just getting off the elevator, pushing a stack of old radiators out on a dolly. Though from the bulk of his chest and biceps, he looks like he could have just picked them up and carried them out in his arms. "He's a salvager."

"I imagine he's been busy lately, then, with all the damage from the hurricane." My shop and Naomi's house had been spared the brunt of this last storm, but other areas of the island hadn't been so fortunate. I gesture at the guy, who waves as he pushes the dolly across the freshly sanded floor, heading for the front door. "So these people just come in and get old junk?"

Aunt Naomi nods. "I don't have to do the work to remove it, and I don't have to pay anyone to haul it away. And the best part? That guy just brought me a collection of framed vintage mirrors in exchange for first dibs on any other metal we're throwing away."

"Cool," I say. "It's nice that all this stuff is getting a second life, too, instead of winding up in a landfill."

"Exactly." My aunt wraps me in a hug. "I'm so glad you're here," she says. "You still need to pick your room. Whichever one you want, we can move your furniture in tonight, along with Knightley."

"Why the rush? You get an offer on the house?" I'm joking, since the house has only been on the market for a couple of days, but Naomi nods enthusiastically.

"For more than the asking price. But they want to move in as soon as we can get the paperwork closed. And they want the bedrooms done in custom colors with matching carpet." Naomi holds out her hand, as though forestalling an argument. "I know I just uncovered all those beautiful wood floors, and it is a crime to cover them up again, but the extra money will be worth it. I can get the painting done a couple of hours at a time over the next couple of weeks, and have the carpet guys over as soon as possible. We won't even get behind here on the hotel."

"That's great!" I'm excited about the move, and the prospect of a room with a bay view. "I already know what suite I want. It's the one with the spiral staircase inside it and the little loft. It will feel almost like having my own place – but I still get to have breakfast with you every morning."

See? I can embrace change.

Aunt Naomi says, "It's going to be a good minute before I get the kitchen here up and running. We might have to start making breakfast at your shop."

I like the idea. But will Carmen?

"Carmen's a little protective of the kitchen at Felicitations," I say. "But I'm sure we can work something out. After I deal with this party I promised Autumn, and this huge order I just took."

"Party?" Aunt Naomi's eyebrows go up. "If you want a plus one, I know this guy from the bank."

"No." I start backing towards the door. "Absolutely not."

Mateo lives in an apartment not far from the ferry station. On the third floor. Which is fine, since I haven't had any asthma symptoms since completing my treatment. Still, I pace myself, walking slowly and pausing briefly between each flight. I'm breathing fine when I get to the top. I'm actually proud of myself for that.

Mateo has a corner apartment. I walk over to the door and knock. "Mateo? Are you home?"

There's no answer. I wait a few minutes, then I unlock the door. "Mateo?" There's tension in my shoulders, and I realize I'm terrified about what I might find inside. Though surely the police have been by here already, and there would be police tape across the door if anything was significantly wrong. Right?

Unless Mateo came back after the police went through here . . .

The tension in my shoulders is back, stronger than ever. I flip on the lights. The living room is spotless, with a brown leather sofa separating the living from the dining space, and a brightly striped rug on the floor. There are geometric patterns in some of the stripes. It looks South American. Which makes sense. Mateo would have collected souvenirs of his travels.

The octopus's tank is up against the far wall, where most people would have had a TV. And the tank is about the size of a TV. It has a weight on top of it, because, as Mateo said, Clive has a Houdini streak in him. But I'll deal with the octopus after I have a look around and make sure Mateo isn't here somewhere, hurt or something.

I check out the kitchen. There's a mess on the floor, with broken glass and spilled clear liquid. Which is alarming. A fastidious guy like Mateo wouldn't have just left that mess unattended.

I peek into the study, where the other fish tanks are. There's also an empty desk. Mateo had had his laptop with him, in the messenger bag he always carried to work, so that's not surprising. There are bookshelves bursting with paper books. It's amazing that he's had time to collect all of these since he moved here – he obviously wasn't lugging them around South America with him. One book is sitting horizontal in front of the others, with a plush alpaca toy on top of it. There's a colorful tassel dangling from the alpaca's neck. The book is HG Wells' *The Invisible Man*. Interesting choice of reading for a man who's since gone missing.

I go into the bedroom, and I'm relieved to find it empty. The closet door is ajar. In case this does turn out to be a crime scene, I use my sleeve to cover my hand as I pull it the rest of the way open. The closet is well organized, and evenly filled with clothes. There's a full set of luggage, along with a backpack and a duffel. It certainly doesn't look like he packed for a trip.

I check out the bathroom. I open the medicine cabinet, again using my sleeve. According to the bottles lined up on the top shelf, Mateo has a medical condition he could have contracted in the rainforest. I suppose it's possible he has another supply of his meds on him. But the fact that these bottles are here and he's not is a bit alarming.

I call Arlo, and I explain my suspicions. "I'm really worried. Haven't you had someone come by and take a look at this place?"

"As a matter of fact, we have. There's no evidence that Mateo came home after leaving your shop. It's looking more and more like he's our killer, and he's in the wind."

I don't bother arguing that it's just as likely that something happened *to* Mateo, and he's in trouble. "So what you're saying is that you're done with this place, and I don't have to be careful not to leave prints while I'm feeding his octopus?"

"Pretty much."

Though he's really saying that if anyone's going to be looking for Mateo's interests here, I have to get involved, promise or no promise. It's going to set me behind even further on the gift basket orders, but I'm going to have to go to dinner tonight with Patsy and her brother – just so I can try to get Arlo to tell me about the case. I grab Mateo's meds and put them in my purse. He can miss a couple of doses and be fine, but after that he's going to be in danger of dying. If he's not dead already.

Logan had said to meet him on the beach to discuss the case. Because, somehow, he knew I would be doing this before I did. Does that mean I'm overly predictable? Or that he pays more than the usual attention to me? I'd like to think it's the latter.

But if I'm going out, that means I'm not going to have time to pack up my stuff tonight. Not that I have much. I'd sold all the furniture and most of the knick-knacks when I'd left Seattle. I text Aunt Naomi. *Something has come up. I have a dinner date tonight.*

A series of excited emojis come squeeee-ing across my phone screen. Followed by bursting fireworks. My aunt has promised to stop playing matchmaker in my life – but that doesn't mean she's ready to give up on the idea of me having a second happily ever after. She recognizes what Kevin and I had was special. But at the same time, she believes I can have something that special with someone else. She texts, *Is it with Logan?*

I roll my eyes. Autumn isn't the only one who thinks that Logan and I still have a chance.

*No.* I don't have the heart to tell her that it isn't a real date. *I'll swing by home later to change, but I'm not going to have time to pack.*

She replies, *Is it okay if I pack for you?*

*Sure.* I don't have anything I wouldn't want anyone to see. And my truly personal things, from my life before I'd lost Kevin, are mostly still in boxes in the back of my closet. *But be careful with my maps.* It's a collection that Kevin and I had put together of all the places we dreamed of going, and places we'd been. But I've added a few maps of my own, from my trip to Colombia, and now to Peru. *And leave out some clothes.* I regret texting that part as soon as I've sent it, imagining her setting out a slinky black dress for me to wear tonight. Or that sleeveless sweater I impulse bought with the v-neckline and the sequins. I quickly add, *BUSINESS CASUAL clothes. This is a low-key date.*

I need to get things taken care of at the shop – and work with Carmen to get things set up for Autumn's party – and then get home as soon as I can. But before I can leave here, I still need to feed and amuse the octopus. After all, Clive shouldn't have to suffer just because his owner has gone missing. I step over to his tank and remove the weight. I peer down into the water, which has that weird reflective optics thing going on. There are a number of pieces of coral in there, and some man-made pieces of decoration, but I don't see an octopus. I lean down level with the side of the tank. There are a lot of places an octopus could hide. I try to inspect each one, from different sides of the tank, but as far as I can tell, that tank's completely empty.

There had been a weight on top of the lid – but I still get the idea that Clive might have gone walkabout. I didn't find him on my tour of the apartment – which is good, since an octopus can't survive indefinitely out of water. I go back into the study.

There are five different tanks in here. I can only assume that Mateo would have left me instructions on how to deal with the sea life in each one, if he'd finished his note. The tank on the wall near the door is obviously the live food tank. It's still brimming over with small shrimp. The others all have different collections of tropical fish – except for the one at the back, near the desk, with plants that look like the underwater version of small prickly pears, and a plastic pineapple like the one from Sponge Bob. There's not a single fish swimming in that tank. But there are a couple of suckered arms sticking out of the pineapple's open front door. I lean down to eye level, and there's Clive looking back at me. He tucks his ungainly arms the rest of the way inside the plastic house, and starts changing color from purple to a dark brown. He knows as well as I do that he isn't supposed to be in there. And I'd be willing to bet that the fish he ate – the former occupants of this tank – were worth a lot more than he is.

"You're not even hungry, are you?" I open the tank lid. Clive moves farther back under the pineapple. He doesn't know me. And if I scare him, he could ink. I looked into it last night, and there's a surprising amount of advice available for new octopus owners. I mime petting the glass, which gets Clive's attention, and then I put my fingers just at the top of the water, wiggling them a little, and encouraging him to come to me. He comes a little way out of the pineapple to see what I'm doing, but doesn't seem interested in coming up to shake arms.

I don't want to push him, and he seems perfectly comfortable where he is, so instead of trying to move him back to his tank, I go get the weight and put it on top of the tank he's in. I know Mateo said not to leave him in view of the fish, but hopefully we'll find Mateo soon, and he can move Clive. Otherwise, I'm coming back here this afternoon with backup. Logan is so good with dogs. I wonder if he's ever handled an octopus.

Probably not, right?

I return to the kitchen and take pictures of the glass smashed on the floor, then I head out to meet Logan.

I'm crossing the parking lot to the area where I parked my catering van when a black car comes out of nowhere and starts barreling towards me. My chest goes heavy, and I'm frozen to the spot. I force myself past the fear. Then I scream and dive out of the way, between two parked cars. The black car goes screaming past, not even slowing when it clips the back end of the vehicle I dived behind.

My pulse still racing, I force myself to calm down, taking slow, deep breaths. My health might not be quite as fragile as it was a few months ago, but it's still not great. I crawl out from between the two cars, and pull myself up to standing – which sets off the car alarm of the vehicle I'm leaning against. I jump, startled, my heart thudding in my chest. I take a deep breath, to calm myself. But I let out a half-hysterical laugh. My touch sets off the alarm, but not the nearby collision?

Ignoring the alarm's racket, I peer in the direction the black car went. Some detective I make. I didn't get any information about the car or its driver, not even part of a license plate. What I did get is a pair of scraped palms and a clear message that someone isn't happy I was looking around inside Mateo's apartment. I keep a first aid kit inside my catering truck, so I grab it and a bottle of water. I rinse off my hands, and then put antibiotic ointment on the scratches. They really aren't that bad. There's only one spot near my thumb that I even bother putting a Band-Aid on.

I take a picture of the dented car bumper. I text it to Arlo, along with a brief explanation of what happened. I'm not about to stay here and wait for the police again. It's not like I can tell them anything anyway. Maybe at least now they'll realize this about more than Mateo having a disagreement with someone.

Arlo immediately texts back, *What color car does Mateo drive?*

I roll my eyes. I text back, *Mateo's car is black.* I give him a second to feel all smug. Then send a second text: *But it's here in the parking lot.*

Which is not surprising. Mateo sometimes takes a bicycle to work. I get in my catering truck. True to his word, Logan's location still shows him at the beach. Only, he's a good way down from Galveston proper – almost down to the San Luis Pass. It isn't that long of a drive, but it is long enough to get nervous. I find myself pulling down the visor and checking my hair in the mirror on the back. Not that it matters. I'm attracted to Logan, but we've stuck each other firmly in the friend zone.

When I get down to the location, Logan's car is in the parking lot on the opposite side of the street from the beach. I park next to it, then cross the street and make my way over the wooden footbridge, down to the sand. Logan is standing with a group of people in golf shirts and khaki shorts. One guy has a tee instead of the golf shirt – but he's still got the requisite cargo shorts.

By contrast, Logan's wearing jeans and his pilot's jacket, holding a bunch of wooden stakes and a roll of orange tape. I can't quite imagine him ever wearing a golf shirt.

Logan's dark sunglasses hide his eyes. But they can't hide the fact that he's six foot four, white with a light tan, and has a strong jaw and messy dark hair. He takes my breath away. But I don't think he realizes that. He waves with the tape roll when he sees me coming, like I'm just another friend. Because that's what I told him I wanted.

I make my way over to the group.

Before I say anything, Logan gestures down at my hands. "What happened?"

"A car tried to run me over." I try to say it like the experience didn't shake me. Though it's not something I can just take in stride. I'm not used to having people try to kill me in the street.

One of the two girls in the group looks at me and says, "Honto da?" She thinks for a second, and then translates, "Really?"

Her hair is in pigtails, and her Asian features are shaded by a brimmed beach hat.

I nod. "I haven't exactly had the best couple of days."

The guy standing next to her says something to her in Japanese that ends with, ". . . satsujin jiken desu." He's the one wearing the tee-shirt, which is adorned with a cartoon muscle man with green hair carrying a giant sword. He tells me, "I just told her you're the lady from the chocolate shop who found the body. And that it is a murder case."

The guy's accent sounds Canadian. Somehow, Logan's found himself in with a group of people collected from across the globe.

The girl's eyes are wide, and she breathes out, "Sugoi!"

I close my eyes for a second. Being a murder magnet is really not what I want to be known for. Internationally now, apparently.

Logan clears his throat. He points to the guy. "That's Nelson Daye. He's a marine biologist." Then to the girl. "Haruka's studying intelligence in marine animals, particularly different species of octopus." Then he points to the other three people, who have been talking amongst themselves as they roped off a small section of the sand with orange tape. "That's Caitlin Murphy, Jeff Daye, and Parker Amdur. Jeff's a botanist, and Nelson's brother. But Caitlin and Parker are volunteers, like me."

Which means this is the group Mateo came here to work with – plus some local volunteers. It isn't surprising that Logan has ideas about this case.

Caitlin's holding a sign that says, *Do not disturb sea turtle nest. Violators are subject to fines and imprisonment.*

I gesture down at the roped off section of sand. "Is that a turtle nest?"

Logan nods. "Probably the last one of the season."

I take a closer look. It really doesn't look like much, just a mounding of the sand. Sea turtle nests are rare enough that I've never actually seen one in person. "It doesn't look like much."

"That's what makes them so hard to spot," Nelson says. "Pretty much if you don't see mamma turtle roll up on the beach, you're never going to find the nest."

I can't tell if he's talking down to me, or if that's just how he talks.

"Then where is she?" I ask. There isn't a turtle in sight.

"Long gone," Nelson says. "Some kid's dog found the nest. It takes almost two months for Kemp's ridley eggs to hatch, so it's possible mamma turtle visited here a month or more ago, when it was more in the middle of nesting season. They don't stay on the beach long, so seeing a turtle actively nest is rare."

Logan says, "It's even more rare that this nest is still here to see. Usually, we report the hatchlings and they get transferred to a facility that protects them, to offer greater chance of survival. They're such an endangered species, we have to try to protect each egg, and the soil here isn't ideal for the eggs to develop so the turtles can hatch on their own. But these guys are studying turtle locomotion and ways to improve survival rates in the wild."

The way Logan says it, I'm not entirely sure he approves.

"It's only one of our projects," Nelson says. "The funding behind this team is extensive, and we're expected to turn in results."

I tell Logan, "I knew you like turtles, with your logo and all." The name of Logan's business is Ridley Puddle Jumping, and the picture is an endangered Kemp's ridley sea turtle – the rarest species of sea turtle, which has been mostly wiped out from poaching and environmental issues, including oil spills in the Gulf. It would be difficult to be in Galveston, and not hear *something* about them – since sculptures of the turtles are up all over town, with plaques about how turtles relate to the community.

Logan says, "I watched a turtle release down in Padre, shortly after I came to Texas. Those hatchlings making their way to the water was the most hopeful thing I had seen in a long time. I joined the turtle patrol first, then took it for my business name later."

Logan, who's from Minnesota but has traveled the world, had put himself in exile here in Texas, after a high-profile client died in his arms, back when he'd been a bodyguard. I can see why he would have been looking for hope after that client – a pop diva that Logan had been in love with – had slipped away. His need to save someone – anyone – would definitely have been triggered by adorable baby turtles.

"I can see the appeal," I tell him.

He grins. "Those little guys were new here, just like me. Well, relatively. Did you know that Kemp's ridleys never had documented nests on the upper Texas Coast before 2002?"

I say, "So this is what you do in your off time, when you're not tinkering with your planes?"

He smiles, and I wish I could see his eyes behind those sunglasses. "Some of it. I have interests other than planes and baseball, you know."

"Yeah, you help me solve murders," I quip – and then I regret it. I just passed up a chance to find out more about who Logan really is, just to get a quick laugh.

Nelson says, "It's a shame what happened. Who could have expected Mateo to just snap like that? The police are saying that poor man was shot point blank, with a silencer."

"A suppressor," Logan corrects. "And they haven't recovered the gun."

And yet, Nelson is just taking the news reports at face value – even though everything connecting Mateo to the case so far is circumstantial. Still, I resist the urge to defend Mateo. If I do that, Nelson will clam up on me. Instead, I ask, "Did you work with him on his project?"

"Not directly. But he was studying the interaction of different elements in marine ecosystems. So he was sharing our lab, and asking lots of questions."

I nod. "Do you know why he suddenly decide to study marine life? Everything he'd been doing before involved botany, specifically the genetics of cacao trees. And when he's been working with me in the shop, he gave every indication of returning to South America as soon as his project ends, to keep studying cacao trees."

Nelson says, "Mateo discovered a new species of river dolphin, deep in the rainforest. It gained him a bit of acclaim, and he got invited to speak at a few conferences. He came back to the States to do that, and somehow he wound up here. I think something bad happened to him in the rainforest, or maybe to the river itself. We had this weird discussion over lunch one time, where he said there's nothing illegal collectors love more than a new, rare species."

Mateo had never said anything like that to me. But those words sound ominous. I believe Nelson is saying that Mateo brought attention to a species of dolphin – only to feel responsible for causing them to disappear. That sounds horrible.

I ask, "Does Mateo have any enemies? Or might anyone have been trying to hurt him?"

"I don't think so," Nelson says. "He seems like a nice guy. A little OCD, but nice."

Haruka gives Nelson a sharp look. "What about the man?"

Nelson says, "That's right. There was a tall man who came to the University looking for Mateo. He said it was urgent that he find him, as something had been delivered to him by mistake."

"Now that's cryptic," I quip.

Haruka shrugs. "That is all we know."

I change tack. "When was the last time y'all saw Mateo?"

"He was in the lab on Friday," Nelson says. "It was just an ordinary morning. He left at noon. Said he had to get to work."

I nod. "Sounds right. He showed up at the shop around one."

So I'd seen him far more recently than these guys had.

"Let's take a walk on the beach," Logan says. It isn't exactly a suggestion. He's already taken off walking.

I hurry to catch up. As soon as we're away from the group, he slows down and asks, "Is this too fast for you?"

"I keep telling you I'm doing a lot better."

"Uh huh." Logan still doesn't believe that my health is improving.

I look out at the water. There's a line of pelicans flying low over the horizon. "So what did you find out?"

Logan pulls out his phone. He shows me a picture of Fabin – very much alive and partying with a couple of girls in sparkly dresses. "This kid was all about buying expensive cars and showing off for the media. Apparently, he would do anything to impress his seemingly endless parade of girlfriends. His family kept threatening to cut him off, but they never did."

"That actually fits with what Enrique said." I explain to Logan about the football-player-chef I'd interrogated. "He told me Fabin came to Galveston for a pop-up dining experience. So you're saying Fabin stopped by my shop to what – buy chocolate strawberries and champagne truffles for his girlfriend?"

Logan shrugs. "That seems a bit tame for him. He has a rap sheet with charges for buying designer drugs, and breaking into stores just for fun. There are also two charges for illegally importing bleu de gex. Which is just weird. Who would risk jail time just to eat unpasteurized cheese?"

"You're not a fan of blue cheese, are you?" I ask, not sure what I'm going to do if he says yes. Because bleu cheese is yeck.

He shakes his head. "You?"

I scrunch up my nose. "It's the only kind of cheese I don't like."

He looks relieved.

"I don't sell anything off the books," I assure Logan, before he can ask. "So there's no reason why Fabin would have been at my shop. It has to be just a coincidence that whoever killed him did it outside my door."

Despite the niggling suspicion at the back of my brain that if those sunglasses were inside my shop, likely Fabin was too.

"You sure Mateo wasn't selling anything on the side?" Logan asks. "It could explain the whole thing."

I consider it. "I haven't known him long, but he doesn't seem like the type."

I show him my pictures of Mateo's apartment, and of the disturbing broken glass on the floor. And I explain what happened in the parking lot. "Whatever happened to Fabin," I conclude, "it has something to do with Mateo's disappearance. Maybe he saw something he shouldn't have-"

Logan shakes his head so emphatically that I stop talking. "That doesn't make sense. Fabin was killed with one shot, directly to the heart. Whoever shot him knew what they were doing. If Mateo had walked into the middle of that, or tried to stop it, the killer would have dropped him too, and you'd have found him on the sidewalk next to Fabin."

Logan's right. But I can't reconcile what I know about Mateo with any other explanation.

"Why do you keep checking your phone?" Logan asks.

I hadn't realized I was doing that. But I look down and realize I'm checking the time. "I took a huge order for gift baskets that need to go out this weekend. I only have enough of my 70% Peru bars in stock to fill half of it, and I left Carmen and Miles at the shop making hot cocoa bombs like mad people."

"Do you need some help?" Logan asks.

"At the shop? Not really. I just need to get the beans roasted and transfer them into the melangers before-" I try to bite back that last word, but it is too late.

"Before what?" Logan asks, the sunglasses coming off, his green eyes suddenly sharp.

I don't want to tell him. But Logan is basically a human lie detector, so pretending I don't have anywhere to go is pointless. I take a deep breath. "Patsy invited me out on a double date with her and Arlo. She's setting me up with her brother."

Logan snorts a laugh. "You can't be serious."

I bite at my lip. "I know it's a horrible idea. But I want to get Arlo to realize Mateo might not be the killer the police are assuming he is. And a couple of glasses of wine and a nice steak might put him in the mood to listen. This is important. I still think Mateo's in trouble."

"Felicity." Logan puts a hand on my arm, and it's like an electric shock through me. His eyes look suddenly soft and concerned. "If Mateo really was abducted, chances are whoever took him needed something from him. And they'll only keep him alive until they get whatever it is. Unless whatever they wanted was at Mateo's apartment, in which case he's probably already dead. Nobody's gotten a ransom note, right?"

"If they have, Arlo didn't see fit to tell me about it. Mateo's family is in Spain. I can try to get ahold of them when I get back to the shop. I think his dad's number is his emergency contact on his application." I hate to worry them more than they probably already are, but they might have important insights that could shed light on this entire situation.

"Make sure you don't wind up alone at Felicitations," Logan says. "Please. The camera feed from the security system I installed for you has been showing blank since last night. I'll come by later and fix it. I know I'm not in charge of your safety anymore, but whoever tried to run you down could try again."

I shudder. "I hope not."

"I got you something. I've been meaning to give it to you." He reaches into his jacket pocket.

I suck in a breath. If he got me jewelry, I'm going to faint right here on the sand.

Logan takes out a canister of hot pepper spray. He holds it out to me. "It'll make me feel better, sending you off on your own."

"Thanks?" I take the canister and look at the label before I put it in my purse. What does this gift mean? He's feeling protective of me, because he cares? Or he's worried about me, because he doesn't think I can take care of myself? I decide to take it at face value: he's just looking out for a friend. Because I've made it clear that's all I want in my life right now: a few loyal friends. My husband died a little over a year ago. I may not be grieving as deeply as I was before I met Logan, but I'm still not sure whether I'm ready to move on. I still have a picture of

Kevin on my bedside table, that I look at last thing at night before I go to sleep. And sometimes I still think about what he would have thought about how the business is doing, about the house my aunt has fixed up, about what I'm doing with my life. But I've been trying to stop filtering everything through Kevin's eyes. I'd had a huge epiphany when my life had been in danger: I have figure out what I want my life to look like – for myself.

Logan says, "Hey. I don't mean the pepper spray as an insult."

"I know," I say, like I hadn't just been thinking it might be.

But now it feels like maybe Logan's been waiting for something like this case to come along – to take us on another adventure together. An adventure that might hold a hint of danger, because let's face it, my little world has to be boring to Logan. But Kevin was the one I always wanted to go on adventures with. Am I really going to let Logan replace him in that role?

Well . . . maybe. Logan hasn't asked me for anything I'm not ready to give. And he is a good friend. I tell him, "Thank you. Really. It does make me feel a little safer."

When I leave Logan and his friends finishing up their work, I find the hairs prickling on the back of my neck. Once I get back up to the top of the seawall, I scan the area, terrified I'm going to see that dented black car.

# Chapter Seven
## *Still Tuesday*

By the time I've gotten back to Greetings and Felicitations, my neck hurts from craning it, trying to keep an eye out for danger. But I didn't see anyone following me. Or anything else out of place. Could that car running at me have just been a coincidence? A stupid teenager out joyriding, or someone not looking where they were going? It would be an awfully big coincidence, but that is a possibility I should at least consider.

I park a few spaces from my front door. I feel safer when I see Carmen inside the shop, wiping down the tables. It's such a normal, quiet thing for her to be doing. When I open the door, the scent of lavender and citrus wafts out at me. Which is instantly calming.

"Something smells nice," I tell Carmen.

"I've been perfecting a cinnamon London Fog for the party tomorrow. Lavender Earl Gray is Autumn's favorite. Do you want to try it?"

"You remembered her favorite tea?" I pull out my phone and take a seat at a table by the window.

"Of course. She always checks to see if there are any lavender-infused baked goods when she comes in here." Carmen hands me a chocolate concha. Carmen has taken the sweet bread to the next level by adding rosemary, cumin, cayenne, and cracked pepper to the topping mixture. "But Autumn is a great listener too. She deserves a great party. I have the decorations under control. Here. London Fog."

Carmen hands me a cup of the foamy hot tea latte. It tastes just as good as it smells, warm and spicy and floral.

I tell her, "We should put this on the regular coffee menu."

Carmen steps enthusiastically over to the menu board and grabs a tape strip. "I'll write it in. How's your part of the party planning?"

I'd gotten Autumn to send me contact info for the people she'd like at the party. She's given me a list with twenty-five names on it. I don't have time to send formal printed invitations, but text messages seem a little too informal. "I'm going to call and see how many of these people are going to be able to make it, and then we can order some tapas from that place Autumn likes. They do catering orders, right?"

Fortunately, most of the people on Autumn's list are available for Thursday night. And the tapas place can give us all of Autumn's favorite appetizers. I just need to make those hazelnut-gianduja-filled chocolate doves to go in the favor boxes Carmen ordered. I'm planning on melting down some of my Madagascar chocolate to make the shells, because the fruity notes will complement the hazelnuts.

I still need to get the Peru beans processed too, and that's going to take longer.

Leaving Carmen to continue tweaking her latte recipe, I take my cup – with a London fog refill – to the bean room, where I roast and winnow the beans for the gift basket order, and then I get the melangers running.

I take a moment to try calling Mateo's family again. Even though no one has returned my calls, despite the seven messages I've left.

This time to my surprise, someone says, "Hola?"

I ask, "Habla usted Inglés?" Because I don't really have the vocabulary to have this conversation in Spanish. Talking about murder and a missing person is a rather delicate undertaking, even in your native language.

"Yes. May I help you?" The woman sounds amused. Maybe she hasn't heard about the murder, after all.

I say, "I am Mateo's employer. He has not come in to work today."

She laughs. "You understand we are in Spain, not U.S.? That he is not here?"

"Si. Yes," I assure her. I'm not sure how to do this, except to just be direct. "There was a murder outside my shop yesterday. Mateo may have been a witness. He has not been seen since. I just want to know if you have heard from him. I want to make sure he is alright."

There's another voice in the background, and then the woman I've been speaking to talking to someone else in the room in Spanish. Then it sounds like the woman has dropped the phone, and I hear snatches of sound from a television.

She picks up the phone. "I am sorry, but we have not spoken to Mateo in several years."

"Oh," I say. "I thought this was the number for his parents."

"Yes, that is us. But Mateo and his father got into a large fight years ago, because Mateo refused to take over the family business. A restaurant is a fine, respectable business, and a good way to earn a living. Now, we have no one to take care of it when we are gone."

That must have been a horrible fight, if Mateo had been either in school or traipsing around the rainforest ever since.

I make the appropriate noises of commiseration. "I agree. I own a bean to bar chocolate making company myself." Though I've never thought about what happens to my business if something happens to me. Naomi has her own thing, flipping property. And I've got . . . nobody, really, to leave it to. It awakens unsettling feelings inside me. But I need to stay focused on Mateo. "So you don't know if he might have spent any time with Fabin Obodozie?"

"What is a Fabin Obodozie?" she asks.

So that's a no. "He's the guy who got killed." I try again. "Do you know if Mateo carries a supply of his medication on him? The main prescription bottles were still at his apartment."

"Mateo is sick?" the woman asks. "You should make soup. Works every time."

"It's not that kind of sick," I tell her reluctantly. I don't want to tell her it is a chronic illness. I've made a blunder here. This is a conversation Mateo should be having with his family himself. If I was still in the medical field, sharing this kind of information could get me into serious trouble.

The woman waits, and when I don't say anything else, she says, "Por favor. When you find him, please tell him to call us. Tell him his father misses him every day, even if he would never say it out loud. Stefan has left Mateo's room just the way it was, hoping that one day he will come home to visit."

"I'll tell him. I promise." And I mean it. I'm going to make sure Mateo gets that message. No matter what it takes. I talk to my parents every week. And to my grandmother – despite the pain of dealing with her memory lapses. I had hurt her feelings by limiting myself to just occasional visits when I had been dealing with the worst part of my grief. I can only imagine the pain it would have caused if I had stayed away for years.

Now, I just have to find Mateo. I brainstorm other leads, while I continue working. I start on the hazelnuts, roasting them and rubbing them to remove the skins.

I'm about halfway done when Tiff walks into the chocolate processing room. She's wearing jeans and a hunter green tee-shirt. Even dressed that casually – rare for her – there's something silky about the fabric of her shirt.

"Hey!" I say. "Taste this." I give her a piece of the Madagascar. "Imagine that with hazelnut paste."

She pops the square into her mouth. "I *think* that will be nice."

"What's up?" Sometimes my friends show up at the shop to grab a coffee or just to hang out. And Autumn comes back here sometimes, and Sonya. But not Tiff or Sandra. I'm not sure why. Tiff usually prefers to have people over to her place, or to hang out at a restaurant, than to join them in the middle of work

"I have a favor to ask you," Tiff asks.

"Shoot."

Tiff hesitates. "You know I've been complaining about how the housing market has slowed down."

I nod, not sure where she's going with this.

She hesitates. "I've only gotten two commissions this month." One of those had been a percentage on what Naomi and I had paid for the hotel. "I want to get Autumn something nice, but an engagement gift wasn't exactly in the budget. I was just wondering if you have any work available, so I can get a quick infusion of cash."

"Before Thursday?" I ask. Tiff is so not a cook, and I doubt she'd excel as a barista.

Tiff gives me a helpless look. "I'm good with advertising. I could cold call potential clients for you."

"I guess you could," I say. Then I have an idea. "But Naomi has to get us out of the house and into the hotel in the next couple of weeks. I'm sure it would be a big favor if you offer to help her. I know she's got a budget for it."

Tiff presses her lips together. "I'd rather not."

"Why? I know you like decorating and arranging furniture. It could be fun to hang out in the big, empty hotel." I try to sound excited, but Tiff looks unimpressed. "Okay, honestly, it's not the world's largest hotel. But the architecture is cool."

Tiff makes a face. "It's not like I'm afraid of painting or moving boxes. But me and Naomi just don't mix."

I stop working the nut grinder. "What? Why?"

They'd seemed perfectly comfortable sitting together at Chalupa's yesterday.

"There was this house up for sale, right after I moved to Galveston." Tiff had moved here when she had gotten married, so her whole life had been in upheaval at the time. "I was nervous, because it was a new job, and I may have been a little too zealous when it came to that particular contract. I was representing a different buyer, and Naomi accused me of buying the house out from under her. Things were said."

"This is ridiculous. I need to go over to the house to change anyway. You're coming with me." I move over to the sink and wash my hands. I can finish making gianduja after my date tonight.

"Felicity, wait," Tiff protests, but I'm already moving to grab my purse and my keys.

"You can either follow me over there, or you can ride in my ridiculous catering truck."

Tiff shakes her head. "There's no point in fighting this, is there?"

"Nope."

I keep checking to make sure Tiff's car is still behind me. When we get to the house, Tiff parks behind me on the driveway.

She stands there for a moment, admiring the gingerbreading on the porch. "It's been a minute since I've been over here. Naomi has done some fantastic work on this place."

"Then tell her that." I head for the back door. Tiff follows hesitantly.

We find Aunt Naomi in the kitchen, wrapping dishes in tissue paper. Some of this stuff's mine. Those plates were a wedding gift from my grandmother. Naomi sees me looking at the pattern.

She says, "Do you think Mom would want to come to the hotel tomorrow? She's been saying how bored she is at her apartment." It's an assisted living facility, actually, because my grandmother has some trouble with her memory. So far it is only mild memory loss, but it still isn't safe for her to stay alone. "She wants to see the place. She keeps insisting she wants to paint the kitchen."

"Then let her. It couldn't hurt, right?" I look from Aunt Naomi to Tiff and back again. These are two people I care deeply about. I need to do this right, so I don't wind up making things worse. I decide to be straightforward. "Look, Tiff thinks you're still mad at her about some old house you didn't get to buy."

"Me?" Aunt Naomi says. "I'm not the one who said I never wanted to talk to me again."

Aunt Naomi and Tiff look at each other. And they both start talking at the same time. It's hard to understand exactly what they're saying, and at first it sounds angry. But then they both sound surprised. And then they cross to the middle of the room and hug each other.

"My work here is done," I say.

"That's right," Aunt Naomi says, as she pulls me into the hug too.

When we all move apart, I say, "This could be perfect. Maw Maw could probably use some help painting the kitchen."

Tiff explains why she needs some extra cash. Naomi says the hotel is such a big project, she could use someone to supervise parts of the work. I leave them to work out the details, saying, "I have a date to get ready for."

I'm wondering if this could lead to them collaborating on other things. See what happens when people just talk to each other?

I'm halfway up the stairs to my room when the doorbell rings. I go down to see who it is.

Sonya is standing on the porch holding a bag.

I usher her inside. "Is everything okay."

"Yes, I'm just out making deliveries." She holds the bag out to me. "I've been making sweaters for all my favorite people."

"Thanks!" I open the bag. The sweater inside is lightweight and soft, but it's a green and brown blend of colors that I never would have chosen for myself. Sonya obviously put a lot of work into it.

"You like it, right?" Sonya asks.

"Of course." It's not that bad, really, once I have time to get used to it. "I'm going to wear it to the engagement party."

Sonya beams. "That's great." She turns to go.

I tell her, "Tiff and Naomi are in the kitchen, if you want to hang out for a minute. But I have to get changed, and then I'm heading out."

"Is that coffee I smell?" Sonya asks.

"It is indeed." Which means that Tiff and Naomi must have made up. My aunt doesn't make coffee for people she doesn't like.

"I guess I could – well hello." Sonya leans over and holds out a hand for Knightley to sniff. The bunny has hopped over and is leaning possessively against her shoe. She pets him on his head. Then she looks at me and says, "Have you ever considered collecting his fur when you brush him? I could spin it and make you a super-soft Knightley scarf."

Sonya really does have a one-track yarn-oriented mind. "I'm glad you found something you're so passionate about, but that sounds like a lot of work."

"Some things are worth the work," Sonya says. "I probably never told you, but I got into doing yarn arts as a result of an anger management class, when I was so stressed out from my corporate job. The assignment was to do a cross-stitch. It was only three inches across, but I didn't have the patience to finish it." She pats Knightley on the head again, then she heads for the kitchen.

I'm not sure what she expects me to take away from that.

## Chapter Eight
### *Still Tuesday*

I walk into the restaurant Patsy picked out for this double date. The place smells amazing. But even that doesn't make me any more excited to be here.

I ask the maître d', "Has Arlo Romero's party arrived yet?"

The guy looks vaguely familiar. It's possible I went to high school with him.

"Are you and Arlo back together?" the maître d' asks.

Yeah. I definitely went to high school with him, if he remembers that. High school was when Arlo and I had been together. He points me towards a table in the back. I can see Arlo sitting there, looking handsome in a dress shirt and tie. And Patsy, sitting next to him, in a sleeveless black dress. They make an elegant couple. And I'll just bet the goofy-looking guy with the big ears and the tie that looks like he's got a flat striped bass hanging awkwardly off of his neck is Patsy's brother, Wallace.

I remind myself that I'm here to fight for Mateo's innocence, and I still have to fight the urge to turn around and go back out of the door. Wallace waves. Which means I'm committed to this – or I'll have to explain to Patsy why I bailed. I force a smile and walk over to them.

I'm not trying too hard for this date – because I'm not actually interested in finding someone right now. If I'm not ready to move forward with Logan, I'm certainly not wanting to move into an even more awkward situation. So I'm dressed in a green cotton blouse and black pants – which I had to rescue out of one of the boxes my aunt had packed, but thankfully not yet moved – with my hair pulled back at the nape of my neck. I catch Arlo giving me an appreciative look – which he then hides before Patsy notices.

I feel heat in my cheeks. How is it that Arlo can make me feel this way, even though it has been so long since we've been together?

I turn towards Wallace and hold out a hand. "It's nice to meet you."

Wallace takes my hand and kisses it – like a guy in an old movie. I can't help but be a little flattered. "I've heard a lot about you, Felicity."

"All good, I hope." I smile at Wallace. Arlo makes a little choked noise.

Wallace grins back and says, "Mostly. Everybody's got to be up to a little mischief, after all."

I sit down. "So what have *you* been up to?"

Wallace laughs. "Wouldn't you like to know."

I look across the table. Patsy is beaming at me. Arlo looks vaguely ill. I remind myself that I'm not supposed to like Wallace, despite his goofy charm.

Wallace says, "Patsy tells me you are quite the gifted amateur sleuth."

I glance over at Arlo. There's no safe way to answer the implied question. "It's more that I keep finding myself in the position to help people."

Arlo says, "You reported an attempt on your life via text. I'd say that this time, you are in over your head."

"Possibly, but someone has to look after Mateo's interests here." I reach into my purse, take out the meds I'd found at Mateo's apartment, and put the bottles on the table.

"Felicity," Arlo says softly, "I cannot discuss this case with you."

Wallace reaches over and picks up one of the medicine bottles. "What is this for?"

I take it back out of his hand. "Mateo has a medical condition. I brought them because I'm trying to convince Arlo that Mateo never would have left town without these. If he doesn't take them regularly, he could die."

"No kidding?" Wallace asks. He looks a little alarmed. His concern for a stranger makes him even more endearing. He turns to Arlo. "What are you doing for this guy?"

"*For* him?" Arlo protests. "He's our main suspect in a murder investigation."

The waiter comes over to our table to take our order. The guy's eyes go wide at the word *murder*. He clears his throat. "Can I get any appetizers for this table while y'all are thinking about y'all's meal?"

"Please," Arlo says. "The lady and I will split the blue cheese fondue." After the waiter makes the appropriate notation on his tablet, Arlo says, "And a bottle of merlot. I have a feeling I'm going to need it."

Wha? Since when does Arlo eat blue cheese? After the conversation I'd had with Logan about cheese preferences, it makes me wonder if Arlo and I had been doomed from the start.

Wallace says, "I will split any appetizer you want – as long as there's no blue cheese involved."

"Deal," I tell him. I tell the waiter, "Give us the crab cakes."

"Nice choice," Wallace says. His phone rings. He makes a face, then says, "Please pardon me for a moment."

Wallace leaves the table to take his call.

Patsy says, "I told you that you and Wallace would hit it off."

I make a noncommittal noise. I turn to Arlo. I do have a reason for being here after all. "Did you realize Fabin's cousin Leslie is in town?"

Arlo blinks at me. "That's impossible."

The crab cakes arrive – super fast. I pick one up and take a bite. It's almost crispy, fried to a golden brown. And the sweetness of the crab is accented by the spicy mustard. After I swallow, I say, "She came in to Greetings and Felicitations this afternoon."

Arlo's lips go tight. "I talked to Leslie Franks this morning. She's on vacation in Switzerland. With no intention of returning any time soon – at least not until the press goes away. She's notoriously camera shy, so most people don't even know what she looks like."

I point with my fork. "Then who did I talk to?"

As my own words sink in, my eyes go wide. If she wasn't a grieving cousin seeking understanding, what was that girl doing in my shop? And why was she prepared with Leslie Frank's card?

Arlo sighs dramatically. "I don't know, Felicity. I can send someone down to get your security camera feeds and we can try to figure it out."

I shake my head. "Logan says the cameras were out since before the murder last night. He just came by a couple of hours ago to fix them."

Arlo stifles a laugh with his hand, while Patsy glares at him. I can just bet that Arlo tried to talk her out of setting me up with her brother by telling her that Logan and I have a thing going on.

I redirect back to the important topic here. "You have to admit, it doesn't make any sense for that girl to come to the shop claiming to be Fabin's cousin if Mateo killed the guy and fled."

"Unless she's working with Mateo," Arlo says, his brown eyes deep with intensity. "She could have come to retrieve a piece of incriminating evidence Mateo left behind. Or she could have some connection to whatever got Fabin killed, and she wants to find Mateo too. Or-"

Patsy puts her hand on top of Arlo's. "Sweetie, you just told Felicity you couldn't discuss the case."

Arlo's jaw snaps shut. "Right. I'm sorry. Let's talk about what's going on with the community garden project."

Patsy beams. She turns that smile in my direction. "Have you thought about participating? It's going to be so much fun."

"It's going to be a pain," Arlo says. "There was a community garden in the town in Arizona where I first got into law enforcement. People stole each other's vegetables. And sabotaged each other's plants. There was even a stabbing, involving a prize-winning pumpkin that had been swapped."

"But that's not going to happen here," Patsy insists, giving Arlo another sharp look. Could there be trouble between the two? Or is Arlo just grumpy today because of the awkward date? "Felicity, the garden will be gorgeous. Plus we're getting the historical society involved."

"Then I'm out," I say. "My aunt wouldn't appreciate me getting involved with a historical society project. The members keep outbidding her on restoration homes she'd like to flip. Besides, I just promised to be matron of honor in my friend's wedding. I have a feeling I'm going to be busy for the next six months or so."

"Wedding?" Patsy's leans forward, and I can practically see images of white lace dancing across her vision. "Do tell."

Okay, so maybe there's nothing wrong between Patsy and Arlo that him popping the question won't fix.

Patsy's phone lights up with a text message. She looks down at it, and then frowns, like looking at it harder will change whatever it says. Finally, though, she looks up. "Wallace had to leave. He told me to tell you he's sorry, and would like a raincheck for another time."

"Oh, heck no," Arlo says. "I am not doing this again." He glances over at me, and then looks a little ashamed. "No offense, Lis. You know I've never been one for setting people up."

"None taken." He knows I'm not a fan of being set up, either. I then settle in for one of the most awkward evenings of my life. Only – it isn't that bad. Patsy is also a Jane Austen fan. We like a lot of the same other books too – and we both share a rule that you have to read a book before you see the movie. She and Arlo seem well suited for each other, laughing at each other's jokes and finishing each other's sentences.

I find myself wondering why he *hasn't* proposed yet. And if – to my shame – the horrific way I'd broken up with him, back when we'd been together, has anything to do with it.

When the waiter comes back to ask about dessert, I shake my head no. Arlo assures me that he's got the check, tells me, "Come on, Lis, treat yourself a little."

"I need to get back to my shop. Carmen is meeting me there to work on gift baskets for this giant order I took. I need to check in on my chocolate, anyway. I had to leave it running."

I never leave machines running when nobody is at the shop – I know chocolate makers who do, and they're always taking a risk. Machines break. Things short out. There are horror stories of what some makers have come back to after letting machines run unattended all night long. But if I don't leave those melangers going this one time, there's no way I'm going to get the chocolate made in time for packaging it to go into the gift baskets. I'll be back before long, anyway.

Arlo looks skeptical. "I know you, Lis. You freaked out the last time those machines got left on and called me in the middle of the night to get my officers to go turn it off."

"It was not the middle of the night," I protest. "You and Patsy were out to breakfast."

They laugh. In unison.

I miss having that – with Kevin. And the overwhelming reminder of my loss hits me so hard it takes my breath and makes my chest literally ache. I bring a hand to my chest, finally manage to pull in air. I haven't had a moment like this in weeks. I can't decide if the sharpness of the grief is making me feel better or worse.

"Are you okay?" Patsy asks.

"Where's your inhaler?" Arlo's up out of his seat, reaching for my purse. He pulls out the pepper spray, and gives me a questioning look.

"I'm okay." I insist. "I haven't had to use my inhaler since I finished my treatments. And the pepper spray is just a general precaution."

"You should err on the side of caution on both counts," Arlo insists. He looks down at me as he hands me back my purse.

"Okay." I lock eye contact with him, and there's that spark again, smoldering hot. And completely inappropriate – especially in front of Patsy.

I have to get out of here. So I make my excuses and look Patsy in the eye. I thank her for inviting me.

I exit the restaurant and make my way out into the parking lot, then I cross it to the only space I'd found big enough to park my giant vehicle. I fumble in my purse for my keys as I walk.

When I look up, I realize there's a person wearing a baggy black sweater and jeans leaning against my catering truck. I consider dashing back into the restaurant. But the figure turns towards me, and I freeze in my tracks. My hand goes to the pepper spray tucked into the front pocket of my purse. I'd gone out into the alley behind my shop and tested spraying it while the beans for the new batch of chocolate had been roasting. It seems fairly straightforward to use.

"Mrs. Koerber, don't freak out. It's just me." It's a woman's voice. She steps out of the shadow of the van into the parking lot's lights.

I take a close look at the woman's face. She had been doing the turtle patrol with Logan, though she looks very different without the golf shirt. "Caitlin? What are you doing here?"

Her shoulders are hunched up near her ears, and at the same time her hands are shoved into her pockets. She's nervous about something. Her accent – she's unmistakably a New Yorker – is more pronounced than before, when I hadn't been able to tell where she was from. "Were you serious when you said you and Logan are going to solve Fabin's murder?"

"You know something about that?" It seems a bit too easy, just to have her come up and offer me information about this case.

"No, nothing like that." She kicks her foot against the pavement. "I just – do you think it's possible that Fabin got killed because he saw something to do with Mateo, and not the other way around."

"It is possible," I say. "Though it seems unlikely."

"I don't know if it means anything, but Mateo got into a shouting match with Haruka and Nelson three days ago, out on the beach."

"Oh?" This still feels too easy. "What were they fighting over?"

Caitlin shrugs. "I didn't hear much. They were mad that he'd been making notes on something Haruka had been doing. And then they realized I'd walked up. It was awkward."

"Why did Nelson get involved?" I ask. Though I have a guess. "He's Haruka's boyfriend, right?"

"I think so. He's kind of obsessed with Japan. And she likes the fact that he's good with animals."

That fight means Haruka has motive. So I'm going to have to find out a way to get into Haruka's life. "I'll come by tomorrow and ask her a few questions about how to take care of Clive."

"Good. Because I don't think she'll talk to me about it." Caitlin makes a face. "If they did something to Mateo, my money's on Nelson. Haruka doesn't seem the type to get her hands dirty."

I need to go check on Clive in the morning. Which will be a perfect time to look for Mateo's notes.

I get a text from Carmen. *When Autumn said her colors are gold and baby blue, does she mean metallic gold or yellowy gold? These flower arrangements aren't going to order themselves.*

I tell Caitlin, "I have to go, before things back at my shop get really out of hand."

As I open the door to my catering truck, I text Autumn, for about the fortieth time today. *Metallic gold or yellow gold?*

*Metallic,* she texts back immediately. *But understated. I want things to be tasteful.*

"How do you make gold understated?" I ask Caitlin. "I'm my friend's matron of honor, and I am so in over my head."

Sympathy in her eyes, Caitlin says, "I feel you. I've never been good at that kind of thing either. Don't ask me to do anything that involves a glue gun. But call me if you need help with your dysfunctional cockatoo."

"What?" It comes out with half a laugh, waiting for the punchline to her joke.

She points at herself. "Animal psychologist."

"Oh, okay." I'm still not sure whether or not to laugh.

We both just stand there awkwardly. Eventually she says, "See ya!" and walks away.


When I get back to the Strand, I park to the right of my shop, next to a cluster of cars taking up most of the close spots. It feels safer. Salsa music wafts on the night air. I get almost to my front door before I realize it's coming from inside – along with laughter and chatter in multiple languages. Is Carmen having a party? I don't really mind – I just wish she would have told me first. I'd been hoping for more help on the giant order tonight.

I go inside and find that all the tables have been pushed together and the chairs circled around them. A bunch of college students are sitting with glasses of chardonnay – and spools of ribbon and stacks of cellophane sheets. There are a couple of dozen finished gift baskets up on the counter.

Carmen sees me and waves. "I hope you don't mind. This is Miles's study group from school. He said they sometimes do community work to get extra credit. I promised them each twenty bucks."

"That sounds fair," I say.

A petite blonde woman in her forties, who is wearing a University sweatshirt, pipes up, "We can only finish 600 of the baskets. The rest of them are missing that Peru bar."

"And the hot chocolate bombs," Carmen adds. "Miles and I worked on them all day, but we only had a few molds to work with."

I'm touched by her loyalty. "Thank you so much for taking this kind of initiative."

Carmen says, "I like Mateo. You proved me innocent. I know you can prove him innocent too. And I don't want you to lose business over it."

I'm touched by her confidence in me – even if I'm a little afraid it's overstated. I move over to her and give her a side hug. "You are the best."

"I know." Carmen starts singing along with the song playing over the shop's sound system.

I take a closer look at the group. There's five people: three girls and two guys. Which means that this is only costing me a hundred bucks – plus whatever Carmen spent on wine. I ask them, "Would y'all consider coming back on Friday night, once the rest of the chocolate is done, to finish up? I'll even spring for pizza."

They all start murmuring assent, except for the guy holding my shrink wrap gun, who says, "Nah, man, Friday's not good for me."

I take a few pictures of the group continuing to work, closeups of the cocoa bombs, everything that will make for a good Instagram post. I need some community-building PR, considering what Ash already said about me. I format one post about the gift basket helpers and get it posted. I can space out the other pics later.

I have to admit, the music Carmen put on does give me the urge to dance, though I only know a few basic salsa steps. I sort of vague salsa my way into the hall and over to the bean room. I go through into the area where my chocolate is being processed. Only – one of my two melangers doesn't seem to be doing anything. I check to see if there's something stuck. The electrical cord has been cut near the base of the barrel. I'm so upset that I can suddenly feel my pulse pounding in my ears. Who would do such a thing? One of Carmen's helpers, maybe?

While I'm leaned over the machine, trying to see if anything else is wrong with it, the lights go out, and there's movement in the dark. The switch for both spaces is in the bean room. Whoever's in here could have been in the hallway, or the bathroom or the bean room – not out with the helpers in the front of the shop. When I came through into the chocolate processing room, I probably walked right past the culprit.

I've still got my purse. I start to reach for the pepper spray, as I say into the dark, "What do you want?"

Someone pushes over the other melanger at me, and as I quickly back out of the way, I hear it crash to the floor. Warm, gritty, hardly-processed chocolate splashes my pants and ruins another perfectly good pair of flats. Even worse, I hear the crack of one of the stone wheels splitting in half.

"No!" I shout.

The intruder rushes past me, carrying something bulky in the dark. Seconds later, there's the bang of the back door slamming closed as the person makes a hasty exit into the alley. The door slams again, as someone follows the intruder.

Seconds later, the light comes on, and Carmen is standing in the doorway between the bean room and the chocolate processing room. She takes in my disheveled state and the mess on the floor, which is even worse than I had imagined in the dark.

"What happened?" Carmen asks.

"Somebody broke in."

"I know that. Corina followed him outside. She used to be a cop, before she went back to school." Carmen gestures helplessly at the toppled melanger. "But why sabotage the equipment?"

"I don't know." I go through the chocolate processing room and into the kitchen, to get a bottle of water from the stock in the fridge.

The door opens, and the petite blonde woman who was sitting at the table five minutes ago making gift baskets walks back in with a fifty-pound bag of cacao beans slung over her shoulder. She drops it onto the floor in front of her. "He got away. But he dropped this before he even reached the end of the alley."

I want to just sit down on the floor and cry. Somebody broke in here and destroyed my equipment as a distraction to cover their escape – all so they could steal a bag of cacao beans? It doesn't make any sense. It's not even the rare Porcelana beans Mateo brought me. This break-in has to be connected to the murder on my doorstep yesterday, and to Mateo's disappearance. But how?

I feel like I'm missing something obvious. But just getting the sense that there is something I need to figure out doesn't help to bring it into focus.

"Should I tell everyone to go home?" Carmen asks. "Without those melangers, there's no way to get the project finished even if we stay all night."

It takes roughly three days of conching to make chocolate. I might be able to push it to two, if I run the machines overnight. The beans have to be broken down into particles that taste smooth inside the mouth, and if the chocolate doesn't spend long enough in the melanger it's going to be gritty. Which is not the impression I want to leave on a thousand potential customers.

"Wait a minute. I need to think." I bring a hand to my temple and feel something sticky. There's chocolate all over my hand – which I just managed to smear into my hair. That's about par for my day. I take out my phone. "The cops might want to talk to everyone. The break-in might be connected to the murder."

And while we wait for the cops, I need to at least try to come up with a solution to this crisis. There's one thing about working with craft chocolate. Everybody tends to know everybody, and we're all on social media. I let one person know I had catastrophic equipment failure – I leave out the miserable details of how it happened – and ask for ideas on how to get replacement machines in time to still meet my deadline. And then I call Arlo. Before the cops even arrive, my phone starts lighting up with commiseration, offers to let me process beans in other facilities, and used equipment for sale. The phone rings, and the ID says Weatherford Equipment. Which is a clearinghouse for culinary machinery. It's way past the time when they should be closed.

When I answer the call, they're offering to waive shipping and get me machines delivered in the morning – if they can send along a media contingent so that their good deed of helping out a small business owner can get plastered all over their feeds. Reluctantly, I agree. I hope they aren't mad at me when it comes out that my equipment was destroyed in a break-in. Although, who knows? The victim angle might make for even more empathy on YouTube.

The chirpy-voiced sales representative offers to take my credit card info over the phone, but this is an unsolicited call, and with the recent rash of credit card phishing fraud, I tell her I'd rather pay through official channels in the morning. The woman I'm talking to seems to understand.

So what could have been a devastating derailment for my business has been turned into a surmountable speedbump. I can get here super early in the morning and get another batch of beans ready to go into the melangers, as soon as the machines arrive. If the engine hasn't shorted out on the smaller of the two melangers, I might even be able to fix it and actually be up a machine at the end of this.

Assuming Arlo doesn't decide to take the rest of my Peru beans as evidence. Could he even do that? Would he? After I had explained at dinner about how much getting this order done means to me? Not that I would expect to be treated differently by the police, just because the detective knows me.

Feeling nervous about what might be about to happen, I ask Carmen, "Can you turn the music down? We don't want the cops to think we were partying too much to be reliable witnesses."

Carmen turns it down. "Are you going to be okay?"

"I hope so." I bring a hand to my temple again, and realize too late that I'm making the chocolate mess worse. I go to the bathroom to try and get myself looking presentable.

# Chapter Nine
## *Still Tuesday*

Detective Beckman shows up before Arlo does. After standing awkwardly for a few minutes, she sits at the table with everyone else, her chair pulled a little way back, waiting for Arlo to arrive before asking any questions. I guess that means he's still in charge of the investigation.

I pour her a cup of coffee. I noticed she grabbed decaf last time, and it is just as late tonight, so I give her the same.

She says, "Thanks." Then after a second adds, "You have a little chocolate-" She mimes an arc over her lip.

"Oh." I grab a napkin and my mirror from my purse and wipe away a faint chocolate mustache. "It's a mess back there, and I got splashed with everything coming right out of the melanger."

"I can see that. Shame about your shoes," she says.

I look down. She's right. These flats used to be pretty cute. "Have you heard anything about Mateo?"

Detective Beckman shakes her head and takes a long sip of coffee before answering. "Mrs. Koerber, personally, I don't think we're going to find Mateo. Not alive at least. That makes two deaths in two months. It seems like it's getting dangerous to be your assistant. Maybe you should take a step back."

It is possible that she's right and Mateo's dead, that trying to find him is pointless. But giving up seems too easy – especially when it seems like the bad guys assume I'm already involved. And they've taken a shot at ending my life too. Even if I wanted to, I couldn't get them the message that I'm off the case – and no longer a target.

I start to ask Detective Beckman what she thinks the intruder was after in my shop's bean room, but there's a squeal of tires outside as Logan's Mustang screeches to a halt. There's nowhere left for him to park, so he proceeds more slowly down the street, then I see him jogging back past the picture window from wherever he finally found to put his car.

When he comes in, I ask him, "How did you even know I was here?"

He jerks a thumb towards the kitchen. "The back-door camera showed that foot chase. And then you didn't answer your phone. I was hoping you *weren't* here, to be honest."

"The pepper spray didn't do me any good in the dark," I tell him. "But whoever it was seemed more intent on getting away than hurting me. He even broke some of my equipment to distract me long enough to kill the lights. I don't think our thief is the same person who tried to run me down in the parking lot."

Logan asks, "You got a look at him?"

"No, but Corina did." I gesture at Corina, who is calmly sipping wine at the table, once again looking completely underestimatable.

She gestures with her glass. "Tall white guy, built like a refrigerator. He was carrying that sack of cacao beans like it was a big pillow, right up until he decided to climb up one of those fire escapes."

"He was bald?" I guess.

"You know who this was?" Detective Beckman asks. She's taking notes on her phone. I guess she doesn't have to wait for anything if we all start offering information.

I nod. "It sounds like the guy who delivered the bean sorting machine. Tell them what you told me, Carmen."

Carmen looks embarrassed to suddenly be the center of attention. "He seemed to know Mateo."

When Arlo gets there, he's still wearing the same shirt he had on at the restaurant. He's not alone. He's got the CSI guy in tow.

Fisk says, "I'm going to have to dust your kitchen for prints again. Sorry."

"He was all over the chocolate processing room too." I make a sweeping gesture towards the back. "Every time y'all wind up here, I end up having to throw things away."

"I'll be careful," Fisk says as he heads into the kitchen. After a few minutes, Fisk comes back. He's holding a plastic bag in his gloved hand. "Do you recognize this cash? It was rolled up in a corner of your stock room."

"I've never seen that much money all together in my life." I look over at Carmen. "Do you know anything about this?"

She shakes her head hard enough to send her ponytail swinging. "You know I'm broke. If I had money like that, I wouldn't be driving such an old wreck."

"Are you still thinking that Mateo was doing something illegal out of the shop?" I ask Arlo. That suddenly seems a lot more plausible. I still find it hard to believe – but maybe I didn't know Mateo as well as I thought I did. After all, he's been working here for less than a month. But even if that's true – and the evidence is circumstantial – I still can't believe he would have killed someone.

"It's the most plausible explanation." After that, Arlo starts asking the questions. Who was here? When? In what parts of the shop? What did we see? He doesn't seem keen on answering questions, though, especially about where the police officially think Mateo might be. Arlo goes to visit the restroom before heading out. When he comes back, he looks troubled. Arlo walks over to me, and asks, "Have you been in your office tonight, Lis?"

"No." Given the expression on his face, alarm is rising in me. "Why?"

"Come see, but don't touch anything until Fisk has a chance to look around in there."

"That doesn't sound good." I follow Arlo down the hall, in the opposite direction from the bean room.

He leads the way to my office, which is past the two bathrooms. The door is open – and it looks like the lock is busted. Objects from on top of the filing cabinet have fallen into the doorway, and rolled out into the hallway. There's paper all over the floor, like someone dumped out the one drawer of my filing cabinet that has paper files – mainly job applications and old order forms. Most everything else I do is electronic. The other things I store in the drawers in here – scratched chocolate molds, party decorations, plastic cacao pods – have been rifled through, scattered, and in at least one case broken.

Our intruder was in here looking for something – in a hurry.

Arlo asks, "Does anything seem missing?"

I shake my head. "No. Just messed up."

"Good." Arlo leads me back up the hallway. "I'll make sure we get the scene here processed tonight, so you can open in the morning. It's the least I can do after – you know."

I do know. After his future brother-in-law had ditched me mid-date.

It feels odd to be driving to the hotel instead of the house, after the crazy evening I've had. I just hope my bed is in one piece, so I can have a shower and then fall face first into it.

Knightley has been closed in in my room – Aunt Naomi wasn't sure it would be safe to give him free run of the entire building, which still has some severely damaged areas.

The hotel isn't huge, but there are easily fifty rooms. The suite I've chosen is on the fourth floor – which is the top floor of this building. It has both a bedroom and a loft.

It's been a long time since I had my own living room. I need to go shopping – when I have the money to afford furniture. The need to budget is hitting me all over the place today.

The lop is hiding under my bed. Knightley has pooped in the middle of the floor, a sure sign that he's nervous. Plus he hates sitting on a bare floor. So much for just going to sleep. I clean up the poop balls, and then I unroll the rug he likes and put it in front of the bed. I sit down on the rug and hold out a hand to my bunny. He comes out and leans against me.

I check in on my social media accounts, while I idly pet Knightley. There have been a ton of likes for the behind-the-scenes shots of Carmen's friends making gift baskets. And I've gotten a couple of messages asking for pricing for more custom gift orders. Despite the recent bad publicity. Which is a relief. I guess since I'm not a suspect this time, people aren't as worried about being contaminated by my shop's reputation.

I check the local news links, to make sure I haven't missed anything else about the case – or about my shop. There's a lot of supposition about Mateo, who remains the main suspect in Fabin's murder. Nobody seems to have a reason for why Mateo would have killed Fabin. I'm convinced there isn't one.

The police are pursuing other leads, though there's no mention of that on the news. Not even of the fake delivery guy who had broken into my shop.

Of course, this murder isn't the only thing the police have to deal with. There was a car accident on the far end of the island tonight. And there was also a break-in at a local pharmacy. Which reminds me of Mateo, out there somewhere without his meds. I can almost imagine his kidnapper breaking into a pharmacy to get the drugs needed to keep Mateo alive. But why would a kidnapper do that? There hadn't been a ransom note.

Or any sign that the killer is even still on this island. Unless Refrigerator, a.k.a. the delivery guy, is also the killer. But somehow, I don't think so. He'd gone through a lot of trouble not to hurt me when he had run through the bean room and out into the night.

Arlo had said he'd talked to the real Leslie Franks – and that he was going to look into the fake one. A woman can shoot someone just as easily as a man, but she hadn't struck me as a killer, either. I could be wrong. Still. She gave me her card. Leslie's card. Or whatever.

I take it out, and I punch the number written on it into my phone. I half expect the number to be disconnected, like in a bad spy movie. But instead a woman answers – the same one I'd spoken to previously.

"Hello?" she says, sounding sleepy.

"Who are you really?" I ask. "Do you know where Mateo is?"

There's silence on the other end of the line for a long time. Then she says, "That money the police found in your shop tonight. What did Fabin buy with it? Was he getting into stolen antiques again?"

"What do you mean again?" I ask. Though if the break-in hadn't been on the news, the only way she could know about that money is if she'd bugged the place.

"Illegal imports. He's done it before. He would see something beautiful at a museum, and pay some idiot guard to make it his." She sighs. "Fabin was just an impulsive kid, acting out to get attention from a father he believed loved his cousin more. He would have grown out of it. Nobody deserves to die over the stupid kind of stuff he pulled."

"Who are you?" I ask again.

"Someone with a vested interest in seeing Fabin's killer brought to justice."

"Good," I say. "We're on the same side."

"Let's hope so," she says. "I'll be waiting for you to prove that. So far, what I've seen hasn't been promising. Especially as reported by your pet blogger. Little Ash. So cute that you can keep him in your pocket."

Then she hangs up.

I guess the pet blogger reference means Ash has another update – though she couldn't be more wrong about my relationship to him. I brace myself, and then I open his blog. This time, he's implying that the police have uncovered a drug ring involving my employees. There's even a photo taken from outside the window showing me scowling at the cops. I'm painted as the victim this time, a femme fatal and detective rolled into one. There's all this bad poetry insinuating that Mateo's hard and fast lifestyle caught up to him. I want to strangle Ash.

But he's right – something had been going on in my shop that I didn't know about. Something that could lead to a roll of cash in the stock room. There has to be connections between all of this. I Google Fabin and Mateo's names together, thinking maybe there will be an article about a former arrest, or some project they'd undertaken together. But there's nothing. And Mateo's background check for getting the job at Greetings and Felicitations had come back clean. He'd even had an excellent credit record.

I do a search for Fabin by himself, and I find a kid who used to love horses and to jump competitively – until he turned fifteen, and his aunt and uncle were killed. There are a number of articles about Leslie coming to live with the family. And suddenly Fabin stopped riding. He started ditching school. He ran away from home and was missing for twelve very tense days, with the news coverage more and more convinced that he'd been killed. When he was found living in a bus terminal in Tucson, his parents had expressed their gratitude to the media for his safe return.

He'd been acting out, quite publicly ever since. Fake Leslie is right. It sounds like Fabin was going through a phase. He was a troubled kid, with something in his past causing him a great deal of pain.

He shouldn't have wound up with a hole in his chest, leaned up against the wall in the dark.

# Chapter Ten
## *Wednesday*

Logan and I are at the shop early the next morning. I'm waiting for my equipment delivery, and he's waiting for results on the ID check he ran on our intruder, who left a very clear print on the back door. The police dusted the whole place for prints while they were here last night, but Fisk had done his best to clean up.

Carmen will be in after the hardware store opens. She's going to try and find a replacement cord for the small melanger. It doesn't look like there was any additional damage to the machine. If the store has what I need in stock, it actually shouldn't be that hard to repair it – and to use a little heat to salvage the partially processed chocolate inside. Too bad it is the smaller of the two melangers.

Logan is using a device to search for the bug we're both convinced Fake Leslie left behind. He finally finds it, taped to the inside of one of the table legs where she'd been sitting. Logan smashes the bug. If Fake Leslie wants to talk to me, all she has to do is call me. Since I called her, she has my number.

Logan continues waving the device around. Finally, he says, "I think that was the only bug she had time to drop."

"Great," I say. "So she was only spying on me a little."

Logan snorts out a laugh. "It comes with the territory. She thinks you know something about Fabin's death that you're not telling. In her situation, I might easily do the same thing."

"You spy on people?" I'm bantering, but Logan takes the question seriously.

"I have, in the past. Most of the time, what you learn is things you'd rather not know."

I gesture at Logan's phone, which is sitting next to his coffee cup on one of the tables. It has been lighting up. "What did you find out this time?"

"Don't know. Let me check." He pulls up the information that came in. He turns the phone screen around, showing me the photo that came back connected to the fingerprint. "This the guy?"

It's definitely the delivery guy from Monday. Refrigerator's real name is Donnie Marks. Logan scrolls through pages and pages worth of information about the guy. "Looks like he specializes in identity creation – and identity theft. You're lucky if all he did was browse your e-mails. But he's got a shop here in town."

"A tech shop?" I imagine a place filled with spy gadgets.

"No, actually it's a doughnut shop. Donnie's Doughnuts. Check it out. The Mixed Plate bloggers did a whole profile on the place while they were here. They left out the part about the whole crime-in-the-back-room business."

The Mixed Platers are a family of bloggers who travel the world, sampling different cuisines and getting to know people. Their kids are adorable. And the whole family had taught me something about living life authentically.

Logan shows me the article. It's good to see Tam Binh's face. She and I still text from time to time, but I need to remember to check in with her blog more often. According to Tam Binh, Donnie's Doughnuts is famous for his maple bacon doughnut breakfast sandwich, which looks gorgeous in the picture. I don't often get doughnuts, but when I do, I go to a different shop, one more about traditional flavors and rich black coffee. I hadn't even realized there was a gourmet doughnut shop on the island.

"Do you think we should go talk to him?" I ask.

"Probably not right now," Logan says. "If we're going to have half a chance of getting him talking, we want to get there when it isn't busy. Otherwise, he'll have an excuse to blow us off."

"So like right before they close?" I ask.

Logan nods.

There's a noise out back, of a truck making its way down the alley. I go and open my door. Sure enough, it's my melangers. Yay! I grab my purse, and then rush out into the alley, literally clapping my hands, I'm so excited.

Logan appears in the doorway, scowling. "Felicity, come back here. You need to exercise more caution approaching strange vehicles. Considering the situation."

I wave a hand at him. "You're not my security guy anymore, now are you?"

He grins in a way that looks mischievous. "Sure I am. I just volunteered."

I roll my eyes. Still, I don't try to stop him when he steps between me and the truck. The woman who gets out is young, and she's obviously been made up heavily for the cameras. A guy on foot has been following the vehicle up the alley, filming. Because for them, it's all about the local color and the humanitarian aid aspect of the story. I try to organize what I will say to them. I need to offer samples of my chocolate, talk up the shop. I probably should have on more makeup myself, instead of just the touch of mascara and lip gloss I'd managed this morning.

The girl has a tablet with an attached credit card reader.

Logan says, "We're going to need to see some form of ID."

The woman breaks into giggles. She's even younger than I first thought – maybe twenty or twenty-two – and she looks absolutely awed looking at Logan. I can practically see a thought bubble over her head reading, *He's cute!*

Logan grins at her – and an unexpected spike of jealousy goes through my chest. I know. I told him I wasn't ready to date. But I just realized that I don't want him going off and finding someone else before I *am* ready. Which isn't fair to him. And is totally confusing. And this is a bad moment to realize something like that, with a stranger with a camera taking random clips and stills. My cheeks feel hot, and I'm sure it must look like I have a fever.

Logan verifies the girl's identity, quipping, "You look young for twenty-three, Trish" as he reads the info off her license.

This woman is here to help me save my business. She hasn't even said anything. And I still have a juvenile urge to pull out her hair, because the guy I kinda like but can't commit to is kinda sorta flirting with her. I'm in my thirties. I need to get past this kind of thing. I need to just suck it up and ask Logan to be my date to Autumn's wedding. But I'm still not ready to do that. Still not ready to admit I want to move on from a lost love and a cold grave – not even to myself, even if Logan is warm and alive and funny and caring.

Instead, because I am an emotional coward, I step between Logan and the woman and tell her, "You are such a lifesaver. Greetings and Felicitations just took one of our biggest orders yet, and this machinery is what I need to deliver it on time." For the benefit of the camera, I add, "We do bean to bar chocolate and orders for custom chocolate gifts. Logan here is one of our regular customers, with a standing order."

The camera guy turns towards Logan, who puts his hands in his pockets and says, "Shop local, you know? The chocolate's excellent, and my logo on the wrappers looks great."

I couldn't have asked for a better endorsement. And there's this little bubble of pride in me because Logan's the one who said it. I am definitely getting way too attached to this guy to pretend I don't care whether or not he's my plus one for Autumn's event.

I need to focus on the cameras right now though. Trish and I make brief small talk, then I take my credit card out of my purse and let her swipe it. She frowns at me, and then swipes it again.

She makes a slashing gesture at the guy to cut off whatever he's doing with the cameras. She says softly, "Mrs. Koerber, your card has been declined."

"That's impossible," I say.

She gives me a *what can you do*? shrug and asks, "Would you like to put it on a different card?"

Embarrassment flows through me. "I only carry one card." If I hadn't just bought the optical sorter, taken the sourcing trip to Peru, and helped my aunt with a down payment on a dilapidated hotel, I would have the cash to cover this emergency handy in my checking account. And once I deliver on the gift baskets, I'll easily be able to pay it off. Even if it was just a different part of the month, I'd have enough cash on hand, and then some. But at this moment, I'm flummoxed. "Just give me a second."

I step off to the side and put in a call to the credit card company. I get put on hold for four minutes – during which I can feel everyone watching me. Then, as the people waiting for me fidget, I have a rather circular conversation with my account representative, who tells me that, due to the story on the news about a second murder on my property, I am now considered more of a financial risk. My credit limit has been dramatically decreased – without notice. When I protest that this purchase is necessary to keep me in business, he tells me that that's the point, and that legally my credit limit can be adjusted at any time.

My neck feels tight, and there's pressure at the bridge of my nose, but I manage not to say anything I'd regret. I just hang up. I look over at Trish and her little swipe device, the only thing standing between me and completing my spa order. She doesn't look like she's going to be willing to negotiate. "I'm sorry. I've just been informed that my credit limit has been decreased." I don't mention that it is because my creditors have decided that my shop is a murder magnet, which is totally unfair.

"I'm very sorry, Mrs. Koerber," Trish says.

The camera guy looks glum. "So you're saying we made a six-hour trip all the way out here for nothing?"

"I'd like to give you some truffles. And I'll call Mrs. Guidry across the street, and arrange for you two to have lunch, courtesy of Greetings and Felicitations." I turn to go back into the shop, trying to keep my shoulders from slumping in defeat. But it feels like there's a bar of lead weighing down my stomach. I just – can't. I tried everything to keep my business moving forward. I'm going to have to call the spa and tell Serena that there's no way I can complete this order. Which will kill the potential for future orders.

Logan takes my arm. "Let me pay for it."

I laugh. Despite the serious look on his face, he has to be joking. "You can't afford that."

"Why not?" He makes a face.

I suddenly feel embarrassed. "Because you don't live like someone who has money to burn. You're a puddle jump pilot."

"Who used to be private security to the stars." He grimaces at the memory. "I haven't exactly had a lot to spend it on."

He's not joking. Wow. I look at his earnest green eyes – and I re-evaluate everything I know about him. "I guess I've made some assumptions."

"Like maybe you assumed that I'd chosen to relocate to Galveston because the beaches in Maui and Santa Monica had been a bit out of my price range." Logan laughs. "I like the beach here. Though my reason for choosing it would sound stupid."

"Try me," I say.

"It's the pirate thing." He looks down at the ground. "After I left the security firm, I was a bit lost. I took a gig salvage diving in the Gulf Coast, and once I started diving near Texas, I got caught up exploring the history of this place. When I found out that the legends about pirate treasure on this island had some basis, I wanted to come check it out. Someone told me about a hanger for sale that was perfect for my planes, and the business just sort of happened over beers one night in a bar."

"That's not stupid." It's actually kind of endearing. Though I still have people waiting for us to make a decision, so I don't have time to dwell on it. "But I can't be in debt to you." Things are already awkward between us. "And I don't need charity. Taking it would mean this business isn't really succeeding."

Logan starts to say something. The he snaps his jaw shut and just stares at me for a good long time. "Fine," he finally says. "In that case, I'd like to invest in Greetings and Felicitations. I'll cover the melangers, and dump in some cash for advertising. And I'll trust you to cut me in for whatever's fair." It's like when I'd hired him as private security. He hadn't wanted to talk specific amounts of money then either – just whatever I decided his services were worth.

It's a reasonable proposition – and yet. Emotion rises inside me, making it hard to swallow. Starting a craft chocolate business had been mine and Kevin's dream. The name of the shop is even a slant reference to Charlotte's Web, one of Kevin's favorite books growing up. He'd given the potential shop that name after his accident, when he'd realized he was going to die. And then it had become just my dream – mine alone. The idea of letting someone into it – even someone as thoughtful as Logan – somehow feels like failure. I'd just been thinking that I want Logan to be a part of my life. But what if that never really happens? Or what if it does and then something goes wrong and we're stuck in a business partnership?

Tears sparkle in my eyes. I try to wipe them away, but Logan has already noticed.

He looks hurt. "Well, if you feel that way about it, forget I offered."

He starts to go back inside the shop. Leaving me to try and negotiate with Trish and her camera guy.

"Wait!" When he turns back towards me, I say, "There's a lot of emotions for me tied up in making Felicitations a success. If you're okay with that, I think you would be a good asset to the business."

He forces a smile, but I can see that he's still not completely sure this is a good decision after all. Still, he goes over to Trish, takes out his wallet and lets her swipe his credit card.

My heart breaks, just a little. There's no going back from this. The business is now mine – and Logan's. When Logan turns, he sees the grief in my eyes, and walks back past me, muttering, "Don't worry. I can be a very silent partner."

"Hey, wait," I say, but he steps into the shop. Eh, boy. This is going to be one awkward day.

I smile and shake hands with the lady delivering the equipment, then the camera guy gets lots of shots of us trundling the equipment inside. I'm a bit surprised Logan doesn't even come into the back to help. And then once the people from Weatherford leave Guidry's – armed with a list of other local businesses they should check out between now and lunchtime – I go to find Logan.

He's sitting at one of the tables in the front of the shop, peering out the plate glass window.

"Who's that?" he asks.

I follow his gaze. Mrs. Guidry is outside her café, sweeping the sidewalk. She pauses and looks over at us. I wave, and she goes back to sweeping. "That's my new neighbor. When the space across the way opened up a few weeks ago, she moved her business from over on Avenue O."

"She looks guilty of something," Logan says.

"Who? Her?" I watch Mrs. Guidry pat her curly gray hair. "She's a gossip, and a busybody, but she's harmless."

"She keeps looking over here. I'm getting a vibe."

"You do vibes?" I'm a little surprised. He always seems so logical.

He shrugs. "Don't you?"

"I don't think so." We're already getting a few lookie-loos hanging out on the sidewalk outside, waiting for us to open. Nothing like the crowd from yesterday, but still, I hope Carmen gets here soon. I've got a lot of work to do in the back. But first, I have to make things right with Logan. I grab a plate and samples of each of my chocolates from the covered dishes on the display shelves. Then I pour him a cup of water, and put the plate and cup in front of him. "Let me give you a taste of what you've gotten yourself into."

"Felicity, you don't have to do this. I feel like I've overstepped my bounds here."

I slide into the chair opposite his, ignoring the fact that one of the girls hanging out on the sidewalk is snapping pictures of us. "Look, Logan. I've spent a long time putting my life together after Kevin died. Change wasn't easy for me before I lost him. And it's worse now. But that doesn't mean that change is bad – or that having a business partner is a bad idea. This could be good for both of us. We could even start booking tours for you out of the shop."

He flinches, and I realize that what I've just suggested would mean he'd have to give me access to his calendar. Which he doesn't look even close to ready to do. I start to apologize, but he puts a hand on mine from across the table. "Okay. I see what you mean. We each have our own ways of doing things. Let's just take this one step at a time, and see how it works. If it doesn't, you can buy me out when you get paid for this order."

"Fair enough," I tell him. "But I'm serious about showing you how the business functions. You've been incredibly generous, and I want to give this partnership a fair chance. First we're going to taste chocolate, and then we will prep and roast beans and get them into those new melangers you just bought us."

I'm almost done teaching Logan how to look for flavor notes in chocolate, and letting him identify the notes he finds in each of the chocolates I've made, when Carmen breezes in carrying a bag from the hardware store.

She shakes it at me. "One cord, just like you asked for." Then she hesitates. "What happened here."

"A lot." I gesture at Logan. "Meet your new boss. Logan just became a partner in the company."

# Chapter Eleven
## *Still Wednesday*

I'm half afraid Carmen's going to be upset about having someone else to report to, but instead, she moves over to Logan and puts a hand on his shoulder. "That's great! I'm going to love having someone new to taste test for me. How do you feel about dulce de leche? I'm going to make these cakes that-"

Logan holds up a hand. "Now wait a second. I don't know how much time I'm actually going to be spending at the shop." When he takes in her disappointed expression, he adds, "But I can make it a point to stop by as often as I can."

That thought makes me giddy, but I turn and ask Carmen, "Why are you working on so many new recipes?"

She grins at me. "I was going to get the project a little farther along before I told you, but I'm working on a Greetings and Felicitations cookbook. I'll make sure you sign off on everything, of course, before I try to sell it. If you're even okay with that."

"That sounds amazing!" It also explains why she's been so proactive with helping grow the business. I would never want to be a pastry chef myself, and I would never want to write a cookbook. I'd been worried I was going to lose Carmen, that she would want to leave to open her own business, or take a high-profile job, but if all she wants is the opportunity to have a more creative role here – I'm excited.

Which makes it confusing why I'm so nervous about letting Logan change our dynamic.

Carmen agrees to man the counter and the coffee station, while I take Logan into the bean room to show him the equipment.

"The first thing we have to do is remove any debris from the beans. Which is easy now that we have this sorter." There's a partial bag of beans left from when Carmen and Mateo had experimented with using this machine. I upend the bag into the hopper. There are rhythmic sounds like puffs of air as the machine starts working, and beans start coming out the other side.

I then turn to the big barrel roaster. "Roasting cacao is a lot like roasting coffee."

Logan steps closer to examine the machine. 'I've never done that either." I know he likes to cook, but that would be a step beyond what most home cooks do. "I have roasted peanuts in the shell before. Is there any similarity?"

"Actually, you can think of it a little the same way. You know how peanuts have a papery skin on the outside of each nut that can be removed? Cacao beans are the same – there's a layer that has to come off after the beans are roasted, or it will ruin the chocolate."

Logan is standing very close to me, watching me speak. I am suddenly aware of how close he is, how good his aftershave smells. Part of me wants to kiss him and see what happens – and part of me wants to flee to the safety of the front of the shop. Because if I try to take our personal relationship to a different level, and I'm not reading his signals right, that could make for an extremely awkward business relationship. Especially since there's no way I can buy him out yet.

There's a spark of tension in the air. I know I'm not imagining that. And I'm not imagining the eye contact that I can't seem to break.

Before I can decide what to do about it, there's a clattering noise, like the sound of more rocks being sorted out than beans. It's normal to have some rocks and other debris, but this is ridiculous. I may have to have words with my supplier. Logan and I both rush over to see what is happening. Most of the lumps falling into the debris bucket are faceted black stones. But mixed in with that, there's also a bullet.

I suck in a breath. There's something so real about seeing that bullet up close. "Odds that that's from the same kind of gun that killed Fabin?"

Logan grabs a paper towel from the roll mounted by the sink. He uses it to pick up the bullet. "It looks about right, but I doubt it. This probably went into the bag when it was packed in Peru."

That sends a chill down my spine. What if someone back in Peru got hurt, so these stones could wind up here? "Well, I guess we just figured out why somebody would risk so much to break in and steal a bag of cacao beans." I gesture down at the glittering rocks. Each one has to be ten, fifteen carats, easily, all finely cut gemstones. And they're still spilling out of the sorter. "If those really are black diamonds, how much do you think they're worth?"

Logan stares into the bucket. Then he groans and brings a hand to his forehead. "I'm afraid that my first act as part owner of this company is going to be calling the police so they can seize more of our raw materials as evidence."

Fake Leslie had said that Fabin was into illegal imports. Was it possible that he had commissioned the theft of the diamonds? Possibly from Refrigerator? Then it would make sense that Refrigerator would be upset about the wrong bag of beans being delivered to my shop. But – if he even was the guy who had showed up at Mateo's other job – why ask Mateo for them back instead of asking him to pass them along? And if Fabin was the client, why kill him?

It feels like all of this was a mistake somewhere along the line – which is having the unintended effect of threatening to ruin my business.

My fists ball up in frustration. After all of this, there still has to be a way to finish this order. I ask, "What if we put the beans from this bag and the debris bucket over to the side, and run a different bag of beans through the sorter? After all, this is the second batch of chocolate I've made from the same stock of beans." Technically the third, if you count the mess that had spilled all over the floor. "Chances are that the other bags are evidence-free."

Logan takes a moment to consider this. Then he gestures to the sorter. "I won't tell if you won't."

Carmen pokes her head into the bean room. "Everything okay in here?"

"Just fine," I tell her. "We're about to call the police again. But we'll try to get them to come in the back way."

"Are you sure?" Carmen asks. "We had a bit of a rush this morning, and several customers mentioned Ash's blog. I'm sure they'd get a kick out of seeing the police."

I groan. "Why doesn't ash have anything better to do?"

Carmen laughs. "You ought to invite him in here to do a formal interview."

"Oh, but no," I say.

But Logan says, "That's not a horrible idea. At least then you'd know that whatever he's reporting about you would be accurate."

I shudder. "But the idea of him in here, touching things."

"This is a business, Felicity," Logan says. "You're going to have to deal with people you don't like."

I sigh. I'm already starting to regret letting Logan have a say in the way things are running around here.

We work for a couple of hours, until finally Logan dusts off his hands and declares, "I need real food for breakfast. Now would be a good time to go bug Mrs. Guidry."

I know full well that Logan wants to question Mrs. Guidry more than he needs to sample her jambalaya.

But we are at a stopping point. We've gotten the beans roasted, cracked, winnowed and into the melangers. All three machines are cranking away in a satisfying manner. We've printed the wrappers for the rest of the Peru bars, so they're ready when the chocolate is. It's been a productive morning. I check my phone. It's close to eleven o'clock. "More like an early lunch. Let me see if Carmen wants us to bring her back something."

I usually have a lunch date with Autumn on Wednesday at our favorite diner, to catch up and share how our lives are going. I call her, but she doesn't answer. So I leave a voicemail, telling her I can't make it today.

As I step out from the back, Patsy's brother Wallace stands up from one of the tables and grins sheepishly at me. I can still see the family resemblance between him and Patsy, despite his gawky ears. I hadn't really expected to see him again, after the way he had bailed at dinner, but I try to hide the surprise on my face and keep my expression neutral. I wonder how long he's been waiting for me.

He heads for the counter.

"Felicity," Wallace says. "I am so sorry about last night. I brought you a little gift to make up for it."

He puts a long, narrow box on the counter.

"Wallace. You shouldn't have," I stammer. I can't believe that he's here, now – with Logan standing right there. Wanting to talk about our failed date. It couldn't be more awkward.

"Go on. Open it," Wallace prompts.

Not sure whether to be flattered he bought me a make-up gift or offended he thinks he can by my forgiveness, I lift the pale pink lid. I'm looking at a diamond tennis bracelet, with little spheres of sapphire in between the diamonds. "Wallace," I say again. "I can't accept this. We barely know each other."

"Of course you can. I can afford it, and I know you like sapphires. And diamonds."

I splutter out a laugh, thinking about the diamonds in the back of the shop. But that's not what he's talking about. "How do you know what I like?"

"I asked Patsy, and she asked Arlo."

Okay. Weird that Arlo had told him I like the same kinds of stones as in the ring Arlo had given me all those years ago. Or maybe not – Arlo had known me well enough back then to have realized his grandmother's sapphire had been perfect for me.

The bracelet is gorgeous, and was just the kind of thing I would have chosen for myself – if I had money to burn. Which is why I can't take it – even if I really want it. I try to close the box, to give it back to him. But he takes the bracelet out and catches my wrist, lightly.

"I told you I can afford it. And I want you to have it, even if you decide you don't want to have anything to do with me." He fastens the bracelet around my wrist.

"What is it you do again?" I ask stupidly. I can't remember if Patsy even told me.

I cut a glance at Logan, who is standing in the doorway between the kitchen and the front of the shop. He has his arms across his chest, leaning against the frame with an impassive look on his face.

Wallace says, "I'm in imports."

Which echoes something Leslie said to me last night, about Fabin being into illegal imports – by which she meant stolen goods. But surely that's not what Wallace is talking about. I should take the bracelet off, tell Wallace I'm not interested in the type of guy who leaves a date without even saying goodbye. But I find myself asking. "What kind of imports?"

"Furniture mostly. It's really boring," Wallace assures me, and I find my smile turning into something real. "I do it because I like to travel. That's why Patsy thought we would hit it off. She told me you have this amazing map collection. I'd love to see it sometime."

"I guess, maybe," I say noncommittally.

"Well, *maybe* we can discuss it over lunch. Patsy has recommended several restaurants for me to try before I leave the island. I'm in the mood to check out an oyster bar."

"I'm sorry. I already have lunch plans." It's not a lie. And I'm looking forward to spending time with Logan.

Wallace frowns. "Okay, it's last minute. That's fair."

I hesitate. I don't want to date Wallace. As charming as he is, he's about to be Arlo's brother-in-law. And if I was ready to date anyone – I have a more exciting prospect glowering in the doorway. But I don't want to hurt his feelings – or Patsy's, now that Patsy and I are becoming friends. Or potentially lose an in to talk with Arlo about the case. Feeling somewhat mercenary, I say, "This has been a crazy week. I have a private party to put on tomorrow night. But I can spare half an hour for coffee."

At least this guy will be leaving the island soon, and life will be that much less complicated. I can give him the bracelet back tomorrow, and make it clear that I'm not interested in a long-distance relationship. Because I'm not. He's dorky and charming – but something about him makes him not for me. Unless I'm just doing the same thing with him that I did with Logan – using my widow's grief to avoid change.

Wallace starts to leave, and I glance over to ask Logan if he's ready to go to lunch. But he's disappeared from the doorway. Surely he has to realize that I only said yes to Wallace because of the case.

The bracelet really is gorgeous. I just wish it was from Logan, not Wallace.

Carmen comes over to me and whispers, "You should have seen the look on Logan's face, when you took an expensive gift from this guy, but wouldn't let him buy you those melangers this morning. If your plan is to make him jealous, I'd say it's working."

I hadn't even considered that. I really am making a mess of this.

But before I can go find Logan and try to make this right, Drake Parker, the love of Autumn's life, comes into the shop. He's a tall lanky black guy, wearing expensive shoes and a tasteful slate gray tie. Smart and a generous dose of eye candy – it's easy to see why Autumn's smitten. He comes up to the counter. "I wanted to thank you for putting together this party tomorrow. I know this has to feel sudden. But I want you to know, you're always welcome to spend time with us. I'm not one of those guys who only wants to have couple friends."

"Um, thanks."

He hangs his head. "I'm making it awkward now, aren't I? I'm sorry. Autumn loves you. She means the world to me. Which makes you important to me too."

"That's sweet. We will have to make a plan to all hang out sometime." I take out a plate and give him a truffle. "Autumn says you like a nice bourbon. I do a whole line of Cajun inspired truffles, and this one has boozed up pecan."

"Thanks." He takes his plate over to a table and takes out his phone. A few seconds later, my phone buzzes with a joint text thread between me, him and Autumn with an initial text that says, *To compare schedules.*

I have to admit, I feel a bit better about him. Not just any guy would have come in to talk to me like that. But that's just a quick impression. I don't really *know* him yet.

And I still think he and Autumn are rushing things.

I go into the back. Logan is talking to Arlo, who came in so quietly I didn't even notice. Arlo's by himself this time, holding the bucket with the diamonds in it with gloved hands. He gestures with it. "We have to stop meeting like this."

"I'm just giving you leads to solve the murder." I pick up a stray diamond which has made its way onto the floor. "I don't suppose you're handing out updates on the case?"

"Not a chance," Arlo says. He turns to Logan. "Hanlon, talk some sense into her. This is dangerous business."

"I don't have any control over what she does," Logan says. I may be imagining it, but I think he sounds a little hurt. Over what, I'm not sure. Me accepting the bracelet, maybe?

We answer Arlo's questions about what we were doing this morning, and where we found the diamonds. Logan talks Arlo out of impounding the rest of our stock – with the caveat that we run the entire shipment of beans through the sorter over the next couple of days. I don't quite understand the subtext running between them. But I'm guessing it has something to do with the fact that Logan used to be into some kind of ops and cops stuff that left him with friends in high places.

As soon as Arlo leaves, I ask Logan, "You ready to go talk to Mrs. Guidry?"

He looks troubled for a moment, then his face clears and it's like the tension never happened. "Sure. I'm starved."

I go to tell Carmen we're leaving. She says she's fine, even if we're gone for the rest of the day. I take a look around the shop. Carmen's right. There's nothing going on right now that she can't handle. Even the death groupies.

We have a small sofa in one corner of the shop, with the intention that people will sit and read, or bring in their laptops and do work. Currently, there's a couple sitting on it, taking selfies. The girl is wearing black lipstick, and the guy has on a spiked dog collar. They're posing with a tabloid newspaper showing a grisly photo of Fabin's body leaned up against the wall outside. Where did that photo even come from? Had someone stopped and snapped a picture between the time I'd called the cops and when they'd showed up? Or had the killer taken it, and then sold evidence of his handiwork? I shudder, thinking about how cold someone would have to be to do something like that.

The guy shifts and makes an unhappy noise. "What's wrong with this sofa?"

Nothing, as far as I know. But he runs his hand between the couch cushions and comes out with a cell phone.

The girl gasps. "Could that be the dead guy's phone?"

That's a wild assumption to make. But they're both staring at it reverently, as though they might have found a sacred artifact.

"If it is, don't you think it belongs in the hands of the police?" Logan asks. He's made his way over to the sofa. He holds out his hand, and the guy only hesitates for a moment before putting the phone into it.

Logan comes back behind the counter, where I'm still standing with Carmen. He spends a few minutes doing something to the phone's lock screen – then it lets him in. The background image is a jaguar, in a very familiar pose.

"This is Mateo's phone," I say.

"The missing guy," the goth girl says, blatantly eavesdropping.

"Yes, the missing guy," I repeat, not really caring if they're listening in or not. "This could help find him."

Logan pulls up the phone's camera roll. "Well, that's ominous."

He shows me a blurry picture of a guy in a dress shirt, a gun held loosely in his hand. Unfortunately, the guy's head isn't visible in the picture, which looks like it was taken by someone sitting on the sofa. With the blur and the bad lighting, it's impossible to tell much about the guy.

But I can't help but imagine Mateo, being threatened and forced to sit quietly, trying to snap a picture of his potential killer, and then shoving the phone in between the cushions, hoping someone would find the evidence. There's no way to know if that picture had been taken before or after Fabin had been killed. If it had been after, then Mateo must have been terrified, knowing he was a witness to the crime. So why hadn't Fabin's killer murdered Mateo too and left a bullet hole in my sofa? Did Mateo know something important? Or did he have something the killer wanted?

It's possible that I had interrupted the killer by coming back, and he could have taken Mateo with him for some desperate reason.

I swipe back a photo, hoping that maybe Mateo got a clearer shot of the guy. But the image is of a heron, taking off in slow motion flight. So obviously something Mateo had taken before coming in to work that day. I still scroll through more of the photos on the phone, trying to put together something that makes sense. Before Mateo's trip to the marsh, he'd been at a party.

There are pictures of random people dancing. Of a table laid out with bowls of soup. And then a shot that makes me gasp. Someone else has taken Mateo's phone to take a picture of three couples posing for the camera – Mateo and Haruka, Miles and a red-headed girl I've never met – and Enrique and a black girl who looks like the opposite of Fabin's vapid girlfriend.

"What?" Logan asks, peering at the picture.

There's a lot to unpack here. Not the least of which is that Mateo has his arms around Haruka's shoulders when Haruka is supposed to be dating Nelson. But I point to Enrique. "That's the guy Fabin was staying with. Funny, when I talked to him, he didn't mention that he knew Mateo."

Honestly, I hadn't imagined that Mateo had any friends, since he'd been in town for so short a time, and seemed busy working two jobs and keeping a home aquarium. I guess I was wrong.

Logan says, "After lunch, I guess we need to go talk to our football playing chef again."

"I agree." I grab a zipper-top bag and drop Mateo's phone into it. We're obviously going to have to make a side trip to the police station, since that picture of the guy with the gun could turn out to be an important piece of evidence. "But I want to talk to Haruka too."

Since Logan's not about to be deterred from questioning Mrs. Guidry, I text Miles and ask him if he can meet us there. He was at that party too. Maybe he has some insight into the relationships between everyone involved.

I see Drake watching us. The plate in front of him is long empty, but he's as rapt as if he was watching a television drama.

Maybe I approve of him a bit more than I did before. But after the weirdness with the death-groupies, I'm not sure he still approves of me.

He smiles, though, and half waves when he sees me looking at him. Carmen brings him a to-go coffee. He tips it at me and then heads for the door.

Logan and I follow close behind, so Drake holds it open for us. He says, "Autumn said you were an amateur detective now. I thought she was kidding."

"Not on purpose," I say.

He laughs. "We don't all find our talents on purpose now, do we?"

He gets in his car and drives away.

# Chapter Twelve
## *Still Wednesday*

I lead the way down to the corner, where we cross the street according to the traffic signal. Logan looks vaguely amused. I guess because it would have been shorter to just cut across the street instead of walking half a block down and then half a block back up.

Mrs. Guidry's café is doing decent business, but there are still a couple of empty tables. She waves us over to one.

When she brings over menus, she says, "Always nice to see two good-looking young people on a date."

I'm about to say something about being flattered that she thinks 32 is still young when Logan says – a little too quickly, "It's not a date."

That stings. But I try not to let it show on my face. I had warned him that Mrs. Guidry is a busybody. He's probably trying to head off gossip before it can get started. I say, "We actually came over to talk to you, Mrs. Guidry."

"Me?" She sounds surprised.

Logan says conspiratorially, "You were over here across the street when the murder happened. You must have seen something."

Her smile disappears. "How do you know I was still here?"

Logan shrugs. "Let's just call it a hunch."

Mrs. Guidry plops her order pad on the table and sinks into one of the chairs opposite us. She drops her voice to a stage whisper. "What if I did see something? Can you follow up on it without telling the police I'm the one who told you?"

"Now that depends on what it is," Logan says. Before he was a bodyguard, Logan was a cop. And I already found out the hard way that there are certain secrets he just won't keep. "But if there's any way we can keep your name out of it, we will."

She nods. "I was over here tidying up after close – just minding my own business – when I heard shouting across the street. There were four people coming out of your shop. I couldn't see them very well, but there was a lady and a man, who seemed to be pushing two other men towards a car. One of them tried to get away, and they left him. They shoved the other guy into the back of the car and drove off."

A guy and a girl. I feel more than ever that we need to talk to Haruka and Nelson. I ask, "What color was the car?"

"It was dark. Maybe dark blue or green. Or black."

A chill goes through me again. Black, like the car that had tried to run me down. Logan and I exchange a look.

"What?" Mrs. Guidry asks. "Did I say something useful."

"Maybe." I fiddle with the edge of my menu on the table. "But why didn't you call the cops? Something was obviously wrong."

She looks down at the table, leaning forward in dejection. "I couldn't. Not after what I did."

"What did you do?" Logan asks. He gives me a smug look, reminding me that he'd had a hunch Mrs. Guidry was guilty of something.

She lays her hands flat on the table. "After the car sped away, I saw that the other man was still there, leaning against the wall. I was worried for him, so I came across the street, just as he slumped down, sitting against the wall. I turned on the flashlight on my phone. I could tell right away that he was dead. And – I recognized him from all the times he'd been on the news." She sounds absolutely scandalized by the thought.

"So?" I ask. "What's so bad about that?"

"I-" she hesitates, like she can't believe she's going to say whatever it is out loud. She looks around at the other tables, drops her voice to an even softer whisper. "I took pictures of him. Even though he was dead."

I gasp. "You're the one who sold that picture to the tabloids."

She looks embarrassed. "You have to understand. My daughter is going through a messy divorce, and it's taking every penny she has just to try and keep custody of her kids. Every penny – and then some. Are you going to tell on me?"

"You should have reported the death," Logan scolds. "But at least your first impulse was to help." Logan obviously doesn't see how stirring up trouble for this grandmother will help bring Fabin's killer to justice. I don't either. "If it becomes relevant, we may have to tell the police, but I don't see that happening."

Mrs. Guidry insists on feeding us for free. She brings us each a thick slice of crawfish pie, with a side salad and a couple of boudin balls. The crust on the pie is light and delicate and the filling substantially spicy. This may be the best version of crawfish pie I've ever tasted.

Boudin is Cajun sausage, made mostly of ground pork and rice. To make the balls, the sausage is removed from the casing, coated with bread crumbs and fried. The trick is to keep them from getting greasy, and Mrs. Guidry has that down pat.

Logan looks trepidatious. But he takes a bite of his pie, then looks surprised.

"What?" I ask.

"I thought I didn't like crawfish. But when you make it into a pot pie, it's actually not half bad."

"Not half bad," I echo. "Admit it. This is awesome."

He makes a noncommittal noise, but scarfs down the rest of his pie. And the second piece Mrs. Guidry brings him.

She puts banana pudding down on the table and reminds us the meal is one the house, but Logan leaves money on the table anyway, when she's not looking.

As Mrs. Guidry goes back into the kitchen, I say, "From the way she described it, it sounds like they were trying to kidnap Fabin to ransom him – only something went wrong and he wound up dead. Which makes Mateo collateral damage."

"And probably dead himself." Logan sounds matter-of-fact. "Unless – maybe Mateo was part of the plot. Those diamonds could have been a payoff for helping them."

I scrunch up my nose at that. "What about that guy Haruka said came by the University? The thing delivered to Mateo by mistake. I think that meant the diamonds?"

"It's possible."

Miles shows up, helping himself to the same chair Mrs. Guidry had just been sitting in.

Before I start questioning him about what he might know about the people in the photo on Mateo's phone, I announce, "Guess what? Logan has agreed to become part owner of Greetings and Felicitations."

"Really?" The grin on Miles's face becomes unexpectedly wide. "In that case, I'm wondering if that job you offered me is still open."

"Why?" Logan asks.

Miles shrugs. "If you're going to be hanging around the shop, maybe you can show me some self-defense."

Logan keeps saying he doesn't plan on spending much time at the shop. I wait for him to explain this to Miles. But instead he looks somber and says, "Whatever you need."

And that's the thing I really like about Logan. I have no doubt he'll follow through on what he just promised. That one way or another, he'll help Miles get past feeling lost.

In the meantime, though, he takes out Mateo's phone, still in the zipper-topped bag. He shows Miles the photo from the party. Miles explains that he's known Haruka pretty much since the researchers arrived on the island – and her and Nelson's supposed romance is one sided. And Miles says that Enrique and Mateo are friends. He thinks.

Mrs. Guidry brings Miles a bowl of gumbo without even asking, and the two of them start talking about some case Miles's dad is involved in. They are still talking when Logan and I leave.

We take Logan's car down to the section of beach where the researchers are studying the turtle nest. It's a quiet drive. It would be the perfect time for me to ask Logan to be my plus one to Autumn's wedding.

"Hey Logan," I start.

"Hmmm?"

"Nothing. Never mind." I chicken out. I'm not really ready for this – I can't even really admit to myself that I *want* to move on from my grief. Although, obviously I do. Otherwise, I wouldn't even be considering asking someone out. But what if I'm rushing it? I was about to cry over Kevin, just last night.

Logan glances at me, then looks back at the road. "That is not a nothing tone of voice. What?"

"I'm just curious," I say. "You told me you'd never go out with a client. But what about a business partner?"

The sudden silence in the car is deafening. I'm not even sure he's breathing. Finally he says, "Is that a hypothetical question? Or are you actually asking?"

"Hypothetical," I say. Because I am a coward. "I'm just trying to understand how you view business relationships."

"I probably wouldn't date a business partner," Logan says. "There's just too much potential for things to go wrong."

"Oh." I try to hide how disappointed I am.

I don't think he's buying it, but he lets it go. I'm really confused by the signals he's sending. He seems to care about me, and wants to look out for me. And at one point, I think he was seriously flirting with me. So either he was never actually interested and I just imagined it – or I friend-zoned him so hard there's no coming back from it.

I can still enjoy spending time with him. I just need to stop thinking about how much I'd like to kiss him. I probably

shouldn't be dwelling on that anyway. We are still in the middle
of a murder investigation and all.

We find Nelson and Haruka together out on the beach.
Haruka waves, looking all happy to see us. Which makes this
even more awkward. After we get the pleasantries out of the way,
I ask her, "You know that Logan and I are trying to find out what
happened to Mateo?"

She nods. "I worry too."

I take a deep breath. I can't exactly ask her if she's part of
a diamond smuggling ring. "I found out you and Mateo had a
fight. Can I ask what it was about?"

"I don't know how to say all of it in English." Haruka
looks at Nelson. He shakes his head, signaling no, they shouldn't
tell us. She gives him a stern look back and says something in
Japanese. She points at me. "Ima."

"Fine." Nelson still doesn't look happy. He rubs his
hands on the sides of the bottom of his tee-shirt, which features a
different anime character. "But this can't go any farther than this
beach."

I don't make any promises, and neither does Logan.

Nelson hesitates, and Haruka pokes him. Nelson says, "It
was my mistake, at first. I mixed up some of the data, trying to
help Haruka with her experiments on octopus intelligence. But
her results started getting attention. And by the time Haruka
figured out what had happened, she was well on the way towards
getting a research grant. So we just kept reporting the data
without changing how it was collected."

"What did this have to do with Mateo?" I ask.

"Mateo got ahold of our notes, and he figured out that the
data didn't all add up. He wanted Haruka to admit that her results
had been faked. Which would have gotten this whole research
project shut down. Or gotten all of us kicked out of academia
altogether. I talked him out of that, but he said he was keeping the
notes, in case we didn't start reporting the correct results. The

way he talked about it, I got the idea that he was keeping notes about something else too. Something bigger."

I ask, "Do you think those notes might have something to do with diamond smuggling?"

Haruka blinks in confusion. "Eh?"

Nelson asks, "Did you just say diamond smuggling? Like Scooby Doo?"

Okay. So he's not involved with what we found hidden in with my cacao beans. If he'd been prepared for the question, he wouldn't have sounded so stupefied trying to answer it.

Logan asks me, "Could he have left his notes in your office?"

"Theoretically?" I ask. "Yes. But I don't know why he would have."

Logan shrugs. "Whoever broke into your office went through your files. You wouldn't have stored diamonds in a file folder."

"You think the killer is looking for Mateo's notes?" I ask.

Logan says, "Maybe. It would explain why someone was at his apartment building. Whoever tried to hit you probably thought you had found whatever they were looking for. They must have realized you didn't, since they haven't tried again."

"Thanks," I say. "You seem disappointed I'm still unharmed."

"No. I'm rather relieved." Logan gives me a grin that melts my insides. Too bad he made it clear that he's not interested.

"I still have one thing to ask," I tell Haruka. "Maybe without Nelson."

Nelson says, "Uh uh. I'm staying right here with Haruka."

Uh . . . okay. I gesture to Logan. "Show her the picture."

Haruka sees the picture of the three couples that Logan had copied off of Mateo's phone, and her eyes go wide. She's so flustered she drops her bag, and it spills open. Two spheres that look like leathery golf balls roll into the sand. I'm fairly sure I'm looking at turtle eggs.

I gesture towards them. "I thought you guys didn't disturb the turtle nests."

Logan says, "Those aren't real turtle eggs. They're decoy trackers. We put them in with the nests we find, so that we can use GPS to track any poachers that take them." He looks pained. "Which is why I would more comfortable if we were relocating the eggs, like we usually do. Best practices are still best practices"

Nelson says, "That would invalidate the results of the one study that's still working out, with Mateo in the wind, and Haruka's project a bust. We need to look legit here, if we want funding for our next project, in Fiji. Besides, what are the odds of poachers stumbling across a nest, way out here?"

Haruka picks up her things, puts the fake eggs back in her bag. She looks embarrassed that we've seen them, though I don't know why, considering they're for the job she's doing. She says matter-of-factly, "Mateo and I are dating. It is atarashi – new. But we have not spoken since our fight on Friday."

Nelson's jaw drops open. "What?" He says in such a hurt tone that I forgive him for being a jerk last time we spoke. He blinks. "Did I completely mis-read your feelings?"

Haruka looks down at the sand. "Not entirely. But you never asked me out."

She looks back up at him. The moment is intensely sad.

It seems mean to just leave Haruka and Nelson looking at each other like that. But what else can we do?

"Come on," I tell Logan. "I still need to go take care of Clive and all of Mateo's fish. If he had any notes, maybe they're in his apartment."

"Sure." Logan doesn't talk much on the way to Mateo's place. We're pulling into the parking lot when he says, "I didn't say I would never date a business associate. But I would have to have a fairly strong reason to believe it would work out and not wreck everything else."

I don't know what to say to that. Is he saying he does have feelings for me? Thinking about what Nelson had missed out on with Haruka, just by not speaking up? I wish I had the courage to flat-out ask him. I say, "That things will work out is a hard assumption to ask someone for, if you haven't gotten to know them."

"True." He gets out of the car, and doesn't say anything else. We go up the stairs to Mateo's apartment. Logan makes me wait by the door while he clears each room. Once again, he's volunteering to protect me. Which only makes his behavior more confusing. Finally, he lets me into Mateo's apartment and we start looking for anything that might be either papers or a digital storage device.

I'm looking under all of the desk drawers in the room with the fish tanks, while Clive peers at me from under the plastic pineapple, but there's nothing taped to the underside of the drawers or hidden anywhere.

Logan comes into the room. Out of nowhere, he asks, "What's your favorite color?"

"Green," I answer, confused. Has he suddenly decided to buy me something? Or is that his way of trying to get to know me better? "About the same shade as your eyes."

My cheeks go hot the instant I say it. But it's true. So I'm not going to try to take it back. Besides, he looks pleased, and I like seeing that look on his face.

He says, "I cleaned up the mess on the floor in the kitchen. I can't figure out what happened. Do you think the octopus might have decided to try to squeeze inside a milk bottle full of water?"

I look at Clive. He's not telling. "It's possible. He was out of his tank at one point. But I had assumed that someone had been in the kitchen looking for something. Like maybe a bunch of diamonds." Which are now in the possession of the police.

"That's possible too." Logan looks at me. I can't read the expression in his eyes. Finally he says, "I don't want to be just somebody's rebound guy. I did that once. It wasn't worth it. She wasn't ready to move on."

Okay. I didn't know about that. It explains why he didn't push to build anything with me, despite the chemistry we'd had when we first met. And why, when he overheard me saying I wasn't ready to move past my grief for my deceased husband that that had completely put the brakes on everything.

"It's not a rebound if the person really is ready for someone new," I say.

"Are you?" he asks, finally direct. This isn't theoretical anymore. And there's both challenge and possibilities in his question.

And suddenly I can't breathe. I want to say yes.

"You're not sure," he answers for me. "I can see that in your eyes."

It stinks, how bad our timing's off. Because we had a moment, right here. And it just passed us by. But it doesn't look like he wants to leave, and if he still wants to be my friend, I'll take it. "Please, Logan," I start, but I'm not sure how to finish that sentence. Please forget I started this, by saying such awkward things in the car? Finally I ask, "What's your favorite color?"

"Black," he says without hesitation. "Look, I don't think there's anything hidden in this apartment. At least not that we're going to find without a demolition team and a metal detector. Let's just feed the fish and look for a more promising lead."

"Okay." I pick up the canister of fish food sitting on a shelf under one of the tanks and turn it around to read the instructions.

"Oh, for crying out loud." Logan takes the canister, sprinkles some of the food flakes into his hand and lifts the lid on one of the tanks. He then sprinkles little pinches of food into the tank, which sends the fish swarming to get it.

I watch him feed all the fish, his face more peaceful than it was a few minutes before. If I told him right now that it wouldn't be a rebound if the two of us got together, what would it take for him to believe me?

Yeah. What would it take for me to believe me? Best to just forget the whole thing.

Logan finds a small plastic tank and dips it into the tank with the shrimp. "Time to get Clive back into his rightful environment. I'm going to lure him out with food. Take that weight off the lid."

I step closer to Clive's temporary refuge and pet the glass. Clive moves partway out from under the pineapple, finally taking an interest in what I'm doing. I open the lid and wiggle my fingers at the surface of the water. He seems to be paying attention, but he's not moving any closer. I move to let Logan approach with the small tank with the moving shrimp inside. Logan holds the plastic by the top edges, submerging most of it into the water where Clive is. Clive starts moving his arms in a way that seems either excited or frustrated, and he changes color, towards tan. Finally, he can't take it anymore. Clive climbs the side of the main tank and maneuvers himself into the smaller one. He grabs onto one of the shrimps.

I catch something glinting in the gravel under the pineapple. It looks like a gaudy rhinestone keychain. "Hey, what's that?"

I start to gesture towards the keychain, but Logan warns me, "Don't make any sudden moves."

Logan carefully lifts the small tank out of the water, and I move along with him into the other room, so I can lift the lid on Clive's actual tank.

Clive willingly climbs out of the small tank and back into the reef structure where he belongs. But then he tucks himself up under part of the structure and practically disappears from view. They say that octopuses are intelligent enough to know their owners on sight, or by the sound of their footsteps. It seems like Clive is sulking because he hasn't seen Mateo in days. I could, of course, just be projecting human emotion onto an animal. But I still wish I knew how to cheer him up.

I go back to the tank where saw the keychain. I tell Logan, "Carmen told me that octopuses like to collect shiny things. Whatever this is, I think Clive might have dragged it in there with him."

I reach my hand into the water. It takes my whole arm and me leaning over, getting my shirt wet, but I manage to grab the keychain, a rhinestone surfboard that says Galveston Surf Shop. And at the end of it, there's a single key. I tell Logan, "Well that's one place no intruder would have thought to look. Under the octopus."

That at least gets me a laugh.

I take the key and wash it off with clean water, and dry it with a towel that's hanging on the little handle on the stove. Then I slip the key into my purse and neatly re-hang the towel.

I make sure the weight is on top of Clive's tank. And then we leave.

As we're getting into the car, Logan asks, "Any idea what that key goes to?"

"A locker. Maybe at the beach or at the gym?"

He nods. "I'll check and see if Mateo has rented anything. Hopefully, he used a credit card."

We start driving back towards the chocolate shop. But I notice the same vehicle behind us for several stop signs. I take a closer look, then I grab Logan's arm. "Look. It's that black car. You can see the dent on the front fender. How long have they been following us?"

"I'm not sure." Logan drives like he hasn't noticed anything wrong. He detours over to the seawall, and grabs a parking place, and then guides me over to the old bath house. He waits until the car is parked, and whoever was behind the wheel gets out. I can't get a good look from here, but I think it's a guy with a hat down low over his face, and sunglasses obscuring his features. "Stay here," Logan says, then he makes his way back towards the parked car. The guy realizes he's been spotted, and takes off running. Logan chases him. I sigh. Of course I have to stay put. With my health issues, I couldn't catch them if I tried.

Logan comes back alone. The front of his shirt is soaking wet, and he smells like soda, which I know he doesn't drink.

"What happened to you?" I ask.

"I ran into a tourist," he says sulkily. "And the subject got away. At least we can pull a plate on the car."

# Chapter Thirteen
## *Still Wednesday*

The car turns out to be a rental, issued to one Janice Joplin. Somebody thinks they're real funny, don't they? Since Joplin grew up in Southeast Texas, and all. The trace on Mateo's credit cards seems to be taking longer than anticipated, so until we know what the key goes to, we're at an impasse.

We stop by Logan's place, so he can grab a fresh shirt. This is my first time seeing his home. It suits him, a luxury apartment with wood and granite, and a spectacular bay view. Logan is just as much of a neat freak as Mateo. Only here, the living room smells faintly of eucalyptus. Now that I've moved into the old hotel, Logan and I share a similar bay view. I move over to the sliding door leading out onto the patio. I'm not sure, but I think I can see the hotel from here, off in the distance.

Logan comes out from his bedroom wearing a black tee, the pilot's jacket he always favors dangling from one hand. I try not to stare at his arms now that I can see his built biceps in detail.

"What do we know about Fabin's girlfriend?" Logan asks.

"Not much," I admit. "I didn't even get her last name. Though I'm guessing Arlo did."

"We may want to go back over there later. Assuming she hasn't already headed home." Logan drops his jacket across the back of his sofa. "Enrique has classes all afternoon, and I can't imagine that girl would be there hanging out by herself, so going by there now would probably be pointless." Because of course he has access to Enrique's schedule.

Logan moves into the kitchen, and I follow. He opens the fridge. I'm curious to see what he keeps in there. I spot a six-pack of craft beer, alongside a half-dozen meticulously labeled containers of high-protein lunches, before the door closes. He's holding a bottle of water.

The apartment's front door rattles like someone's trying to open the lock. I freeze. Logan hands me the water bottle. He gestures me into the pantry, as he goes to stand beside the door. His hand dips into a decorative bowl on a table nearby. I expect him to bring out a gun, put he pulls out a cannister of pepper spray, angled and ready to hit whoever comes through the door.

This pantry is huge for an apartment, so there's plenty of room for me alongside Logan's canned goods and high-end olive oil and artisan pasta. I leave the pantry door gapped, just enough to see what's happening. The rattling in the lock seems to take forever. Whoever it is is not great at picking locks.

Finally the door opens. It's Fake Leslie.

She sees Logan, who hesitates. Maybe he doesn't want to pepper spray a woman. Maybe she just doesn't look dangerous. After all, she's not holding a weapon.

But she doesn't hesitate. She hooks her leg around his, and suddenly Logan is on the floor. He doesn't stay down long, bouncing back up in a sort of flip-jump. He manages to grab Fake Leslie's wrists and bring them together behind her back.

He growls, "Who are you?" as he takes a zip-tie out of his pocket and fastens her wrists. He still keeps ahold of her arm.

"I'm Fabin Obodozie's cousin Leslie," she says. "Please. I just want to find out what happened to him."

I come out of the pantry, since Logan has her subdued. "You already tried that act on me."

She looks from me to Logan. She asks him, "You two are together?"

"We're colleagues," he says.

She nods, like that's the only thing that makes sense. Like she thinks Logan is out of my league. "None of my research revealed that."

"It's a new arrangement," Logan says.

"In the chocolate shop or the flight business?" she asks.

"What are you doing here, anyway?" I ask, frustration building inside me.

"I could ask you the same thing."

"Logan invited me in." I sound defensive, which is stupid. "I could call the cops and report you for breaking and entering." I gesture over at Logan. "And possibly assault."

Fake Leslie rolls her eyes. "Fine. Look. I work security. Fabin's father asked me to find out who had killed his son. I know it doesn't look like it on the news, but Graham Obodozie really cared about Fabin. They were really close until Leslie showed up. I've been trying to prove for years that Leslie did something to Fabin that made him run away."

"So you work for the family," Logan verifies. "You weren't just hired because of this case."

"That's correct," Fake Leslie says.

Logan takes out a pocket knife and cuts the zip tie off of her wrists. But he keeps hold of one of her hands, and opens an app on his phone. He presses her thumb down against the screen. I'm guessing he's verifying that she's not lying about who she is again.

"I figured I would blend in better in a small town if people thought I was Leslie." She nudges Logan's shoulder. "You've been under cover. You know I'm right."

"Exactly how much did you research about me?" Logan asks.

"Enough to know you're bad news," Fake Leslie quips, smiling at Logan. "And I like bad news."

Logan is grinning back. "What exactly are you suggesting?"

Oh, good gawsh. I hadn't expected Logan to wait around until he wasn't going to be a rebound for me. Or I don't know – maybe I had. And the way we'd left it back at Mateo's apartment – I'd assured him that I'm okay with us being just friends. But I can't believe that he's flirting with someone else right in front of me.

I clear my throat. "That still doesn't explain why you have a mock-up of Leslie's business card with your phone number on it. That seems a little – premeditated."

Leslie nods. "I told you. I've been trying to prove for years that Leslie was responsible for her parents' car accident. There's something not right with that girl, even if the Obodozies can't see it. I had those cards made a long time ago, when I was following a different lead."

That sounds logical enough.

"But what were you looking for here?" Logan asks.

"You ran Fabin's name through a ton of databases. I was determining your interest in the case."

Logan finally lets Leslie go. "Same as Felicity's. Now that I'm part owner in the chocolate shop, I need this case closed before it disrupts Greetings and Felicitations' reputation in the community."

"Not exactly the same," I say. "I want to find Mateo. He's a nice guy, and I think he's in trouble."

Both Logan and Leslie give me identical sympathetic looks. Because they're both assuming that Mateo's dead. Then they look at each other.

Leslie puts a hand on my arm in passing as she heads for the door. "I should go."

After Leslie leaves, Logan puts his jacket on, but instead of heading for the door too, he moves over to the sliding glass, watching the water sparkling on the bay. "Statistically, if they don't find someone who's gone missing within the first twenty-four hours, the chances of finding them alive is very small."

"But it's not zero," I insist.

"No, it's not. And if I talk you into giving up, and it turns out we could have found him, you'll never forgive me. But I have to be honest. I think we're investigating two murders here." He looks at me, the green in his eyes even more intense by this light. "What do you want to do now?"

I run both hands across my face. "I still have three dozen chocolate hazelnut doves to make before tomorrow. I should probably head back to the shop and work on that, while we wait for information about the key."

"*We* have three dozen doves to make," Logan says.

"Are you sure?" I ask. "I know you have your own business to take care of."

"And I have a flight scheduled for tomorrow morning. But today I'm all yours."

So we go back to my tiny chocolate factory, where Miles is in the chocolate making room, finishing up the hot cocoa bombs, and Carmen is out front, dealing with customers.

"Here," I tell Logan, handing him an apron. "You're going to want to trade the jacket for the apron. Working with chocolate tends to get a bit messy."

The noise from the melangers all grinding away is comforting. Things are going right, for once.

Once he's got the apron on, I lead Logan over to the nut grinder and give him the container with the roasted hazelnuts. "I like to do a rough manual pre-grind. Have you ever made gianduja before?"

He shakes his head. "I'm not even sure what that is."

I'm not surprised. A lot of people have eaten it without ever knowing the word.

Miles looks up from his work at the counter on the other side of the small room. "It's hazelnut chocolate spread. It was originally created as a way to extend the chocolate supply in Italy when the country was facing a shortage. Without that shortage, we'd be missing out on any number of confections."

Miles has obviously been paying more attention when I've been talking about chocolate making than I had realized.

"That's fascinating," Logan says, but I can't tell if he means it. He gets to work pre-grinding the nuts, while I pull out the old workhorse food processor from under the counter.

"We will combine the hazelnut butter and the chocolate in the processor to make the filling. Ordinarily, I'd do this in the small melanger," I tell him. "Because it would make a creamier result. But that would make a huge batch of gianduja, and we're just trying to get enough doves made for the party. Besides, the melangers are all busy making chocolate."

"Yeah," Logan says. "I can certainly hear that."

He doesn't seem as happy about the noise as I am. But he doesn't complain. And it doesn't take long to get the chocolate melted to go into the spread and then to get the gianduja processed.

Logan is good with projects involving his hands, so once we get more of the chocolate prepped in the tempering machine, it isn't hard to show him how to fill and empty the molds to make the outside of the doves.

With all the work we need to get done today, and the follow-up we need to do in trying to find out what happened to Mateo and Fabin, having Logan and Miles help is a big relief. Maybe letting both of them into my business wasn't such a big mistake after all.

"That's the last of them," Miles says, as he holds up one of the hot chocolate bombs. The seam where he's melted the two halves together is still wet and glistening.

"What's in there?" Logan asks.

"Mini marshmallows, sugar and cocoa powder made from the beans I bought for my Colombia chocolate," I say. "Plus cinnamon and nutmeg, and just a hint of cayenne."

"You make your own cocoa powder?" Logan sounds impressed.

I show him the cocoa butter press and the hammer mill. "I just started experimenting with it. And just in time too, or we would be using somebody else's chocolate in our baskets – and I wouldn't want to have to put that on the label. Pressing the fat out of the beans takes a bit of doing. It's actually one of the most time intensive processes in chocolate making. You put the ground cacao in a canvas bag and the hydraulic press presses the cocoa butter out of the cocoa liquor. Then you get this solid cake that has to be ground."

"But now that we're done with today's projects," Miles asks hesitantly, "Maybe you have a minute to show me that self-defense stuff?"

"We still have to have to wait for all the shells to set before we can fill them for the doves," I tell Logan. "So it's not a problem."

Logan nods and gestures towards the kitchen. "Come on. Outside."

I hope this is a good idea. I know Miles needs *something* right now, to get him back on track. And it feels like Logan is the right person to help him. But I'd hesitated to even talk to Logan at first, when I found out he carried a gun. And now, who knows what he's going to show Miles.

I follow them out into the alley. I feel responsible for this, and I don't think they'll mind me coming out here to just watch.

Logan hands Miles a canister of pepper spray, just like the one he gave me. I think it's the one he had handy when we were at his apartment. "This is your first line of defense. Any encounter where everyone walks – or limps – away is a good one."

I remember how flippant Logan had been when he'd thought I might have killed Emma. It wasn't a dealbreaker for him for working with me. Because violence didn't scare him. And yet, he's showing Miles a more compassionate side, because he can tell that Miles is a sensitive kid.

Ironically, this incident, more than anything that has happened so far, makes me fall in love with Logan Hanlon.

Logan shows Miles a few moves that are meant to use the momentum of someone swinging a punch or trying to grab you against them, by throwing them off balance. And he talks about a last-ditch knee crunch, if there is an aggressor that you really need to run away from. None of these are techniques you would use to start a fight, which makes me feel better. And by the time they're done, Miles looks so much more confident. So much closer to his old self.

Logan tells him, so softly I can hardly hear, "What happened before wasn't your fault, you know."

"I know." Miles squares his shoulders, and turns towards me. "I'll clean up the workstations, and then is it okay if I bail so I can study? I have a test in the morning, but then I'll be in all day to prep for Autumn's party."

"You're staying for the party too, right?" I ask.

"You don't think she'd mind?"

"After all the work you've put in? You really ought to be there. Logan and Carmen are staying too, so it will be our whole crew."

There's a look on Mile's face when I talk about being part of something that puts a little bubble of joy in my heart.

"Thanks, Mrs. Koerber." Miles starts to go inside. Then he turns back and says, "And you too, Mr. Hanlon."

After Miles walks away, I tell Logan, "You keep talking about how little we really know each other. And just now, I think I saw a whole other side of you. But I don't know which version is the real you. So I have a blunt question. You don't have to answer if you don't want to."

"I'll tell you whatever you want to know," Logan says.

"Okay. What's the worst thing you've ever done?"

He squints at me. "Other than get people killed because I blew an op? Which I already told you."

I wince. "I'm not talking about a tactical mistake. I mean real regrets."

If there's something even worse about him that's going to be a dealbreaker, I want to know it now, before I get any more attached.

Logan says, "When I was hiding out in Europe, I didn't know anybody. And I was short on cash, after paying for the falsified documents that got me into France under an assumed name. My alias had a right to work in the country, and I was trying to start over, so I built a fake resume, and tried to get hired as security at a local bank. The manager was so condescending, and so downright mean that I keyed his car on my way out."

"That's it?" Other than having gotten people killed, keying a car is the worst thing he can come up with?

He looks upset that I'm not upset. "Felicity, that's the kind of thing an impulsive teenager would have done, not someone with tactical training and years of dealing with high-stakes situations. I was 30 years old at the time."

"But you were obviously under a great deal of stress."

"What about you," Logan asks. "What's the worst thing you've ever done?"

My face goes hot. I guess I should have expected him to turn the question back at me. "Probably the worst thing I ever did was break Arlo's heart."

Logan shakes his head. "You don't get to choose a tactical mistake either."

I pause, trying to understand the correlation. Is he saying I shouldn't feel guilty about Arlo anymore?

"You just want me to confess something you don't already know." I try to put the banter back in my voice. "Okay. When I was a teenager, my dad told me I couldn't go to a concert in Houston. But I really wanted to go. Arlo had invited me, as part of a group of friends from school, and I had the biggest crush on him. I was afraid that if I didn't go, he'd never invite me anywhere again. So I stole my Mom's minivan to take us all."

Logan shifts his head, looking at me skeptically. "You don't approve of J-walking. You seriously stole a car?"

I nod. "The whole thing was a disaster. We never made it to the concert. We got hit by a drunk driver coming the wrong way out of the venue's parking lot. It could have been worse, but several of my friends were injured. Arlo wound up having to do physical therapy to get his shoulder working right again. I went with him to some of his appointments, and we got to know each other, sitting in the waiting room."

"Which explains how you got interested in physical therapy," Logan says.

I nod. "And also why I'm so big on following the rules. Having to call your dad from the hospital and explain that you've totaled a car you weren't supposed to be driving because you're too young to have a driver's license tends to leave a lasting impression. Rules are there to keep you safe."

Logan grins. "Yet you're willing to bend them when it is necessary for the greater good. Like with the chocolate melangers. You told me you never run them overnight. But you're willing to do that to get the spa order done."

"I know I shouldn't," I stammer. "It's too much risk. Maybe I should sleep up at the shop-"

"No," Logan says. "That's not what I'm saying. I'm just saying that that kind of seeming contradiction is what makes you intriguing."

Intriguing? Nobody has ever called me that before. I guess that's a good thing?

"Ready to finish up the chocolate doves?" I ask. I'm not sure what else to say. I stammer, "And then we can go talk to Donnie?"

"Sure," Logan says. "But before we go, we need to talk about something."

"Okay." His tone of voice has me nervous. "Shoot."

He takes out his phone and opens a browser tab. He has an article from *Gulf Coast Happenings* already pulled up. There's Ash, with his rectangular black-rimmed hipster glasses, skinny tie and smug smile, as part of the banner at the top. The headline says, *Local Chocolate Shop Embarks on a Sweet Partnership*. And there's a picture of Logan and me at Mrs. Guidry's, looking cozy over our lunch plates. Given what I've learned about Mrs.

Guidry – and the fact that Ash pays top dollar for photographs – my guess is that the sweet old lady took it herself. Come to think of it, she may well have taken the last one too, of me with the police inside my shop. There are some serious downsides to having such a nosy neighbor just across the street.

The article is once again done in the noir story style, and implies that the business partnership Logan and I have embarked on is a matter of convenience, to cover the fact that we're either setting ourselves up as private detectives – or deep in a romance. It is all clearly speculation, full of probabilities and maybes, nothing he could get in trouble for saying. And again, there's nothing truly malicious. Just embarrassing, and potentially able to cause problems between me and Logan. Or me and the rest of the community.

I sigh. "Maybe Carmen's right. I'll invite Ash into the shop tomorrow, and explain what we really do for this community. I'm sorry you got dragged into his obsession with Greetings and Felicitations."

"I didn't get dragged into anything," Logan says. "And this is hardly the worst thing the press has ever written about me. I'm more worried about protecting your reputation."

"Don't be," I assure him. "If this doesn't embarrass you, I won't let it bother me."

I take out my own phone and text Tam Binh. She had helped me the last time I had wound up in Ash's sights. Her Mixed Plate blog is a big deal, with more followers than I could ever dream of for my own social media. Ash had been intimidated enough by what she might say about him that when he'd found out I was a friend of hers, he'd written a positive post, after all the ones insinuating that I might have murdered one of my employees. And he'd actually apologized after I had been proven innocent. *Hey!* I ask. *Do you have a way I could contact Ash?*

She immediately texts back, *What did he do this time?* Then, *Never mind. Let me look.*

While she's looking at his blog, I text her, *I'm going to invite him to come into the shop in the morning, to do an actual interview with me, where I can give him some real facts. Do you think that will be a disaster?*

Logan is looking over my shoulder as I type. "Not in the morning. I told you I have a flight."

"I know," I say. "But you're this big intimidating-looking guy. If you ask him to cease and desist, you'll just scare him. And then who knows what he will write about us."

"Miles won't be here either," Logan says.

"Well, it's not like Ash has ever put me in physical danger. Carmen and I should be able to handle him."

"If you're sure," Logan says, but he sounds anything but certain.

We go inside, and I show Logan how to fill the shells. We're just putting them in the fridge to set when my phone dings with a text. It's from Tam Binh. *Ash will be there at 9 AM sharp. If he's late, call me. XOXOXO*

I show the text to Logan.

He says, "I guess that settles that then."

# Chapter Fourteen
## *Still Wednesday*

Logan goes out into the front of the shop while we wait for the filling to set. He's doing something on his phone, but I'm watching him, and he's actually watching Carmen, getting a feel for how the shop runs, nodding to himself as she makes recommendations to customers, and outright staring when she makes lattes and dirty horchata. I have to say, I like his subtle approach. After all, Carmen might get insulted if he was looking over her shoulder asking questions.

And yet – I still can't get used to the idea of him being here long term. Of having to consult him on decisions I want to make for Greetings and Felicitations. The shop has been just my thing, from when I chose the location, to when I made the first bars of chocolate. I can see how easily Logan fits here. I had been content inside that little workspace with him and Miles – but I'm still not sure how much I'm giving up.

Autumn texts me, *I just realized we missed our weekly lunch date today. But Drake wanted me to meet his mama before tomorrow night's party, and I was so nervous I forgot it was Wednesday.*

There's way too much information there to unpack in a text message. So I go into my office and call her. When she answers, I say, "You got engaged before you met his family? What if they're awful? You could get stuck with a deadbeat brother-in-law and a mother-in-law who wants to run your life."

Autumn laughs. "Drake's mamma is absolutely adorable. She raised him all by herself, so of course he wants to take care of her. I'm okay with that. And his brother's a cardiologist, so if

141

anything, we're the deadbeats, with a university salary and a freelance income."

What can I say to that? "Well, as long as you're happy."

"I feel like there's a hint of judgement in that," Autumn says, a shade of hurt in her voice.

"This is the most important decision of your entire life. I'm not saying that marrying him someday might not be a good idea. But right now? When you don't know whether something about him might be a dealbreaker? Autumn, that feels downright irresponsible. Which is not like you at all." I sigh. "There isn't some reason why it has to be so sudden, is there"

"No!" Autumn sounds offended. She hesitates. "I just want a winter wedding, and I don't want to wait until next winter. You've seen my dream wedding book." Autumn has been building her wedding binder since high school, even though she's never dated the same guy for more than a couple of months. As far as I know, her dream wedding dress still looks like something that would be appropriate on one of the princesses out of *Frozen*. "You can't exactly wear a white fur stole in July."

"I can see that," I say. "But is fashion really a basis for life choices?"

Autumn laughs in my ear. "It's also when the University gives library staff insane amounts of vacation. We've both always wanted to go to Tanzania, so we're going to take the trip of a lifetime for our honeymoon."

I can see the appeal in that. And in wanting to believe in everything Library Guy seems to be at face value. But how can a month between meeting and getting engaged be long enough to know if he is really Prince Charming? "Drake came by here. He seems really sweet. But how do you know that's not just a façade? People tend to show their best side when they're dating, in order to make a good first impression."

Autumn sighs. "I've dated a lot of losers already. I've learned a little bit about how to spot somebody who's faking."

"I'm sorry," I say. Because what else is there to add?

"Drake's a genuinely good guy. I'm going to hold onto him." She sounds upset.

And I realize she's right to be. "I am sorry. Truly. I want your relationship to be a success. I want you to be happy. And I'll do everything I can to help make your perfect wedding happen."

So we talk more wedding ideas, then I let Autumn go and return to the chocolate finishing room, with Logan and Miles. We finish the doves and leave them to set. Carmen promises to put them in the gift boxes later.

There aren't any customers around, so Logan and I decide to head for Donnie's doughnut shop. I tell Carmen, "We think Donnie may be involved with the diamonds."

Carmen's eyes go wide. "That means he killed Fabin, right?"

I take a couple of chocolate bars off of the shelf. Bringing chocolate often serves to get people talking. "We don't know that."

Logan brings his Mustang around to the front of the shop. I hop in, and we head off to follow our clue. This is starting to feel like a normal way for us to spend time together.

Donnie running whatever his real business is out of a doughnut shop is kind of ingenious, actually. All sorts of people go into a doughnut shop, it's not unusual for them to stay to hang out and drink coffee, and the whole shebang officially shuts down at 2 PM.

When we get there, it's just after two, so I'm worried the place will be closed. But we go up to the door anyway, and when Logan pulls on it, it opens.

"Hello?" I call. It smells nice inside the building, but I still can't see anyone in here. Donnie must be in the back. Though, even as we cross the room to the order counter, I can't see him back there either.

There's a clatter behind the counter, and from the floor, a croaked, "Help!"

Logan dashes around the counter, and when I start to follow, he pushes me back. "Stay there."

I follow him anyway, just a little more cautiously.

Fake Leslie is crouched on the floor, her hands around Donnie's neck. Somehow, I'm not really all that shocked. Logan tries to pull her away, but her hold on Donnie is strong. She shoulders away from Logan.

Her showing up here when we did isn't a coincidence. Fake Leslie has to have left us another bug, back at Felicitations. And the only time I'd talked about the doughnut shop in earshot of any public area was with Carmen, right before we left.

Fake Leslie gives Logan a dirty look, then goes back to staring into Donnie's eyes. "Ignore them. I said I want to hear a confession."

Donnie shakes his head vehemently. "I didn't kill nobody. Ever. I left Mateo and that girl still playing with the sorting machine, and I went home."

Logan finally pries Fake Leslie's hands off Donnie's neck. "I believe him."

Fake Leslie lets go. "Fine. I wasn't getting anywhere anyway." She stands up and leans against the wall.

Logan helps Donnie up to sitting. The poor guy's coughing. But he doesn't look embarrassed about having been overpowered by a 110-pound girl. I go over to the refrigerator case and take out a bottle of water, which I hand to Donnie. He breaks the seal on the cap and drinks big, heavy swallows.

Logan shoots Fake Leslie a disapproving look. "I did a sweep for bugs. When did you get another one in?"

She shrugs. "Yesterday."

Donnie gets to his feet and goes to wash his hands at a nearby sink. "Help yourselves to some coffee." He seems okay with talking to us, now that nobody's trying to choke the life out of him. He gets us each a maple-espresso-glazed chocolate doughnut – even Fake Leslie. She looks surprised, but she takes it, staring down at the pecan pieces studding the top.

"Carmen said you and Mateo had a fight," I say. "What was it over?"

"Mateo came to me, because he heard I had done some documents for people coming into the country through the cruise terminal. He thought it might be the same people he'd been looking for. I refused to discuss it with him. It's bad for business if you go around telling people who you made papers for," Donnie said.

"Then why were you there at the shop if you weren't wanting to talk to him?" I asked.

"I didn't even know he worked there, but my payment for the cruise terminal job got shipped in inside a container of cocoa beans."

"Which just happened to be a container I'd bought part of," I say. I'd split the order with three other chocolate makers in different part of the country, because a full container of beans is extremely expensive. But since I'd initiated the deal, I'd had the beans shipped into the port here in Galveston, and arranged for the main stock to be transferred to my warehouse in Waco, while the others had made their own arrangements. "So why didn't you collect your payment before it got split up?"

Donnie says, "The guy who was supposed to pull out the special sacks of beans got arrested for something else, two days before the container showed up. The regular guy didn't know anything about it."

"So you hacked into my e-mails to find a reason to get into my stock room?"

Donnie looks hurt by the accusation in my tone. "It seemed more civilized than just breaking in. Which I wound up having to do anyway. When Mateo recognized me, he wasn't about to give me the room to look around." Donnie points at me with the doughnut still in his hand. "I did save you the shipping cost on that sorter. You should thank me."

"After the damage you did to the melangers? Do you have any idea how much those cost to replace?"

"You should have taken it out of the diamonds." Donnie takes a bite of his doughnut. "There's no way the cops would have known how much was there."

Logan stage whispers to me, "This guy's moral logic's fascinating."

"It's creative at least," I stage whisper back.

"So why did you steal that particular bag of cacao beans?" Logan asks. "Out of all the ones in the storage room."

Donnie puts the remaining half of his doughnut down on the counter and takes out his keys. He shows us a little flashlight attached to it, and when he turns the beam on, it emits a purplish light. "There were two bags, with smiley-faces on them with black light paint. I found one of them."

"Which means the bag the police took as evidence also has diamonds in it," I say.

Donnie nods, "Unfortunately."

"How did Fabin know about the diamonds?" Fake Leslie asks. She doesn't care about the rest of the case. Her concern is simply finding Fabin's killer. I'm still a bit unclear what Fabin's father is paying her to do once she does.

"I doubt he did," Donnie says. "I never met Fabin, and I certainly didn't see who killed him. I was just there that night to collect my property, and Mateo was still there when I left. I came back looking for a better opportunity."

"Then why did you trash my office?" I ask. "It had to be obvious your diamonds weren't stuck in my file folders."

"I did what now?" Donnie picks up his doughnut and stuffs the rest of it into his mouth.

"Felicity's office was searched – rather sloppily," Logan says. "The same night you broke in."

"I don't know anything about that," Donnie says.

We all look at Leslie.

"What?" She picks a pecan off her doughnut's surface. "Don't look at me. If I'd searched the place, you would never have known I'd been there."

"You searched Mateo's place, didn't you?" I ask.

She doesn't deny it. "I'm surprised you could tell."

I huff out a disbelieving noise. "You broke a milk bottle, and left glass and water all over the kitchen floor."

"I most certainly did not!" Leslie sounds offended. "That bottle had a Siamese fighting fish swimming around in it on the counter, and it was still fine when I left."

Logan splutters a laugh. "I told you the octopus did it."

I give him an exasperated look. He smirks back at me.

But Clive really does have a problem. It's a miracle that he managed to eat that fish without injuring himself on broken glass. Maybe he grabbed the fish before the bottle fell – the logistics doesn't really matter.

I focus on Fake Leslie. "So you had a look around, put everything back, and didn't even leave a bug in the apartment?"

"What would have been the point? Mateo obviously wasn't going back there. And it wasn't like eavesdropping on the cops was likely to be helpful – I already had more information than they were starting with."

The point is that Logan and I were in Mateo's apartment, talking about the key we'd found – which could be the key to the whole mystery. I still have it, on the shiny keychain in my purse. Said purse is currently slung over my shoulder. And Fake Leslie doesn't know about it.

I still haven't figured out whether we are on the same side. But if she did know about the key, she probably wouldn't hesitate to use force to take it away from me. It's that arrogance that makes her not want to be a team player. The same arrogance that made her feel like she had nothing to gain from bugging Mateo's place once she searched it.

We need to break away from her, so that when we figure out what the key goes to, we can check it out on our own. Once we figure out what information Mateo is hiding, then we can decide if it is a good idea to share it with her.

Fake Leslie flashes Logan a smile. "Maybe we should go grab a drink and discuss the case." She hands him her doughnut. "You can have mine. I'm not much of a sweets person."

"We don't have time," Logan says. "But maybe later. Should I give you my phone number?"

She puts a hand on his forearm. "You think I don't already have your number?"

Logan watches her for a moment as she walks out. And I have an intense urge to smack him.

Almost as an act of defiance, I take a huge bite out of my doughnut. It's lighter than I thought it would be, and the maple-espresso glaze is less sweet. I may have a new favorite doughnut place – if Donnie doesn't wind up in jail after all this.

We go outside. Pulling out his phone, Logan says, "Shame about this place."

"Why?" I ask.

"As soon as we leave this parking lot, Donnie's going to be in the wind. He has to realize we're going to share our evidence with the police."

I wince. "Arlo's not going to want to hear that I was involved with this. Can you call your contacts at the station instead?"

Logan shakes his phone at me. "Way ahead of you."

As we get back into the car, I can't think of anything to say to Logan. He hasn't done anything wrong. I've made it clear I have no claim on him. Still. How am I supposed to compare to someone like Fake Leslie, who has so much more in common with Logan than I do? He wouldn't have to be careful with her, the way he would with me and my grief-scarred heart. It isn't fair, this thing with the timing between me and Logan. Why couldn't I move forward with him when we had that moment back at Mateo's place? Now it feels like I've lost any chance.

I say, "I guess this means the diamonds are a dead end."

Logan considers that. "Maybe. It just seems like an awful big coincidence."

Logan's phone lights up. He looks at it. "We've got the info on Mateo's credit. He's got a monthly payment going to Blue Heron Fitness. Chances are, that key goes to a locker there."

Which just happens to be the same gym that both Logan and I go to. I've been trying to keep up with my low-impact exercise regimen, even though my drug treatment is over. I've never seen Mateo on a treadmill or lifting weights or anything. It is possible he only got the membership to use a locker. "Then let's go."

# Chapter Fifteen
## *Still Wednesday*

I put the key on the counter and ask, "Does this go to one of the lockers here? It should be one of the long-term rentals."

The girl behind the counter gives me a disapproving look. "I can't give out that information."

She is all of eighteen years old and wearing a lime green tee-shirt, but sure, judge me.

"Please," I say. "This key belongs to Mateo Alvarez. They guy who went missing. We're trying to find him, and we have reason to believe he might have stored information in a locker here."

Her eyes go wide. "Are you private investigators?"

"Yes," Logan says, before I can get my mouth open to say no. He flashes her an ID from his wallet. I'm pretty sure it's his pilot's license.

She doesn't ask for a better look. "In that case, I guess I can look up the record." She spends a few minutes fiddling with the computer. Then she says, "It's locker twelve. Men's locker room, obviously."

"Obviously," Logan says, scooping the key up off the counter.

Which means I'm going to miss the excitement of opening the locker and discovering what's inside. I wait for Logan by the water fountains near the locker room door.

This really built guy walks out of the locker room. He gives me a funny look for loitering. I look away, not sure why I'm suddenly so embarrassed.

It doesn't take long for Logan to come back. He's carrying a slate gray messenger bag. We take it out to his car.

I gesture at the bag. "Did you take a look already?"

"No." Logan looks amused. "There were several guys back there getting changed."

This embarrasses me too, probably because it doesn't feel like he's taking me seriously. I clear my throat. "Well. Let's see what was so important to Mateo."

Logan flips over the flap of the bag. He pulls out a binder full of papers, complete with tabs and color-coordinated highlights. I don't understand some of what I'm looking at. There's a whole stack of papers with what looks like GPS coordinates. And then a tab with copies of e-mails. He's intercepted information about river dolphins, and rare birds, and big cats, and endangered reptiles – all of which are being brokered for astounding prices. It doesn't sound like they're going to any sort of legal zoo either.

Mateo was doing an investigation of his own. It had started in South America, with the dolphins Mateo had discovered. A number of them had been brokered, and Mateo had followed the trail – which had led him, on a circuitous route, to Galveston.

Unfortunately, the investigation detailed in the notes is incomplete. There's info on the endangered animal poaching ring, but not on who is actually in charge of it. Mateo just keeps calling this person The Mysterious Z.

While I'm sorting through the binder, Logan is doing something on his phone.

I tell Logan, "I had wondered why Mateo suddenly developed an interest in marine animals instead of cacao trees. He was probably only on the research team so that he could track the poachers."

Logan shrugs. "I'm not sure that matters. It still feels like this is about Fabin."

"You're right," I tell him. "But what connects Fabin to the diamonds? Because why else would he have been at the shop?"

"Not sure." Logan's phone lights up. He looks down at the screen. "Hmmmmm."

"What?" I try to get a look at what he's looking at. But I'm still thinking about the diamonds. "If Donnie was told that the diamonds were his payment, only he had to retrieve them – could somebody have told Fabin the same thing? Or maybe even told a third person, who killed Fabin?"

"That's possible. But whyever Fabin actually came to Felicitations, it's obvious Mateo saw him." He reads off his phone screen. "Fabin Obodozie owns a number of exotic animal pets. He's recently put out feelers about trying to buy a Sumatran tiger cub." Logan looks up. "Aren't all tigers on the endangered animals list?"

"I think so." I remember something Kimmy had said. "Fabin's girlfriend claimed that he had promised her an exorbitant present while they were here on the island. And when I met her, she was wearing a tee-shirt with a tiger on it. Fabin could have been trying to get a tiger cub for her. But why would he have come to Galveston to do it? It's not like tigers are native here."

"But it is a port town," Logan points out. "And not a huge one, at that. If you're looking to smuggle something in, it wouldn't be a bad place for it."

"That would explain why Fabin decided to drive all the way down here instead of fly."

"I hate to say this." Logan looks at me, troubled thoughts muting his green eyes. "But Fabin might have been involved in whatever Mateo was investigating. Which could mean Mateo has a motive for murdering him. Did Mateo ever strike you as the type to be an environmental extremist?"

"You think Mateo might have killed somebody for trying to buy an endangered tiger?"

Logan just shrugs. "I never really talked to the guy. I don't know what his priorities were."

I run my finger along the edge of the window. "But what about what Mrs. Guidry said? Somebody forced Mateo into a car and drove off with him."

Logan says, "She was watching from across the street. Maybe she misinterpreted what she saw. Mateo could have been embracing that girl. Or Mrs. Guidry could have imagined the other people altogether."

"It's possible. I guess." I skim through the rest of the binder. There's a lot here. How had Mateo had time to do all of this? "I just thought-"

"What?" Logan looks at me with concern.

"I just thought we would find some straightforward answers. Instead, we're out of clues. After we found that key that everybody else had missed – I wanted – I don't know-" It's stupid, but as I'm trying to form the sentence, I realize exactly what I'd wanted. "- to prove that I'm just as smart as Fake Leslie."

"Hey," Logan says. "You don't have to be like her to be smart. You passed your classes to become a physical therapist, didn't you? And watching you this morning, making chocolate – you have the instincts of an artist."

He really thinks of me like that? "I'm flattered."

Logan says, "In my world, straightforward answers are hard to come by. You learn to take fragments of shattered puzzle pieces and put them together. Sometimes, they lead to a truth. But not all cases get solved, not all clients can be saved. And you have to learn how to live with that."

"I'm not sure I like it in your world," I tell him.

"That makes two of us," Logan says. "Look, let me take you back. Get a good night's sleep, and we can think about this fresh in the morning."

Logan drops me back off at the shop. I go in to check on things before heading home. Carmen is just closing up. She tells me, "The surfing's going to be good tomorrow, so I'll probably come in late."

"What?" My stomach sinks. If she's not here, that means I will have to deal with Ash by myself.

"Kidding! I know that guy's coming tomorrow." Though there's a wistful look in Carmen's eyes. "The surf report really is nice, though. I wouldn't kid about that."

"Any day but tomorrow," I tell her. She's been doing so much at the shop lately. And both baking and surfing are typically early-morning activities, so I'm sure she hasn't had as much time for the waves as she would like.

"What's tomorrow?" Arlo asks. He's been sitting quietly on the sofa, a bag with my shop logo on the cushion beside him. I hadn't even noticed him there – obviously waiting for me.

I don't really want to go into the details, so I just say, "There's a blogger coming to profile the shop."

"Nice." Yet, Arlo presses his lips into a flat line. "You want to tell me what you and Logan have been up to?"

Carmen says, "I'm heading out."

I wave at her, "Be safe." Then I move over to the drip coffee station. I'm afraid Carmen has emptied it, but she must have forgotten, because hot, strong decaf comes out of the appropriate spout. I pour Arlo a cup that's fully leaded, and gesture him over to a table. "We found some papers Mateo had been keeping in his locker at the gym. Logan has them, so you should ask him for the details."

"I'll do that." Arlo takes a single paper-wrapped truffle out of the top of the bag – probably a sample Carmen had given him. He unwraps it and bites into it. Which doesn't feel like professional cop behavior.

"You're not here about the case, are you?"

"Not exactly. Though I'm glad you gave me the information on those papers." Arlo gestures with the other half of the truffle. "This is good, by the way." Then he sighs. "Patsy sent me by to get the inside scoop on what you think about her brother. I told her you probably wouldn't tell me anything, but she insisted."

"She's really okay with you coming in to see me like this? Considering our history?" And how attractive Arlo still is.

"She trusts me. And I don't intend on ever giving her a reason not to." He pops the rest of the truffle into his mouth.

"You always were one of the good guys," I tell Arlo. "I just wish I had appreciated what I had with you at the time. I hope Patsy realizes how lucky she is."

"Can I quote you on that?"

"Sure. You and Patsy make a good couple. But how did you even meet?"

"Patsy's an elementary school teacher. She deals with special needs kids. I went out to do a campus-wide presentation on bullying prevention. Afterwards, she came up to me, and asked me for some tips on how to help one of her students that she suspected was being bullied electronically. I gave her my card, but when she called it was to ask me out."

"*She* asked *you* out?" Actually, considering the type of person she is, that's not hard to believe.

Arlo nods. "I really like this girl, Lis. She is one of the most caring people I've ever met. With the kids she teaches, with her family – with me."

"Does that mean I need to put another wedding on my social calendar?" I ask. I'm more on board with this match than with the other wedding on my events list.

"I don't know." Arlo looks all embarrassed again. "Maybe. It's just – I'm not sure we're at that point yet. She's independent. And it takes a lot to blend two lives. I learned that the hard way, a long time ago."

So had I. My breakup with Arlo had been messy – and the fact that I'd hurt him so deeply is one of the reasons that I'm hesitant to step into love again.

But I'm glad that Arlo and I can talk like this now. Like old friends, who have put the past behind them. We chat for a while about other things, then I empty and clean the coffee urns, and Arlo walks me to my catering van. Before I can get in, he says, "You never did answer the question. What do you think of Wallace?"

"I haven't decided. So for now, just tell Patsy no comment."

I pull my catering truck up to the hotel, ready to turn into my usual spot. Only – there's a police car parked just outside the front door. And an ambulance. And a gray truck marked Animal Control.

My heart freezes. I keep looking at that ambulance. Nobody's in it. Could something have happened to my grandmother? Her memory issues are only partial, but there are a lot of unfinished surfaces and staircases.

I rush towards the front doors. When I open the right-hand one, Aunt Naomi and Tiff are standing just inside, looking scared, and leaning against each other for support. Like old friends, instead of sort-of enemies.

"What happened?" I ask.

Naomi points towards the hall that leads to the modestly-sized hotel restaurant. "Mom is trapped back there."

Her mom – i.e., my Maw Maw.

"Trapped? By who?" I hope this doesn't have anything to do with me butting in on Fabin's murder investigation. I hadn't exactly been discreet about looking into it. But for someone to threaten my family is just a step too far.

"It's not exactly a who," Tiff says.

Not sure what she's talking about, I take off across the room and down the hall.

"Felicity, wait," Aunt Naomi says, but I keep going.

There's still water damage here on the first floor, and the floor is soft in places, so I slow down enough to make it safely. I reach the entrance to the restaurant dining room. There are still tables and furnishings that the old owner left behind. Up on top of one of the tables, two uniformed police officers and two EMTs are doing their best to all stay in the center of the surface.

On the floor next to them, there's a ten-foot-long alligator. The alligator isn't focused on the table, though. It seems mostly interested in the guy with the lasso on a stick trying to get a rope around its neck. There's already a rope around its jaws, holding its mouth closed.

One of the cops, a short red-headed guy, is holding a tranq gun, but the dart is lying on the floor, like it might have bounced off the alligator. Or maybe he missed.

I back carefully away, then move quickly back up the hall. I jerk a thumb in the direction of the unexpected spectacle. I demand of Aunt Naomi, "What exactly does that have to do with Maw Maw?"

"She saw it coming and locked herself in the storage room," Aunt Naomi says. "We couldn't get her to come out." Naomi puts a reassuring hand on my arm. "She should be perfectly safe in there."

I shake my head in puzzlement. "How did this even happen? Alligators usually stay over by the marsh, closer to the state park."

"One of my Craigslist guys had it in a U-Haul – who knows why. The guy went to put some old beds in there, and the alligator jumped out. The minute it escaped, the guy took off."

I'm not even going to ask about the series of events following that that led to the alligator being in the hotel. But then I remember what Naomi had said, about bringing Knightley down for Maw Maw to pet before they got to work. My poor lop would barely make a snack for an alligator. I turn to Aunt Naomi, "Knightley-"

"Is back upstairs, away from the paint fumes. I know how sensitive bunnies' little systems are."

I heave a sigh of relief.

"Ladies, watch out!" A guy's voice echoes down the hallway.

The alligator comes barreling up the hall. Aunt Naomi, Tiff and I quickly cross the space to the main desk and leap behind it. The alligator doesn't care about us. It has spotted the open door, and is making for it at full speed.

The guy with the lasso comes chasing after it.

We head towards the restaurant, where the cops are down off the table. The EMTs are gone – presumably into the kitchen to help my grandmother. I ask the red-headed officer, "What happens if your animal control guy can't catch it?"

The officer looks troubled. "With its mouth tied shut like that – that animal wouldn't have much chance of surviving. Which is why we're headed out to help."

I never thought I'd feel sorry for an alligator. I hope they can capture it and get it safely back to where it belongs. I go through into the kitchen. My aunt has been busy in here over the past few days. The old drywall has been replaced. And it looks like Maw Maw and Tiff had started painting one of the walls a calming sky blue. There's a roller someone dropped in the middle of the floor, splattering paint across the linoleum.

The two EMTs are standing by the storage room door. One of them, a woman in her thirties with dark hair and blue eyes, knocks – presumably not for the first time. "Mrs. Lavergne?"

"Stop knocking." I can hear Maw Maw's voice coming from the inside. "I'm not coming out until it's safe."

"But it is safe, Mrs. Lavergne," the EMT says.

"Here," I say. "Let me try." I move over to the door. "Maw Maw, it's Felicity."

She opens the door a crack. "Is that alligator gone?"

"They chased it back outside."

I brace myself emotionally as the door swings open the rest of the way. I love my grandmother. But her memory issues relate to not being able to hold onto painful memories. And one thing she cannot ever remember is that Kevin's dead. So every time I see her again, she asks about my late husband. And I have to tell her all over again that my husband is gone. She's going to ask, *Where's Kevin?*

"Felicity, I'm so glad you are here." Maw Maw is significantly shorter than me. She looks up into my face, then moves forward to wrap me in a hug. With her forehead still against my shoulder, she asks, "Where's Logan?"

I freeze and murmur a confused, "What?"

She's meant to be asking after Kevin. She only met Logan once, at my make-up grand opening party.

"Where's Logan? The guy who always keeps you safe."

"He's not here." I feel heat from my face all the way down into my chest. I've spent so long dreading each time of having to explain the pain in my heart to her – so why am I even more upset that she *didn't* ask. Tears spring to my eyes. But I'm not going to let them fall.

I'm doing better, these past few weeks. I'm moving past the rawness of my grief. I'm able to function as a human being. But right now – just for this minute – I can't let go of my grandmother. I picture Kevin's face, remember how it felt each time he embraced me. He was my everything. How is it okay that everything in my life keeps changing, leaving him farther and farther behind?

Maw Maw pats me on the back. "Let me make you some coffee. And we can talk. After all, I keep missing so much of your life. When are you and Logan going to get married?"

"Oh hold on now," I splutter. "I'm not even sure I like Logan, Maw Maw."

The other EMT, a young-ish guy, snickers. "I'm sure you can take it from here."

I pull away from Maw Maw and turn to address the EMTs. "Thank you for your help."

Maw Maw, who has stepped over to one of the kitchen countertops, blinks in puzzlement and asks, "Kit, where's the coffee maker?" Kit being a family nickname for me, from when I was a small child. She adds, "I'm sorry. I must have forgotten again."

That's the most heartbreaking part of all of this. Maw Maw knows her memory is flawed, and it bothers her. "You didn't' forget. There isn't one yet. Naomi's bringing it over from the house this weekend."

"No coffee maker?" Maw Maw moves over to the EMTs. "Please. Take me with you."

Naomi and Tiff enter the room just in time to catch this exchange. Aunt Naomi starts snickering. She tells Maw Maw, "We can stop at Starbucks on the way back to your apartment. I think we've had enough excitement for one day, don't you?"

The two cops come into the room. The animal control guy is with them. He's older than I thought at first, with gray hair at his temples. He's cradling his arm, which seems injured.

The female EMT moves over to him and gestures for him to hold out his arm. "Let me see."

I feel a wave of nostalgia as she tests the joint and declares it a sprained elbow, pending x-rays to rule out anything worse. Once upon a time, she would have recommended he come and see me afterwards for physical therapy. I have to remind myself that that's not my job anymore. Someone else will have to put this guy back together.

"We got the gator into the van," he says, even as he winces in pain. "I'm about to head down to the state park and release her back where she belongs. Parks and Wildlife has a couple of folks waiting to help out."

"That was a brave thing you did," I tell him.

He waves his good hand dismissively. "Pssht. It's all about confidence. Most of the time wild animals would just as soon escape from you as attack you."

Tiff shudders. "That's easy for you to say. I chickened out of a trip my company organized for team building because they were going out on the boardwalk at Sea Rim. Just the thought of being out on a wooden plank with an alligator was enough to freak me out."

Tiff moved to Galveston less than two years ago, and she's already had to deal with a hurricane and the Gulf's capricious weather. I doubt she's ready to explore Southeast Texas's wild side.

The animal control guy says, "You would have been fine, even if you did see a gator. Like with any wild animal, you face it, because prey runs. Then you avoid eye contact, because that's aggressive. And then you back away. When you've got a safe distance between you and the animal, then you can run."

"That's how I approach most things in life," I quip.

Everybody laughs – except Tiff. Her eyes are still round like saucers. I wonder if she ever regrets moving to Texas.

Once we've thanked everyone for helping us, and the emergency vehicles have left, Aunt Naomi says, "What do you think? No more Craigslisters?"

I consider it. "Nah. They still seem useful. Just be cautious."

"And if they turn feral," Maw Maw says, "Slowly back away."

We all laugh. Tiff gives me a quick hug. "I need to go tell my husband what happened. Don't be surprised if I call you later to corroborate, because he is never going to believe it."

Aunt Naomi says, "Once I drop off Mom, I'm going to call Greg out on the offshore rig. Only he will believe it – because crazy things always seem to happen to me."

And with that, they all leave, and I am alone in the not-yet-functional kitchen. Seriously, if we're going to be living here now, we at least need a microwave.

I go upstairs to check on Knightley. I know Aunt Naomi said he's in my suite, but I just need to make sure.

When I walk in, my living room is just as empty as it was yesterday, with nothing in it but Knightley's crate. Which has hay and food and water – but no Knightley. He doesn't usually hang out in it anyway, unless I'm in the same room. When I go through into the bedroom, my little bunny is asleep on the bed I put for him next to my bed. He lifts his head and looks sleepily at me.

I go over and sit on the bed, dangling my hand down so Knightley knows I'm offering to pet him. He hops over and starts chinning my shoe, reminding me that I'm his human. I've hardly been home the past couple of days, while he's been adjusting to the new space. I feel guilty about that. Knightley was the only constant left in my life after Kevin died and I moved half way across the country, back to my hometown to start a chocolate shop. He's been there for me. But I haven't been there for him.

"I'm sorry," I tell him. "I'll get you some parsley tomorrow. I promise."

Parsley is Knightley's favorite food. It's been too long since I'd gotten him any. A good second best is his treats. I dig through the moving boxes until I find the container.

"You have no idea what I've been dealing with," I tell him as I hold out a treat. "Do you think Mateo might really be a murderer? Arlo could be right on this one. I don't want it to be true, though."

Knightley is silent on the matter.

"I hope I'm not that bad a judge of character." But how much do I really know about Mateo? I'd learned next to nothing from his family. And only a few bits and pieces from the people he was working with on the research team. There had been that incident in the rainforest. I have a sudden urge to talk to the people who might have been involved.

I'd called to check Mateo's references, so Hector Rivera, the director of The Heirloom Review Foundation is still in my phone. I hadn't saved it under his name, but it's the only call I've ever made to Bolivia, where the foundation has its headquarters, so it isn't hard to pull his number back up. I explain who I am and what I want.

Hector says, "Mateo was a good kid. Not what the media is saying he was like at all. I don't believe he had it in him to kill anyone."

"Did he ever show any signs of aggression?" I ask. "Get into fights with anyone? Or have things unexpectedly break around him?"

"No," Hector says. Then he says, "Well." The he hesitates. "There was this one thing that happened. It was right after the men came through and took the dolphins. Mateo got into an argument with a girl on our team, accusing her of having something to do with it."

"Did he strike her, or anything?" I ask, though I have a hard time picturing Mateo hitting a girl.

"Of course not."

"That's what I thought," I say. "So the problem didn't escalate?"

"No. But the girl left our group, and Mateo left soon after. So there's that."

Which implies Mateo was right – the girl had been up to something illegal. "Who was the girl?"

"Her name was Caitlin Clement," Hector says. "I don't have any follow-up contact information."

"Caitlin," I repeat. I've just met a Caitlin. But her name is Caitlin Murphy. On one level, that seems like an odd coincidence. But on another, when you think about how many Caitlin's there are in the world – I had gone to school with two of them – you're likely to know multiple people with the same given name at the same time. Still, I ask, "What did she look like?"

"Thin, long dark hair, insisted on wearing mascara in the rainforest. Spoke Spanish like she'd been raised in a bilingual household. Favored wearing lots of bracelets and pendant necklaces."

So it's not her, then. The Caitlin I'd met had been a blonde, without a speck of makeup or jewelry in sight. So I shift the conversation to the other question I've been wanting to ask.

"We're assuming Mateo has been abducted. But if he wasn't –
would he be capable of going off the grid and becoming
untraceable? If he saw the murder and was trying to make sure he
didn't wind up being next?"

"He's a capable camper," Hector says. "And he's smart.
In theory, he could be hiding out somewhere. Before he left here,
he told me there were a couple of spots he wanted to visit while
he was in Texas. The one he kept talking about is called
Enchanted Rock."

"I've been there," I tell him. "It's beautiful."

I text Logan, *A source says that if Mateo is hiding out, he
could be at Enchanted Rock. Of course, that park is huge. IF he
went somewhere of his own accord, instead of being kidnapped.
And IF he didn't decide to just keep going until he got out of the
country.*

Logan texts back, *I'm dropping my client off in Austin, so
I won't be far from there. I can check in with the park staff, and
do a flyover to see if there are any campsites set up where they
aren't supposed to be. Even if it is a longshot, at least it is a lead.*

# Chapter Seventeen
*Thursday*

I know Ash is coming at 9, so I make sure I'm at the shop by 8. Carmen has already been there for a while by the time arrive, and she has sweet bread dough rising and ready to bake – and more about to come out of the oven.

"What's with all the bags?" she asks.

"I want to make sure that everything looks perfect." I stopped by the grocery store to pick up fresh flowers and little vases to do arrangements on the tables. And I remembered to get parsley for Knightley, and a packaged salad bowl so I can have a healthy lunch. I tuck the parsley and the salad into the fridge and find a spot Carmen isn't using on the counter and quickly trim the stems of the flowers.

I know I said I wanted to deal with Ash on my own, but that doesn't mean I'm not nervous. Especially because I'm starting to convince myself that maybe I'm wrong, and Mateo is the killer. That Logan will definitely find him at the park. Wouldn't Ash love to get ahold of that story?

Ash shows up at 8:30.

Carmen rolls her eyes when she spots him outside, cupping his hands, to better peer in through the plate glass window. "He's already trying to catch us off balance, and he hasn't even stepped through the door yet."

"I know." I wave at Ash and gesture him inside. We have a couple of customers hanging out and eating chocolate conchas. But none of them even give Ash a look as he makes his way up to the counter, taking pictures of the inside of the shop as he goes. This is the first time he's ever actually been in here.

The first thing he says is, "Where's Logan?"

I gesture vaguely towards the ceiling and thus the sky. "Logan is off doing a flight."

"Oh. I thought he was going to be here."

I put my hands on the counter and lean forward slightly, trying to come across as confident. "None of this really has anything do with him, now does it?"

"It does if I'm going to do a profile of the new dynamic at your shop. That is what you want, right?"

"Yes, but I really just want to talk to you first."

He looks wary. "What do you mean?"

"I want to understand this obsession you have with me. All these stories about me keep popping up on your blog. Is this because you resent that Tam Binh made you write something nice about me? Because this is starting to feel a bit personal."

"Personal?" Ash busts out laughing. "Look, Koerber, you take a pretty picture and all, but I could care less. This is all about the likes. And the comments. None of the other stories I've ever posted have gotten so many people talking on my blog as that first one I did about you. I'm trying to be a bit nicer about it now, but people are still wanting to know what happened over here at the Murder Factory."

"This is you being nice?" Carmen asks.

"I haven't said anything about you yet, have I?" Ash counters.

"And he refrained from calling it the Murder Factory in print," I say. Though that's still not saying much. If he was a good person, he wouldn't even consider doing that.

"Clever headlines get clicks," Ash says. "You can't argue with the algorithms."

He's not even ashamed to say that.

I force a smile. "I was thinking I could show you how to roast cacao beans this morning. You can take all the pictures you want. Or video."

"Sure. Just answer me one question. Are you in love with Logan Hanlon?"

I'm taken aback by his bluntness.

Now Ash looks smug. "Well, that face says it all."

"No, it doesn't," I protest. "I honestly don't know how I feel about Logan."

"Uh huh." Ash snaps a picture. Of whatever face I didn't realize I was making. Great. That's probably going to be front and center on his next blog post.

Carmen asks, "What turned you into this . . . whatever?" She waves her hand at his phone.

"My grandfather was a newspaper reporter," Ash says. "I grew up wanting to be just like him."

"And you couldn't get a job at a real newspaper?" Carmen asks. I want to tell her to be careful and avoid the sarcasm. If she upsets this guy, he *will* start writing about her. Not that there's anything embarrassing in Carmen's life – that I know of. But Paul's ex-wife could try to use bad publicity as a reason to deny Paul custody of his kid – or to make Paul and Carmen break up.

But Ash doesn't seem offended. "Everybody says that you should build a platform if you want to be a real writer. Put together some articles, so you have clips later. So I started doing that, when I was still a teenager. But the blog took off. And it started making money. So now I'm a decade in, and adding onto the platform is basically my entire job."

"That's actually kind of commendable," Carmen tells him. "If you weren't hurting people in the process."

"You think I really hurt Koerber here?" Ash gestures to the Jane Austen volumes on display, commemorating how I'd solved a murder. And then at the section of my shelves holding my Sympathy and Condolences line of bars – which came about directly because of one of his articles. "I've said it before. No publicity is bad publicity."

"What if I asked you to stop?" I ask.

He gestures at the books again. "I doubt deep down that you really want that. And besides, no. Your click conversion rate is just too good." Ash takes a good close look at the last concha under the glass dome on the counter. "You know influencers are often offered freebies, right?"

"Do you want a concha, Ash?" I ask. "The topping is made with cacao grown by a collective in Venezuela."

Concha in hand, Ash follows me to the back. He nibbles delicately at it as he watches me sort and roast beans. All the while he asks questions like, "How many countries have you visited?" and "Is it true your late husband was the inspiration for your shop name?" But then he balls up his napkin, wipes his lips and asks, "Why is it so hard for you to let new people into your life?"

"Excuse me?" I ask, standing frozen over the beans in their long cooling tray.

He says, "You and Hanlon have been through a lot together, and you're still not sure how you feel about him. You don't really want to talk to me, even though I'm being perfectly civil. You apparently tried to give Wallace Nash back the bracelet he'd given you." Ash's spies are everywhere. "Where does that kind of pattern come from, psychologically?"

My first thought is, *how dare he!* But rather than shout at him, I take a deep breath. I'd promised myself I wasn't going to let him rattle me. "I don't think it is a bad thing to be cautious who you let into your life, and in what capacity."

"Even if it means letting the possibilities of new friendships just pass you by?" He looks genuinely curious. And I don't sense malice in the question. He sounds like my aunt, honestly.

"I'm trying to deal with change, as best I can. The past is safe – it's already happened. Even the bad things. They're part of you. But if you don't make the right decisions in the present, change can turn out to be bad. Even if I'm missing things – I just want to keep myself from getting hurt." My face is going hot. I hadn't meant to be so honest. "I hope you're not going to print that."

"It would make a great quote for the little homework assignment Tam Binh asked me to write," Ash says. "But I'm not sure it's true. I think I'll watch a little more and see if it really represents who you are. I'd rather print something about the progress of the case. Since I've been highlighting your skills as a detective."

I decide to tell him *something*. But what can I share without making someone's secrets the next target of Ash's laser? I say carefully, "We know Fabin was in Texas to impress his girlfriend with an extravagant gift and an amazing meal."

He keeps asking follow-up questions, trying to get more information. But I keep deflecting back to harmless topics, about how the shop runs.

Ash is still there when Carmen calls me to the front, saying there's someone here to see me. It turns out to be Enrique. I do a double-take. Instead of another expensive button-up shirt, Enrique is wearing a thin sweater, just like the one Sonya made me.

I gesture at the green and brown patterned yarn. "How do you know Sonya?"

Enrique straightens the sweater's cuffs. "I helped her out with a cheesecake emergency."

Well, that raises more questions than it answers. But Sonya doesn't make things for just anybody. Which strengthens my impression that Enrique's not really a bad guy.

Enrique asks, "When you were over at Mateo's place, you didn't happen to see a copy of *The Invisible Man*?"

I nod. "There was one on his bookshelf."

Enrique looks relieved. "I loaned it to him, but now a friend of mine wants to read it, so I need it back. Could you grab it for me when you go over there?"

"Sure," I say. Is he expecting me to bring it back by his place? If Kimmy's going to be there, I'd rather not step back into that situation. "Are you planning to come back into the shop again soon?"

He takes a chocolate bar from the central bin and puts it on the counter. "I'm sure I'll need another one of these by next week. I can get the book then."

"Fair enough." I ring up his purchase. I get the distinct feeling someone is watching me. When I glance behind me, there's Ash, phone in hand, taking my picture. I smile and actually pose for once.

"Are you in the middle of a website redesign?" Enrique asks, nodding with approval. "People love those behind-the-scenes shots."

My first thought is, *Why? Is something wrong with my website?* But really, Enrique probably hasn't even seen it. "Ash is a blogger," I say. "He's doing a profile on Greetings and Felicitations."

"Really?" Enrique says. "I've been thinking about starting a blog."

"Good," I say. "I've been showing Ash how I make chocolate. I have a batch that's ready to go in the molds. You should come watch his process as a reporter."

Ash gives me a dirty look. Which gives me a little passive-aggressive moment of satisfaction. I don't care if the last thing he wants is answering some noob's questions about the best blog platform to use – if it deflects him from asking more questions about what Logan and I are doing to solve the murder.

"Check this out," I tell the two guys. "This is the melanger that survived the break-in. Carmen and I fixed it."

"You like tinkering with machines?" Ash asks. He's making a note. Clearly, I've surprised him.

"It's a fun part of the job – unless the machine that's not working is needed urgently. We were able to reheat that chocolate that cooled inside the machine and get it going again. This chocolate has been processing since Monday. It should be just about done."

I get them each a sample, and explain how you can tell chocolate is ready by the mouthfeel. You stop processing it when it ceases to feel gritty, but before it becomes gluey. It's all about the micron size of the particles. I start laying out molds. I line them up, all the way across the counter, three deep. Each mold makes four bars. I turn and tell the guys, "I usually mold the bars myself. It feels like part of the artistic process to finish the bars I started by roasting the beans. But Carmen is a whiz at working the wrapping machine. And she takes the chocolate I've made and works it into the baked goods and coffee drinks. She does some amazing work. You know she's working on a cookbook?"

"I have a cookbook," Enrique says. "It's self-published, but I'm still proud of it."

"Really?" Ash asks. He opens a search window on his phone. "What's it called?"

"Recipes on the Fly." Enrique looks pleased with himself.

Ash studies his screen for a few moments, then says, "I thought Felicity said your name is Enrique. Why does this say the author is Ray Fines?"

Enrique says, "Plausible deniability."

I listen to them banter, while I transfer quantities of chocolate into the tempering machine, and then into the chocolate molds, smacking each filled mold repeatedly on the counter to remove air bubbles that could ruin the look of the bars. I'm about half done when my phone rings. It's Logan.

I tell the two guys, "Excuse me. I need to take this."

I go through the kitchen and head outside, where I lean up against the wall. "Hey. I see you landed safely."

"Thanks for the concern," Logan says, but it sounds like he's bantering again. "Look, I did a thorough flyover, and I talked to some of the park staff. There's no sign that Mateo is or ever was in Enchanted Park."

"So you think maybe he's hiding out somewhere else?" I try to sound hopeful.

Logan sighs. "There's been no hits on his credit card or his bank card. Or any other sign that he ever left the island."

"You think he's hiding out *here*?" There's a squeak in my voice.

"I mean, it could be possible." Logan sounds hesitant.

"But you really think he's dead."

"Isn't that better than him being a murderer?"

I'm not sure what to say. *Is* that better? I consider it. He would at least be innocent, and his family can grieve in peace. But it would mean he's dead.

Logan's logic just feels a little too cold.

When I don't say anything, Logan finally says, "Look, I'll get back as soon as I can. How's it going with Ash?"

"Better than I expected," I tell him. "But it's Ash. So who knows, until it shows up on his blog."

I let Logan go and head back inside. The rest of the molds are filled, and there's a note from Enrique, saying, *I have to go. But let's catch up next week.*

Ash says, "I should probably head out too. I've got a lead on a new story to work on."

I'm nervous about having had someone who's not an employee working with my chocolate. But at least Enrique is a chef. Surely he observed the proper cleanliness standards. I check over his work, banging the filled molds on the counter, at least making sure he's gotten all of the bubbles out of the bars.

After Ash leaves, I take my salad out of the fridge and eat a quick lunch. It's still early, but the way this day has been going, who knows when I will have another chance for non-chocolate sustenance. Then I throw the plastic bowl and spoon in the trash and go out and see how Carmen is doing. There's brisk business in the shop, so I take over the register, freeing Carmen to focus on the specialty coffee station. I get to talk to several people who are more interested in chocolate than in murder, and a couple of regular customers who are excited to try my newest bar. It's a nice, normal moment after all the recent craziness, exactly what I want my business to be like.

Miles's girlfriend comes into the shop. I recognize her from the picture on Mateo's phone, but she doesn't know me. As I wait on other customers, I track her progress as she checks out the book section, and then makes her way over to the shelves with all the gift sets.

She picks up one of each of my single bars and gets in line to check out. There's no one behind her, so when it is her turn to check out, I say, "You're Miles's girlfriend, right?"

She nods. "I'm Ariel." She gestures around. "I've never been in here before. But I wanted to see the place where Miles said he's going to be working. It's really nice."

"Thanks," I say. But I don't get the idea that she's really enthusiastic about the place. Her hands kind of flutter as she fumbles her wallet out of her purse. "Hey, are you okay?"

"Yeah, fine," she says. But then she looks more directly at me. "But is Miles? He's a really sweet guy – most of the time. But sometimes he gets in these moods. We haven't been together that long, but I think we really have something. I don't want to give up on that if there's a way to help him."

"You know about what happened to him?" I ask. "With the guy who tried to kill me?"

"Yes," she says quickly. "He doesn't want to talk about it, but it was all over the news."

"It was a trauma I don't think Miles was prepared to handle. But he seems like a resilient kid. I think he'll be okay – eventually."

"So you know him well?" Ariel asks.

"Maybe not as well as some. I never met him before I moved back here from Seattle last year." I start putting her chocolate bars into a bag. "He's been good friends with my cousin Wyatt, though, for a long time, and he thinks of my aunt as a second mom."

"He didn't mention that." She looks troubled.

That is odd. But come to think of it, Miles hadn't been around nearly so much in the month since the incident with Emma. "I'll ask Wyatt to call him."

"He said something the other day, when we were watching an old Spiderman movie. He said he understood how Peter Parker felt, that the only way to keep people safe was to avoid getting too close." Ariel hands me her credit card. "Honestly, I thought he was about to break up with me."

"I'm glad he didn't. You seem to really care about him."

She signs the receipt, then twirls the pen between her fingers. "Just don't tell him I came here. Guys think that kind of thing is nosy or clingy or whatever."

"Then you'd better get out of here. Miles is supposed to come in today as soon as he gets out of class."

Her eyes widen, and she scoops her bag off the counter. "Then he should be here any minute." She rushes out the door, calling, "Thanks Mrs. Koerber!" back over her shoulder.

I like Ariel. I hope Miles can trust her enough to let her in, to find that being close to people doesn't mean that they won't be safe. Surely, these two will get there. Really, who should a guy be able to trust, if not his girlfriend?

And it hits me. Mateo wasn't close to his family. But if he is on the run out there somewhere, he could have turned to his girlfriend to help.

I go back into the kitchen and call Haruka and ask her bluntly, "Has Mateo attempted to contact you since the night of the murder?"

"No. Why?" Her voice sounds urgent. "Have you heard something? Is he okay? Onegai, please tell me."

I wince. I hadn't meant to give her false hope. "No, I'm sorry. I'm still looking for him. I was just hoping that maybe he had reached out to someone."

"Our relationship is very new. He might have tried to trust someone he had more of a-" She hesitates, maybe searching for the word she wants to say.

"History?" I guess.

"Yes. You have his phone," she says. "If you scroll through, the profiles of every girl he's dated have a heart by them."

"He told you that?"

"No." She laughs into the phone. "But I was smart enough to figure it out."

"Makes sense." If only Logan hadn't insisted we turn over Mateo's phone, then I'd have something to go on right now. "Thanks for the info." I hang up.

Logan comes into the shop. He looks tired. Without even asking, Carmen pours him a cup of coffee. He starts to take it to a table, but I gesture him back towards where I am. He heads back behind the counter. "Everything okay?"

I explain what Haruka had said about Mateo's phone.

Logan looks at me like I'm a bit dim. "That's not a problem. I cloned the data before we handed it over."

Of course he did. "You should have told me."

"Do you want the data or not?"

Together, we sort through the entries in Mateo's contact list. We call every one of Mateo's former girlfriends. None of them have heard from him. And none of them seem particularly like potential accomplices. Two of them don't even know about the murder, or that Mateo has gone missing. The girl back in Spain tells us that, if we find him, we should tell him that she's sorry – apparently, she needs closure, even though she's the one who ended the relationship. And one of them says she hopes he *is* dead, and hangs up.

"I'm beginning to think Mrs. Guidry was right," Logan says. "Mateo really was abducted." He doesn't add, *and killed*. But it's there in his expression.

"I just wish we knew why. Why kill Fabin, but not him? Fabin had so much money – it still feels like it should have been the other way around."

"Criminals don't always do the logical thing." Logan yawns. "I had an early flight, and it's been a really long day. I'm going to head home and take a nap before the party tonight. Unless you have time for a quick lunch first."

I feel disappointed – even if I'm not sure Logan was asking for an actual impromptu date. "I already ate, while I was working. I'm sorry. I'm so short on time today."

"Right." His smile droops into a frown. "You already have plans for coffee. I forgot."

I sigh. "I wish I didn't."

But I'm not sure he hears me. He's already headed for the door.

Part of me wants to rush after him, tell him I'll drop everything for him. But I'm sure that would be a mistake.

## Chapter Eighteen
### *Still Thursday*

I still feel a bit subdued, with the shadow of the murder hanging over the shop, even as my friends start showing up to help set up Autumn's party. A couple of them are planning to spend the whole afternoon here, even though it won't take nearly that long to set everything up. It makes me feel better about leaving briefly for my coffee date with Wallace – and to take care of Clive.

Sonya comes into the shop, carrying two bags. One of them is silver and white, and all covered in glittery bells – obviously her engagement present for Autumn.

The other bag is plain brown craft paper. Sonya puts the plain bag on the counter.

"What's this?" I ask. I peek inside the bag. It's another sweater.

"That one is for Mateo," Sonya says. "I want you to leave it here for safekeeping until he comes back."

"That's very sweet of you." At least there's one person who shares my hope that Mateo is out there, somewhere, alive.

"He will come back," she insists, even though I haven't said anything to the contrary. "And he will prove himself innocent. Someone like him couldn't be a killer."

"How do you know Mateo?" I ask. Sonya runs a yarn shop. Other than in my shop, it's hard to think where the two would have come into contact with each other.

"We did a couple of beach clean-up events together. In our little group, I held the bag, and he put trash in it. He's reserved, but once you get him talking, he just does not stop. Did you know that he was engaged to a girl, back in Spain? She left him for his best friend. I think that a broken heart was the real reason he left home, not whatever happened with him and his dad."

It still amazes me how Sonya just knows things about people. I guess that happens when you're a great listener. Mateo had been working with me for almost a month, and I hadn't found out anything about his life back in Spain – until after he had disappeared. Maybe Ash has a point about me being reluctant to let others in.

I gesture down at the bag. "I'm sure Mateo's going to love this."

Sonya beams. "I hope so."

Carmen asks for help frosting all the tiny cupcakes she's made for the party, so Sonya heads into the kitchen to help her.

It doesn't take long for me to get into a more festive mood. Part of it is the music. Autumn loves Jazz. It's something she's always shared with her mom, as they go to live concerts multiple times a year. When Autumn and I used to hang out back in high school and college, sometimes I'd go with them. Autumn is even named for *Autumn Leaves*, her mom's favorite song. So for the party, I've pulled together a playlist of jazz standards that I get going through the shop's sound system. Which makes for an elegant feel to the evening, with wine, tapas and lots of chocolate.

Oh no! I forgot about the wine. And now that my funds are nonexistent, that could be a problem. Good thing the tapas are already paid for. I hesitate, but then I text Logan, *Any way you can pick up wine for the party? I will pay you back, as soon as I can. Autumn prefers champagne. Get plenty of that and a couple bottles of a decent merlot.*

He's probably home asleep already, which makes the request pointless – champagne takes time to chill. And I'm afraid he's going to take the instructions part of the text as a bit presumptuous.

But he texts back, *Don't worry about paying me back. Consider it part of my gift to your friends. I'll swing by in a couple of hours.*

Which means that if I hurry, I should be back in time to thank him personally. I rush to get myself together.

I have my purse in my hand, and I'm heading for the door when Sandra walks in. She's carrying a giant box which she sets down on the nearest table with obvious relief.

"What's that?" I ask.

"Autumn has the world's oldest microwave. This was the perfect chance to get her a new one, so I don't feel like we're irradiating ourselves every time we're over there making popcorn."

"That's great. She'll love it." I pat the box, and come away with glitter off the wrapping paper all over my palm.

I take a closer look at Sandra and realize she's covered with the stuff. She sees me looking and wipes at her cheek. "This has just been the craziest day. It's everywhere, isn't it?"

"Yep." I'm in a hurry, so I tell her, "I'll be back in about an hour and a half."

"I haven't told you the crazy part."

I hesitate. I want to get back before Logan comes in later. But I don't want to just ignore my friend. "What was so crazy?"

"You know that guy I kind of like, the pharmacist at the Underdog Drug Store? He saw me over at the Top Notch and just slid into the booth opposite me." Top Notch is the same café Autumn and I usually do lunch at. Sandra says, "He started telling me about his day, and how his boss is still upset over that break-in the other night – even though nothing turned up missing."

"That is weird," I agree. "Why break in, if you're not going to take anything?"

Sandra shrugs. "I don't know. Maybe if they didn't have whatever it was that you were wanting to take after all? It would still be odd not to take anything else, considering the street value of some of the things pharmacies keep in stock. But that's not the crazy bit."

"Oh? What is?" At first I was waiting just to be polite, but now I'm getting drawn in to the story.

"It turns out that he thought I was Sonya. It's not the first time someone has mistaken me for my sister, especially since I let her dye my hair with the same shade she uses. But it was super embarrassing, because I really like him, and apparently my sister has been chatting him up. He was embarrassed too, when he figured out he was talking to the wrong twin. Apparently, Sonya never even told him she has a sister. And she never told me she had an interest in the same guy. I am dying my hair back to its natural color tomorrow."

Sonya comes out of the kitchen, holding a tray of cupcakes. I'm pretty sure she heard everything her sister just said. Sandra sees her, and her cheeks instantly go red.

This is going to take them a good minute to sort out and I don't have time to stick around.

So I just smile a bit too big, wave at both of them and head out.

On my way to keep the coffee date with Wallace, I stop in to take care of the octopus. Clive is fortunately still in his tank. I spend some time petting the glass, and this time, he comes out from the reef to see what I'm doing. He's still sulking, but he puts an arm up against the glass. I take the weight off his tank and open the lid. Then I wiggle my fingers at the top of the water. He climbs up the reef structure to see me.

I flinch when he reaches out and wraps an arm around my finger. He immediately withdraws it and just sits there looking at me. I move my fingers a little closer, and he grabs on, pulling himself up to sit in my hand. He's kind of big to fit there, and most of his disproportionally long arms are hanging over the edge of my palm, though he's got one wrapped around my wrist.

"I'm sorry little guy," I tell him. "I really wish we could tell you we are going to find Mateo. I know you must miss him."

It's the first time I've admitted, even to myself, that I'm starting to give up hope.

Clive just looks at me. Obviously he can't understand what I'm saying, but maybe he's picking up my tone of voice. I don't want to think about what happens to him if Mateo is dead. It's not likely that Mateo's family will want Clive shipped to Spain.

I try tapping his other arms, like Mateo's note had instructed, but Clive doesn't seem in the mood to play. He lets go of my wrist and lowers himself into the water. I put the weight back on his tank and go to fish out some shrimp for him to eat. The note had been very clear about the order in which to do this – the last thing you want is to handle an octopus with the scent of its food on your fingers.

I pour the live shrimp into Clive's tank and replace the weight. I don't wait to watch him hunt. There's very little chance that he'll go hungry.

I move over to the bookcase and pick up the Enrique's copy of *The Invisible Man*.

This book just seems so apropos for the middle of a murder investigation. The Invisible Man himself is a practitioner of wonton violence – who appears able to disappear without a trace. Who is our invisible man? Who appeared only in that single, blurry photo Mateo took, and then disappeared?

He must have left something behind, some clue that would make all of this easier. If only I could figure out what it is.

Why had Enrique thought it was so important to get this book back? It doesn't look like there's anything special about this copy. I flip through it. Someone has annotated it in pencil. It looks like Mateo's handwriting. I stop on a random page. He's circled the name Dr. Kemp. And the note out to the side says, "What an odd coincidence."

Even then, was he thinking about the sea turtles? It wasn't a doctor who discovered the Kemp's ridley, though, but a fisherman off the coast of Florida. So maybe he was thinking about something else. I do a quick search on my phone, but there's no Dr. Kemp with a practice on Galveston Island. Nor one listed at any of the universities.

There's a piece of paper tucked inside *The Invisible Man* as a bookmark, and the notation marks stop on the page where it is stuck. It's a receipt for a MacBook. Since Mateo's laptop is a PC, I can only assume that the receipt is Enrique's and Mateo was just using it because it was handy. Could Enrique have incriminating information on that computer? Something that implies he might be a killer? But why not just wipe the info? What could be the significance of the receipt?

I sigh out a breath, trying to release the tension building in me. I'm at the point where I'm jumping at shadows and looking for clues everywhere. How can I figure out which ones are real?

It's been a long time since I've gone anywhere for coffee other than my own shop or the diner over by the seawall. Wallace has chosen a quirky little shop called Keen Beans. It's next door to Island Breeze Books, which my former nemesis owns. My repaired relationship with Kaylee is still fragile, and the fact that I haven't taken the book section out of my own shop is still a point of contention that could easily explode. I find myself tiptoeing past Island Breeze, keeping my face turned away as I pass the double glass doors.

When I look to the sidewalk ahead of me, I realize that Wallace is already at the shop, sitting at a small table, watching my approach with curiosity.

"What was that all about?" he asks.

"Nothing important," I lie. "Let's go inside."

"Sure." Wallace stands up and opens the door for me.

It takes a second for my eyes to get used to the shop's dim lighting after the brightness outside. But once I can focus, I take in a lot of warm brickwork and solid wood tables. There, at a table in the corner, is Fabin's girlfriend. She has an iced coffee and a photo album, and it looks like she's been crying.

As much as I've been hoping to avoid her – I can't just leave her there in that state.

I turn to Wallace. "Would you mind ordering me a decaf soy latte, and I'll be over in a second?"

Wallace looks at Kimmy, takes in her disheveled state. I can tell he gets it. "You know her?"

"Sort of," I say.

"Okay, well, I'll be waiting." Wallace sounds flustered. Which makes sense. After all, I'd told him I have limited time for this date, and it looks like it is getting derailed.

I walk over to Kimmy. "You okay?"

She crumples a tissue in her hand. "Not really. It just hit me today. I didn't realize it when he was alive, but I actually loved Fabin, you know?"

"I know that love is complicated," I tell her, sliding into the chair opposite hers. "And I know what it is like to lose someone. But I also know the loss gets easier to deal with, over time. You may not believe it right now, but you will be okay. Eventually."

She blinks her mascara-smeared eyes. "Why are you being nice to me? I was horrible to you the other day."

I gesture at her photo album. "Because pain is something that equalizes us all. You two look happy there."

"He'd just bought me a car. I thought I was happy because of the money he'd spent – but really, it was so sweet of him to remember that my dad had had a car just like it." She turns the book around and flips the page. "And here. Look at the earrings. They're worth a mint. But Fabin knew that roses are my favorite flowers. So he had those specially made with white and pink diamonds."

I get hit by a wave of nostalgia. It takes me a second to realize it's because what she's saying makes me think about the bracelet around my wrist. And it's not Wallace I credit for it –

though he may have paid for it – but Arlo. Arlo was my first love. And now he's starting to be a friend. I'm actually happy that Patsy set up that dinner date. Because things are less weird between us now.

But Kimmy won't get a chance to figure out what she really could have had with Fabin, if the relationship had had time to develop.

"I'm sorry for your loss," I say. It's a cliché, and it's empty. I hated it when people had said that to me. But what else can I say?

"Thanks. I would have gone home, only that detective told me he might have more questions." She closes the book and clutches it to her chest. Something falls out, hitting the floor with a plastic thunk.

"What's that?" I ask.

"Ugh. I have it upside down again. That thing is always falling out." She reaches under the table to retrieve a thumb drive. "It's just something Fabin asked me to hold for him."

"Have you looked at what's on it?" I ask. "Or mentioned it to the police?"

"Why would I do that?"

I stare at her, incredulous. "Because it could relate to why he got killed."

"Ew!" She drops the thumb drive on the table, like it might itself be toxic. "You take it. If there's anything dangerous on there, I don't want to know."

"You still need to be careful." I pick the drive up and slide it into my purse. My phone lights up with a text from Wallace. *You almost done? Your coffee is ready.*

I roll my eyes. "My date's getting anxious."

"You should go. But here's my card, in case there's anything on that thing that I *should* know about. Like if he left me everything in his will or something." She's kidding about that last bit. I think.

Kimmy goes back to looking at her photos, and I make my way over to Wallace.

He gives me a lopsided grin. "So what was that all about?"

"That's the girlfriend of the guy who was killed. She doesn't have friends in town, so I was just trying to make her feel better."

Wallace says, "You have a very kind heart."

"You're the one who's big on generosity." I hold out my wrist. "I really shouldn't accept this."

He crosses his arms. "Well, I'm not taking it back."

To lead into my I don't do long-distance relationships speech, I say, "You said you were leaving soon. How long will you be in town?"

"I was planning on heading out on Friday, but I don't know. Patsy is very serious about this detective guy. I kind of want to stick around and watch him solve this case."

I take a sip of my coffee. "I guess that will tell you a lot about how Arlo thinks."

"Arlo seems to be a pretty straightforward guy. I'm honestly more curious about you. Arlo said you'd gotten involved in one of his other murder cases. That you didn't know when to leave well enough alone."

"Is that exactly how he put it?" I ask, trying not to be too offended.

"Well, no," Wallace admits. "What he said was that he tried to get you to let the police do their jobs, but you wouldn't let it go, and you nearly got yourself killed."

"You don't have to worry about that this time," I say. Because this time, I'm not in Arlo's way at all.

"Good," Wallace says. "I don't want to see you get hurt. I'm sure Arlo will catch that Mateo guy soon. He's going to have to go somewhere to refill his prescriptions, and they'll be able to track that."

I say, "We don't know for sure that Mateo was the killer. But I'm sure the right person will be brought to justice."

I'm not sure how to get back from that to the I-don't-do-long-distance thing, without sounding petty.

"Enough talk about dark things," Wallace says suddenly. "This is supposed to be a date. Tell me why you opened a chocolate shop."

I start talking about my desire to travel, about that chocolate class I'd taken with my late husband – and Wallace doesn't give me pitying looks at all, the way most people do when they find out I'm a widow. I find myself actually enjoying talking to him.

I ask Wallace, "What have you been up to since you got into town?"

"I only arrived on Monday," he protests. Then he takes a deep sip of his coffee.

"Then what did you do on Monday?"

"Oh, stuff." He waves his hand vaguely. But his jaw tightens. Which I take to mean that Patsy had drawn him into something embarrassing.

I lean forward and tap his hand from across the table. "So like a marathon session of watching Patsy's favorite musicals or something?"

"Something like that." He takes another sip of coffee. "I haven't spent a lot of time in Texas. Patsy and I grew up in Florida. She took a job here, six years ago, and then, when I graduated high school, I moved to New York. After a few misadventures involving attempts at breaking into the music industry, I started my own business.

"You wanted to be a musician?" I don't even try to hide my surprise. "Like for the Philharmonic?"

"Hardly. I wanted to be the next Van Morrison."

I half-choke on my coffee. "Seriously?"

He starts crooning out a few smooth lyrics. His voice isn't half bad.

I say, "Tell me about the import business. It doesn't sound like the thing you just fall into on the rebound from record label rejection."

"It's not an interesting story." Wallace sets his coffee cup on the table. "I took a job working for someone else, learned the ropes and eventually started my own company. We're based out of New York, but we do business with companies all over the world. We work with a lot of high-end interior designers. Indonesian teak Java furniture is especially hot right now."

"So you got to go to Indonesia? I would love to go there."

"I've never visited the suppliers there in person. Just over Zoom." He leans forward, coming a little closer to me, though he's still across the table. "Maybe we could go together some time."

He waggles his eyebrows, obviously joking. I laugh. "Sure. Right."

"Or," he amends, "maybe we can choose something more modest for our second date. I assume Houston has a Philharmonic."

I scrunch up my nose. "I'm not actually a fan of classical music."

# Chapter Nineteen
## *Still Thursday*

Even after I'm safely back at Greetings and Felicitations, I'm trying to decide if I'm being fair in discounting Wallace, if things might be different if he wasn't Patsy's brother. Or if I might be more open to the idea of Wallace if things weren't already so weird between me and Logan. And I decide, though we have a lot in common, and we should match up, given our interests, there's something about Wallace that I empirically do not click with. I can't put my finger on it, exactly, because Patsy was right – it seems like we would work well together. I managed to be noncommittal enough to avoid agreeing to a second date. Though I'm not sure he's given up on the idea.

"That's not centered," Carmen tells me.

I look down, and focus on getting the centerpiece even on the mirrored plate.

The centerpieces Carmen and I chose are these old books that have been hand carved into hearts, so that when you bring the two covers together, turning the book inside out, you get a 3-D heart sculpture. They're perfect because Drake is a librarian and Autumn used to be a mystery writer. It is the one thing so far as matron of honor that I feel like I have really nailed.

I'm just balancing the last one on a table, on top of the mirror strewn with glass beads and pearls, when Miles walks in. He apologizes for being late. "I'm sorry, Mrs. Koerber. I ran into my girlfriend, and she wanted to talk."

I'm glad he took the time to talk with her, instead of citing work as an excuse to further distance her. "Don't worry about it. It's been a weird week for everyone. Good talk, though?"

"Well, yeah. It helped. A lot."

"Good." I don't want to grill him about something private, and Miles knows a bit more than I do about computers, so instead of following up with the personal thread of conversation, I ask him, "Can you make sure I'm not going to give my computer a virus looking at this?" I hold up the thumb drive.

"Sure," Miles says.

We go into my office, which still has a hint of the break-in about it. My paper files are still a mess, even if everything has been stuffed back inside the filing cabinets. Some of the chocolate-themed decorations didn't fit back the way they'd been packed, so they're stacked in the corner. And the carpet in here could use a good vacuum.

At least it doesn't seem like anything has happened to my office computer, which boots up like normal. And all the settings are the same as they were before. I usually use my laptop for day-to-day stuff, so I haven't used this computer in weeks anyway.

Miles has me put the thumb drive into the USB slot, and walks me through how to scan it for viruses. From what we can tell, it seems safe. So I open the list of files.

There's one marked *Leslie's Diary*. I click on it, and it opens a word document, which as promised, is pages and pages of Fabin's cousin rambling about life, about her trip through various parts of Europe, about horses she's buying and breeding. I'm just making supposition, but maybe Fabin had stopped riding because horses were Leslie's thing, and he didn't want anything to do with her.

The entries go back for years, and there's way too much to read. But the latest one mentions Fabin going to Texas. She's gotten the information from a PI, who'd hacked Fabin's e-mail – at roughly the same time Fabin had been hacking Leslie's diary. Which means the two of them had been spying on each other.

There's a ton of other files, including videos. One of them is labeled *Proof for Safekeeping*, which stands out, so I click on it. There's a video of the real Leslie Franks, who is obviously very drunk and giggling, about to fall out of her chair. She's sitting next to Fabin. She has on glasses and her hair is cut into a blunt bob. Real Leslie looks much less glamorous than Fake Leslie.

This video must be fairly recent, because Fabin looks much the same in the image as he had when I had found him dead. Only, you know, breathing. This is the first time I've actually seen him alive and in motion. He was a handsome young man, with a baritone voice. In the video, he has a glass in his hand too, but he seems to be more just swirling the ice around rather than drinking anything.

Leslie seems oblivious of the camera, which was sitting on the table in front of them, though Fabin looks at it a couple of times, as he speaks.

"Tell me what you want, for you to leave Kimmy alone," Fabin says.

"I want you to break up with her," Leslie says. "You're dating a woman who could be your mother. It's bringing shame to our family. You don't want that. Trust me."

"Is that a threat?" Fabin asks. He glances nervously at the camera again.

Leslie gestures at Fabin with her glass. She asks, "Did you put something in here?"

"Maybe," he admits. But he doesn't sound sorry for it.

"Look," she says, staring skeptically at the contents of her glass. "If you're trying to kill me, you'd better succeed."

"Don't worry. I didn't poison you. I'm not a killer," Fabin says. "Unlike some people."

Leslie grins, and it's like a whole different person has taken over her face. Someone who is ice cold, despite the inebriation. "You know what happened to my parent's car could just as easily happen to your car. Or to that little hotrod you bought Kimmy. You'd better have a talk with her."

Fabin nods miserably. "I'm taking her out of town. If it's the only way to keep her safe, I'll break up with her at the end of the trip. But at least give me this last time with her."

"Don't ever say I'm not generous," Leslie says. And then she falls asleep in her chair. Fabin leaves the camera on her for a while, as she starts unattractively snoring.

He grins, either because he's finally got her to admit that she did something to her parents' car – or because the camera is capturing an unflattering view up Leslie's nose. Finally, he reaches towards the camera, and then the video ends.

I just sit there, staring at the black square on my screen.

Miles, who is after all a lawyer's son, says, "That would never hold up in court."

I nod. "But I think Fabin wanted this for blackmail. Maybe to let him keep seeing Kimmy."

"That seems elaborate," Miles says. "But everything about this feels over the top."

I need to show this video to Logan, get his opinion on where this bit of evidence fits into our investigation, but in the meantime, I copy the video and send it to Arlo.

I add a text. *Mateo's not looking like such a strong suspect now, is he?*

Arlo texts back, *We are considering this from multiple angles, Lis. Mateo's either part of what happened – or he's another victim. We've had divers out looking for his body since yesterday, but the Gulf is a huge place with unpredictable currents. So is the bay.*

I stare at my phone. I guess Arlo forgot again that he isn't discussing the case with me. But this time, I wish he had kept the information to himself. It's chilling to imagine that divers might find Mateo floating amidst the seaweed. The image is far too vivid.

I ask Miles, "You don't think Fabin's cousin might have decided to have him killed, do you? If she found out he'd taped that confession."

Miles is still staring at the computer. "Why are people so cruel to each other, Mrs. Koerber?

I'd forgotten who I'm talking to. Miles has already been traumatized by a killer for hire. My theory has to be reminding him of that experience. "I'm sorry, Miles. I shouldn't have said that."

"No," Miles says. "I really want to talk about this. It keeps going round in my head, and showing up in my dreams. I'm always back to being unable to move, so sure that I was going to die. But I'm lucky, compared to Fabin. You and Mr. Hanlon saved me."

Miles wants me to explain something I don't really understand myself. But he's basically still a kid. He's looking to me, the nearest adult, to be reassuring. "Most people aren't like that. We have a basic sense of right and wrong, and it tells us that taking a life is definitely wrong. But sometimes people lose sight of that, or there's something wrong with their minds."

"So how do you stay safe? How do you know that you won't wake up tomorrow, and walk straight into a knife?" He gestures at the black rectangle on the screen. "If I had taken Mateo's job back when you first offered it to me, I would have been here that night. If you're right, and someone came to kill Fabin and Mateo tried to stop it, that could have been me."

My mouth drops open, but words don't come out. "Oh, Miles." I give him a hug. He remains tense. I let him go. "Every day, you just have to appreciate that it's another day that you *are* alive. And over time, it will get easier. You'll start to trust people again."

"I really hope so," Miles says. "Because there are days when I have a tough time leaving the house."

"Have you talked to your parents about it?" I ask.

Miles looks away. "I don't think they'd understand."

I put a hand on his shoulder. "You won't know unless you try."

"Try what?" Logan asks, stepping into the doorway. It's a small office. There's not a whole lot of room for him to come in.

"Nothing," Miles says. "Excuse me."

He steps past Logan, out of the office.

"What was that about?" Logan asks. He is a lot more dressed up than the last time I saw him, in slate gray slacks and a fine-gauge darker gray sweater. He's gone all out for Autumn's party.

"Miles is still having trouble," I say. "I really wish I knew what to do for him."

"You're doing it," Logan says. "You're listening to him. And taking what he has to say seriously. A lot of people would tell him to just suck it up." The look on Logan's face tells me he knows this from personal experience.

"I hope we can figure out about Fabin soon. I think knowing what happened, and seeing whoever did it brought to justice will go a long way towards helping all of us." I take a deep, calming breath. Because we don't seem to be any closer to being able to solve this thing. "Miles will be at the party tonight. Maybe it will at least be a distraction for him."

Logan says, "I might be late. I'm meeting Cheyanne for a quick drink first." But he's standing close to me, looks like he regrets even saying that. Though it explains the real reason he's so dressed up. "Don't worry – I left the wine with Carmen. She's getting the champagne chilled as we speak."

But that's not the significant point here. "Cheyanne?"

"You call her Fake Leslie."

We both laugh. There's another moment here, and if I let it go, it might be the last one. Yes, we're business partners, and no matter what he says right now – even if it's a stinging rejection – I'm going to have to face him again in a couple of hours at Autumn's party. And again in the morning at the shop.

But I suck up all my courage and I ask him, "What if I told you it wouldn't be a rebound?"

His eyes go wide. "When you agreed to go for coffee with Wallace, I assumed that meant you wanted me to back off."

I flop my hand up in the air. "I'm not sure what I want, but it isn't Wallace. I only went out with him because Patsy wasn't going to let me hear the end of it if I didn't."

"Really?" He sounds skeptical.

"I've been trying to ask you all week if you want to be my plus one for Autumn's wedding. As a friend, as something more, as business partners – whatever we might be in six months. Because I don't know what that would be. And I can't promise that I won't break your heart, or that I'm really ready to move on." I take a step closer to him. "But I'd like to try. Only – now it's too late, isn't it."

He just stares at me. I feel like crawling under the desk so he can't look at me, but I maintain the eye contact with him while he thinks. Finally he says, "I can't make you any promises either. And I'm not in the habit of standing people up, so I'm still meeting Fake Leslie for that drink. But after Autumn's party, let's talk."

"Okay." I'm not sure whether or not I'm ready to hear whatever he's going to say. And I have a feeling what he says may depend on how his evening goes with Cheyanne. I want to play fair here. I take the thumb drive out of the USB port. The computer makes a sad little beep. "Give her this."

By giving him something Cheyanne has spent years of her life looking for, I've pretty much ensured his date with her is going to go well. Which means I may just have ended any chance I had with Logan.

But as he leaves, Logan leans in and brushes his lips against mine in the lightest kiss I've ever had in my life.

I just stand there, holding my hand to my lips, long after he's walked away.

## Chapter Twenty
### *Still Thursday*

I sit down at the computer, since it is already up. Maybe I'm missing some obvious clue someone else has already uncovered and reported on. There's a lot of coverage of the murder. Especially about Fabin's family, and the effect his death has on the family's business and dynamic. Leslie is now the sole heir of the family's fortune. Which strengthens the theory that she found a way to eliminate her cousin from the equation. But if she's not here, who could she have gotten to actually pull the trigger?

It could have been Mateo – who had then fled, just like the cops supposed. Or it could have been Enrique, who could have dropped his own sunglasses at the scene. Which would finally give a logical reason as to why he had been looking for them. Or it could even have been Donnie, lying about what those diamonds had been payment for.

Finally, I give it up and shut the computer off.

More people are arriving, and I need to greet them.

Naomi and Tiff show up together to help set up, and they walk in talking about drapes. With a real estate agent and a house flipper -- there will be no stopping that conversation. Tiff's husband Ken is in tow, but he's more focused on a baseball game streaming on his phone. He just happens to find a seat at the corner table, the most out of the way of being asked to rearrange furniture or chip up ice blocks. I can't really blame him. He did put in a full day today at his job, going in early so he could leave early and drive over with his wife. I, for one, plan to give him a break.

Tiff is holding a square white box, with a giant bow on top that is hanging over the edges.

I gesture at the gift. "What did you wind up getting Autumn?"

"You know how Autumn loves funky one-of-a kind jewelry?"

"Uh, yeah," I say. Autumn makes her living selling vintage jewelry on Etsy. She wears some of the pieces she finds for a time, and then when she gets bored with them, she adds them to her inventory in her store. There's always a story behind the maker, and where she discovered the piece, and what people should love about it. I think those entries are where she channels her need to keep telling stories, since she stopped writing new novels.

Tiff lifts the lid on the box, and just about everyone who's been setting up comes over to take a peek. "This is a replica of a historical piece worn by a Duchess in England, shortly after Queen Victoria's diamond jubilee. Those are opals instead of diamonds, and I got them to do a picture of Drake and Autumn holding hands for the central cameo. She should be able to wear it with her wedding dress."

No wonder Tiff had needed the extra cash. The rush shipping on this thing alone cost more than the gift card for dinner out that I'd gotten Autumn. It's a gorgeous piece, choker style with inch-high silver segments linked together and adorned with silver flowers and leaves surrounding diamond-shaped opals. Below the central image of Autumn and her true love, there's a larger opal teardrop dangle.

She *has* to wear this with her wedding dress.

And it hits me hard. Autumn really is marrying Drake. She's always been a good friend to me. And she deserves so much happiness. And yet-

Sandra puts a hand on my shoulder. "Are you okay?"

I try to force my expression back to neutral, but Sandra gestures towards my office, so we can have a quiet moment for conversation. Which means I must still look heartbroken.

"You're still not sure about this wedding, are you?"

"It's not the wedding per se," I admit, to her and to myself. "Autumn's been the one constant in my life, when we were kids, even over social media once I'd moved to Seattle – and the dynamic of her life is about to change. I know it's selfish, but I resent that. And I just realized that's why I've been so resistant to the whole thing. I need to get past my own fears about our friendship changing."

"Now that you realize that, I think you'll be okay." Sandra gives me a quick hug. "Not all change is bad. Remember that."

She leaves me standing there, contemplating what change really means. I've had so much happen that's out of my control. My friends – my whole life – are going to move on without me if I don't start making some more active choices.

I'm expecting Ash's follow-up story to show up at some point, and I remember his promise not to quote what I had said about vulnerability and change. But what did he say – if he even mentioned the topic?

I check his blog, and there are several new stories. There is a straight-up profile piece of Greetings and Felicitations, but anyone could tell that Ash's heart really wasn't in it. The photos are nice, though. He's got the one of me posed at the register, with the shop behind me, and one of me loading beans into the roaster. And he's got one of Carmen, with a tray of chocolate chunk cookies fresh out of the oven. She's still got the mitts on her hands. I don't even remember her making those, I was so preoccupied. Ash talks mainly about Carmen, who he claims is keeping the shop running while Logan and I are busy solving the mystery – which he just had to mention, to tie in with his other pieces. Ash isn't far wrong. He paints Carmen as a hero. I'm glad of that. It's one less thing for Paul's ex to use as ammunition.

But that's not the story Ash really spent his time on. Oh, no. He's written about someone he met in my shop – though not someone who actually works there. The new target in his sites: Enrique. The title above Enrique's head is *The Hottest Plate in Town – Literally*.

Somehow, Ash has come up with a picture of Enrique in chef's whites, standing behind a table placed directly on the sand, grating cheese onto a dozen plates of pasta. The article starts with, *It's hard to get an invite to one of the most exclusive dining experiences in the whole Houston area when the chef specializes in "plausible deniability" for an appetizer and changing locations as a main course. I haven't even been able to verify for 100% certain that the man in the picture actually is the chef for the experiences in question.*

He goes on to describe Enrique's pop-ups and insinuates that the events use illegal ingredients to create showstoppers. Things like cheese with unpasteurized milk, and unlicensed preparation of fugu. Things that would have been right up Fabin's alley. I know firsthand how shoddy Ash's reporting can be, and how he's willing to guess and make things up, if he thinks it will get him more clicks. But this time, given the circumstances of the case, I think he may be onto something.

This could be what connects everything. The animal trafficking ring Mateo had been looking into – Fabin's appearance in Galveston – and Enrique. Who is starting to look less like a chef – and more like a murderer.

I take out the card Kimmy gave me. It has a tiger on it, with faded tiger print stripes as a background. This girl seriously has a thing for big cats. I find her cell number amidst all the cluttered printing.

There's music in the background when she picks up – soft, and elegant. Something classical I don't recognize. But I'm not into classical, so that doesn't mean much.

"Where are you right now?" I ask.

Kimmy says, "I'm getting a pedicure. I was lucky to find a place open this late, on this island. But pedicures always cheer me up. And since I shouldn't leave, I figured I might as well do something other than grieve."

Darn. She's probably not going to want to answer my questions in earshot of other people.

"Hey," I say. "Would you call me back when you get finished in there? I want to ask you something."

"Sure. I'm almost done." She hangs up without waiting for me to say goodbye. But it is only a few minutes before she calls back and announces, "I'm in the car, but my toenails are still wet, so I'm not going anywhere for a bit."

"Great," I say. "I just saw the article on how Enrique always advertises outrageous main ingredients for his dinners, and I know Fabin was arrested more than once for purchasing unpasteurized cheese. I just want to know what Enrique promised y'all as the special dish at this party. I figure it was something rare, and hard to import. Queen conch, maybe? Or fugu?"

Kimmy says, "I have no idea what you're talking about."

I tell her, "A local blogger just did an article on Enrique. And his alter ego Ray Fines. I don't care what part you had in all of this. I just think Enrique might have been in touch with all the wrong people to get his ingredients."

"You think he really had something to do with Fabin's death?" Kimmy asks. She sounds scandalized.

"I thought you were the one who accused him of killing Fabin in a fit of jealousy over you. I remember you shouting something to that effect the day we met."

Kimmy huffs into the phone. "I was just being noisy. Guys expect that from a girl like me. If I'd thought Enrique could actually have killed someone – do you think I would have spent another night under his roof?"

I can't tell if she's being honest. I mean, it is possible that she and Enrique were the two kidnappers Mrs. Guidry saw. Or what if she's the one who killed Fabin, and Enrique has been covering for her? That would make her attempt to throw him under the bus extra over the top.

"So about that special ingredient . . ."

Kimmy lowers her voice, even though she said she's alone in her car. "It was sea turtle eggs."

"What?" I wince. I had been trying to play this cool, but I can't hide my surprise. Given her personality, I can see Kimmy wanting to hatch a sea turtle egg. I can't imagine her wanting to *eat* one. "Are you serious? I thought you loved animals."

"Animals yes, reptiles, no. They creep me out. But the whole thing was Fabin's idea. He was so excited that night when he left here with Enrique to go get the turtle eggs. He told me the night of the dinner was going to be the best night of my life. I didn't care what we were eating. I was just hoping he meant he was going to propose."

Although, from what was on that thumb drive, that wasn't going to happen, even if Fabin hadn't been killed. But Kimmy doesn't need to know that Fabin was planning on breaking up with her at the end of the weekend. "Where were you, after Enrique left that night?"

"I stayed at his house, just hanging out and watching TV with a couple of Enrique's friends. When Enrique came back alone, he said that Fabin had decided to stay out and collect a few souvenirs. Which wouldn't be unlike him. So I wasn't worried. I tried to wait up for my Boo, but I fell asleep. And in the morning, it was all over the news."

Which means she has an alibi – assuming Enrique's friends can be trusted. "So what happened to the turtle eggs?"

"They're at Enrique's house, in a bag. He showed them to me, the night he brought them home. He seemed to think they were hilarious, but I don't know why. I really did kiss him. I know I shouldn't have. But he just seemed so happy. And now you're saying I kissed him because he was happy he'd killed my boyfriend?"

"I hope not," I say. But I'm afraid that that's exactly what happened. "Where are you going now?"

"I was planning to head back to Enrique's place and watch a movie. But now I'm not sure I want to see him. What if I freak out?" She sighs heavily into the phone. "I think I'm going to take myself to the theater and think. Want to join me?"

"Can't. I'm about to throw an engagement party for my friend."

"That sounds nice. Have fun."

Kimmy sounds so sad, I almost invite her. But that would just make everything awkward. So I let her go, and then I change into the sweater Sonya made me.

I head back out to help finish setting up the party – by which I mean starting to hand out wine to everyone who came to help set up, as we transition into the pre-party cocktail hour.

I've just managed to uncork one of the bottles of merlot when Logan shows up. He puts a bulky bag on the gift table. I gesture with the glass in my hand, asking if he wants wine, but he shakes his head no. He really is more of a beer guy. Which explains the six pack I saw in the shop's fridge next to the champagne.

Logan half-dances his way over to me, moving in time to the smooth sax crooning through the sound system. "Nice music."

I pour wine into the glass and take a sip of it myself. "I thought you were more into European techno."

He gestures at his chest. "What? I can't have more than one side to me?"

"I get that. I like a lot of different kinds of music, too." I touch his arm. I'm not sure if that's a problem, since he hasn't said anything yet about what might have happened between him and Cheyanne. "Just wait. One day, I'll teach you how to do the Cajun waltz. When my family gets together, Cajun music is a thing."

"You mean like Wayne Toups?" Logan says.

"So I'm too late. You've already been introduced to Cajun music."

"Afraid so." He touches my arm. I try not to read anything into that. "One of the guys I worked with on the dive team was a fan. He had a whole Spotify channel. I thought it was pretty cool. Just don't ask me to do the Cotton Eye Joe. Because that is not happening."

I snort out a laugh. "I didn't figure you'd be much for something that close to line dancing. But I need to tell you something. I talked to Kimmy again. She said that Enrique's involved with stealing sea turtle eggs. Which are just the kind of thing Fabin might have been trying to buy. I'm thinking he's our prime suspect."

"That brings things a little clearer into focus." Logan taps a finger against his lips. "But it doesn't necessarily make him a murderer."

I try not to feel too disappointed. I still feel like the information is important.

Aunt Naomi is sitting at a table near the window. She turns to me and says, "Do you know the old lady with her face up against the window? She looks lost."

I glance over and see a figure standing outside, peering in. But whoever it is notices us all staring and turns away.

Logan rushes outside, leaving the door open behind him. I move cautiously into the doorway, close enough to hear Logan call out, "Mrs. Guidry? Are you okay?"

I step out onto the sidewalk. It's Mrs. Guidry, all right. She freezes, half way into turning the corner. She's been recognized, so running away is pointless.

"Please," I call out. "Come back here, so we can talk."

She hesitates, but finally makes her way back up the sidewalk. "I can explain. I was just checking in on your shop. Aren't you usually closing about now?"

Logan frowns. "Be honest, Mrs. Guidry. You were trying to get photographs of the party, in case Ash might pay to print them."

She flushes bright pink in the streetlights. "I told you. I need the money."

I put a hand on her shoulder. "I understand that. Look, why don't you come inside and enjoy the party. I'm sure Autumn won't mind."

"The novelist?" Mrs. Guidry says. "Who mysteriously quit writing?"

"Just the one. She's getting married, and we're setting up for her engagement party. She might even pose for a picture when she gets here."

Mrs. Guidry follows us inside. "Oui, sha, that would really help. Ash didn't buy the last round of photographs I tried to sell him. He said the man wasn't a local, so the story wasn't interesting enough."

"Which man?" I ask.

"The one I saw leaving the pharmacy over on Postoffice, not long before it was broken into."

"You saw something that night?" I don't even try to hide my surprise. "Why didn't you tell someone?"

"I did. But when I reported it, they said I didn't give them enough to go on. They said a sandy-haired man wearing a dress shirt and a fish-shaped tie going into a pharmacy wasn't exactly suspicious behavior."

"A fish-shaped tie?" I ask. It sounds like she's describing Wallace. And the pharmacy in question isn't far from where Wallace and I had part of dinner together. There are a million legitimate reasons for him to have been there. Mrs. Guidry had said he'd looked nervous. Maybe he'd had an unexpected stomach issue. That would explain why he'd left dinner so suddenly – and why he hadn't wanted to offer an excuse. But it still feels like a weird coincidence.

After a while, the guests start arriving, including
Autumn's parents and Drake's mom. I move closer to the door, to
start greeting guests as they arrive. When Autumn walks in, there
is a round of applause.

She comes straight over to me and hugs me so hard that
for a second I can't breathe. "Everybody's here! I can't believe
you got them all together on such short notice."

Maybe I'm not so bad at this matron of honor thing after
all. Once she let's go of the hug, I grab her hand. "I want you to
know, I really am happy for you."

Sudden tears glitter in her eyes. She wipes one away from
the corner. "Girl, you had better not make me cry at my party."

Drake walks in. Autumn squeezes my hand as she turns
to look at him. And the look on his face when he sees her – that's
the way Kevin used to look at me. This is the real deal. I know
love when I see it.

Maybe they *are* being impulsive. But – it feels like they
have a chance to really make this work. As matron of honor, my
self-appointed job is to give them best chance possible. Because
I've never seen Autumn this happy.

Everyone seems to be enjoying the party, and they settle
into groups for conversation. Miles and his girlfriend start
swaying to the music, over in one corner. Sandra and Sonya, who
seem to have made up their differences over the pharmacy guy,
are standing together near the buffet table, debating the merits of
each type of tapas on offer. I'm sitting with Tiff, who is
commiserating with her husband because the team he was rooting

for lost the baseball game. Logan comes up to us. I know he's a huge baseball fan, too.

"Tell Ken it will be okay his team lost."

Logan grins at me. "You know I can't do that. They were playing the Twins. And we won."

"You act like you personally helped out the team," Ken says.

"Fan support always helps morale." Logan takes the empty seat at the table, pointing with the neck of his beer bottle. That may be the least logical thing I've ever heard him say.

"You got another one of those?" Ken gestures at the bottle. "I'm not much of a wine guy."

"Coming right up." Logan turns to me. "What's up with the parsley in the fridge? Is that supposed to be a garnish for something?"

"No. That's for Knightley. It's his favorite snack, and I feel like I've been neglecting him lately. I'm basically his whole world, you know."

"I get that." Logan leaves his beer on the table, and heads to the back to get another bottle out of the fridge. It seems so natural, him doing that. Like he's been part of this business all along. I don't know how to feel about that. But I kind of like it, despite my fears and reservations.

The front door opens again, and a guy I don't recognize walks in. He's built like a boxer, somehow lean and muscular at the same time. Sandra and Sonya both swivel towards him, in unison, identical expressions of shock on their faces.

Tiff puts a hand on mine to get my attention. "That's the pharmacist they were fighting over earlier. Tobias."

"That guy's a pharmacist?" There's nobody who looks like that at the pharmacy I go to. I can see why both twins were interested in him.

I have never seen the two sisters fight over anything before. I hope they are not about to ruin Autumn's party. Tobias stands frozen. I can practically see him not being able to tell which twin is which. And I have no idea which twin invited him.

Sonya walks over to him. "Tobias, I thought I told you not to come."

He says, "You were serious about that? You're breaking up with me because your sister has a crush on me?"

Sonya looks over at Sandra, who is just standing there, her eyes wide. Finally, Sandra says, "You did that for me?"

Sonya replies, "You remember the time we let a guy come between us. It wasn't worth it."

"*He* wasn't worth it," Sandra says.

Tobias advances towards Sandra. "Did you just call me worthless?"

"No, that's not what I meant," Sandra says. "I was talking about the guy my sister and I fought over."

Tobias says. "I really liked your sister. You ruined everything."

Miles steps over and puts a hand on the guy's shoulder. "I think you should go. Please."

"Or else what?" Tobias, who's taller than Miles, looks down his angular nose at him. "You're going to make me?"

"I'm not looking to fight you," Miles says.

Tobias turns towards Miles, shrugging the kid's hand off his shoulder. Sandra moves backwards, to stand next to her sister.

Tobias swings at Miles, who ducks. When Tobias takes another punch at Miles, who is still ducking, Miles uses one of the grabs Logan taught him to catch the guy's arm, using Tobias's own weight against him. Tobias winds up sprawled on the floor. He looks both angry and embarrassed. But he doesn't say anything as he gets up, dusts himself off, and leaves.

Ariel steps over and grabs both of Miles's hands. "Are you okay?"

"I'm fine," he says. He sounds a bit in shock.

She pulls his hands to her face, holding him like that for a moment. Then she lets him go. "If you hadn't been here, someone could have really gotten hurt."

"Yeah," Miles says. Then, with more meaning, "Yeah."

There's a lot tied up in that single word. And from the look on Mile's face now, I think maybe he's going to be okay. It's too simplistic to think that this one event will reverse all of the fallout of the incident that made him feel like a victim. But it's certainly a start.

Logan never came back from the kitchen. I look over and find him standing in the doorway between the kitchen and the counter, looking very pleased with himself. I remember thinking he might be the influence Miles needs right now. I'm still not sure if I'm right – but I really hope so.

Sandra comes over and gives Miles a hug. She asks Ariel, "Do you mind if I have a thank-you dance with the hero of the party?"

"Go right ahead, Miss Popescue." Ariel looks at me. I think she's as happy as I am that Sandra called Miles a hero.

Far from being ruined, the party takes on more energy. Autumn's mom gets Miles to hook her phone up to the projector we use for presentations and chocolate tastings. And I fumble my way through setting up the screen. In the short time since we'd announced the party, Autumn's parents have pulled together a slideshow of her as a kid. There's a picture of her at maybe three or four years old, dressed as a princess, with a pink polyester fur wrap. It makes sense now why she wants the grown-up version of that costume for her wedding gown.

Autumn looks mortified, and asks her mom, "What. Have. You. Done?"

"Don't worry," her mom reassures her. "Drake's mamma made one too."

"I'm not sure that makes it better," Autumn says.

A few images in, there's a picture of me and Autumn in middle school, probably not long after we'd met. We're both wearing these green tee-shirts that say, *I'm with stupid*, with arrows that point towards each other. I was going through a heavy eyeliner and smoky shadow phase, which didn't quite go with my thick hairband and bangs. It was, after all, the 90s.

Logan leans over and whispers, "That was you?"

I feel my face going hot. "Middle school was awkward for me."

"Middle school was awkward for everybody," Logan says. Though *he* doesn't seem willing to offer any photographic evidence.

After Autumn's slideshow, her brother stands up to sing a song.

Midway through it, my phone rings. I silence the ringer immediately. I look over at Autumn and mouth, "Sorry!"

Then I head into the kitchen to take my call.

It's Haruka. "Apologies please, Mrs. Koerber. I did not know who else to call."

"Haruka. What's wrong?" The tension in her voice has my heartbeat going up a notch.

"I am outside the house of Enrique, Mateo's friend. I went to ask about something Mateo had borrowed that might have been a clue as to why he was taken." I assume she's talking about the copy of *The Invisible Man*. I knew there was a clue in there somewhere. "But Enrique did not answer the door. I heard muffled shouting. I think maybe someone needs help."

I look up, and Logan is already standing in the kitchen doorway. "We're going somewhere, aren't we?"

I tell Haruka, "Don't go inside. We'll be there as soon as we can."

"I am sorry," Haruka says. "I drove home before I called you."

That's actually a more reasonable response than what Logan and I are about to do.

"I'm glad you're safe," I tell her before I let her go. I tell Logan what she said happened, and add, "Should we call the cops?"

Logan says, "We don't really have much to give them. A girl who probably won't even admit to having been there says she heard a noise. I doubt it would be enough to get a warrant to search the place."

"There's the sunglasses," I say. "Enrique said Fabin borrowed them, but I think Enrique had them in his pocket and dropped them inside my shop. Which puts him at the scene of the crime. Which he then lied about."

"Do you have these sunglasses?" Logan asks.

"No." My shoulders slump forward in defeat. "Enrique says he picked them up out of the lost and found. But surely, if Haruka heard someone calling for help – that has to mean he's holding Mateo inside the house. Right?"

"She also said Enrique's car is gone. So it's the perfect time to go have a look around. It might be the best approach anyway. The cops might spook him, and then who knows what could happen to Mateo. *If* he's really there. It's odd that no one heard anything before now."

In the main part of the shop, they've started on Drake's slideshow. It's on a picture of him mugging for the camera with two missing front baby teeth. I go over to Autumn, who is staring at the slide, enraptured. Which makes sense. She probably hasn't seen any of these pics before. I tap her on the shoulder. She stands up and whispers, "What's wrong?"

I whisper back, "We think we know where Mateo might be. I – I had a speech planned. I'm sorry."

"You have to go. It's okay. Go." She sits back down, obviously not wanting to miss any more of the slide show. She doesn't look upset. But I still feel like I'm failing in my promise to her – right after I'd decided I'm on board with the wedding.

But there's nothing else to say. I head for the door, Logan trailing me. We haven't gotten more than a few steps outside when the door opens again, and Miles comes out.

Miles asks, "Where are you going?"

Logan says, "We're following a lead on Fabin's murder."

Miles says, "Do you want me to-"

"No," Logan interrupts. "Stay here, and keep the party organized. If you don't hear from us in an hour, call the police. Felicity will text you the address where we're headed."

Miles nods. "Thanks, Mr. Hanlon. For everything."

Why does he sound like he might never see us again?

# Chapter Twenty-Two
## *Still Thursday*

Logan is driving fast, urgency in his tight grip on the steering wheel.

The whole way over to Enrique's place, there's a lead ball building in my stomach. I had been to this very house, right after Mateo had disappeared. If Enrique has been holding Mateo hostage inside the whole time – while I was right there – it just makes me feel so helpless.

"You okay?" Logan asks.

"Not really." I look out the window, at the houses and palm trees and oleander bushes flashing by. "I never expected to make a habit out of breaking and entering."

"I was going to ask you to stay in the car. This could be dangerous."

I wince. "Then why bring me at all? You should have brought Cheyanne." I bet no one ever asked her to stay in the car in her life.

Logan glances at me, then back at the road, but the surprise on his face is unmistakable. "Do you not want to stay out of danger? Because I got the idea that car chases and bullets are very much not your thing. You kind of freaked out watching me push Miles using passive defense tactics. It's the kind of techniques they teach medical staff to use when patients get out of hand, to stop someone but keep from hurting them. And still, you should have seen your face when he hit the ground."

"Never mind," I say. What I want is to fit with Logan, somehow. And if that's how he sees me, I'm not sure that's possible.

212

We lapse into a tense, uncomfortable silence.

Finally Logan breaks it. "Nothing happened with Cheyanne. And it's not going to. She's leaving on the next possible plane to follow up on the information on Fabin's cousin. I told her I wasn't sure where my life is at right now. That I'm already exploring other possibilities. And she told me she understood. She said that you're beautiful, inside and out, and it's hard to compete with that."

It's my turn to wince. I have plenty of flaws. And Logan gave up something that could have been great for him – for something that is possibly a mismatch. "Even if I can't make any promises?"

"Who makes promises, in the beginning of anything?" He stops at a stop sign and looks at me. It feels like he's looking into me, really seeing me, flaws and gifts and all. "I don't know what we have here, Felicity. But I want to find out. It just didn't feel right to pursue something else in the meantime."

"Thank you," I say. I know that's an odd response, but I feel grateful to him for letting me be where I am, without pushing me towards even faster change.

His eyebrows go up. "You're welcome?" It sounds like he's laughing inside.

Logan parks in the driveway across the street from Enrique's place. I guess he's not taking any chances. Before he tells me not to, I open my door. Logan looks at me skeptically.

I tell him, "I'll stay outside until you check it out. But if Mateo's hurt, I want to be there. I can help."

Logan's eyebrows go up. "I tend to forget that side of you."

"Most people do, when they mainly see me making coffee and running a register."

"There's nothing wrong with that side of you either," Logan insists.

Enrique's car isn't in the driveway. Which means he probably isn't home after all.

We cross the street and go straight up to the porch. Logan peeks into the windows first, to make sure there's no one visible inside. He knocks and waits for an answer. I hear the muffled shouting Haruka was talking about. Could Mateo have heard us coming? Or has this racket been going on since Haruka left? You have to be close to the house to hear it, so I'm not surprised that no one else seems alarmed. But how could Kimmy have been staying in the house and not noticed? Something here just doesn't make sense.

I put a hand on Logan's jacket sleeve. "Be careful."

He smiles. "Always." He moves his hands away from the lock and opens the door. He makes opening a lock look a lot easier than it is – just look at all the trouble Cheyanne had.

He goes into the room, and his hand is close to his jacket, keeping a weapon in easy reach. I wait until he's cleared the hallway, moving towards the noise, before I go inside. This door leads into a small sitting room, with uncomfortable looking furniture and a small reception desk that makes it feel like Enrique is running more than a simple catering business out of his house.

"Felicity," Logan calls from down the hallway. "False alarm."

I follow the sound of his voice, towards a sunken living room, where there's a television playing a Gordon Ramsey show on streaming marathon. It's the one where he helps people renovate restaurants – so obviously there's a lot of shouting and crying. Logan switches off the TV.

"I've checked everywhere," Logan says. "Mateo isn't here. Unless there's a secret room or a basement."

"This is Texas. Nobody has residential basements."

"Yeah," Logan says. "There is that."

Mateo's not at Enrique's place after all. The whole thing is another dead end, and now I'm worried that Autumn is going to be mad at me for leaving her party over nothing. Because I can't lie to her about it.

I glance down, and there's a flier amidst the clutter on the coffee table. I pick it up. "Logan, look at this. It's all in code, but this is an invite to Enrique's pop-up dinner."

"You think he's still having it? Without his guests of honor?"

"He's not here, is he? It wouldn't hurt to check it out."

"If we can find him." Logan moves over and points at the picture on the flier. It's a blue heron, running, wings outstretched. "What's that about?"

"It's not uncommon to see herons in the state park, but I doubt Enrique would hold a party there." It takes me a second, but then it clicks. "Blue Heron Fitness. They have a couple of sand volleyball courts back behind the building, with some picnic tables. It would be enough space for a small pop-up."

"That could make sense. Mateo had a locker at the gym. He could have spotted the location and told Enrique about it."

"So what are we waiting for?" I ask.

"Nothing." Logan bounces his keys in his hand. "Let's go."

The whole drive over, I'm worried that I'm wrong, that we'll get there and it will be an empty volleyball court and Logan will think I'm silly for following a hunch.

But when we pull into the gym's parking lot, the smell of outdoor cooking hits us before we can even get out of the car. Something in the air is rich and roasted, and it is making me salivate – even though I'm horrified to find myself hungry, now that we know he poached some of his ingredients.

I exchange glances with Logan.

"I'd say he went ahead with the pop-up," Logan says.

We walk around the building. The area behind it is lined with citronella torches, to keep the mosquitos at bay. There's a portable kitchen setup with a long metal counter with a range set into it. Enrique is at the counter, unwrapping steamed packets of banana leaves and sliding tamales onto plates already thick with black beans and garnished with fried plantains and sour cream.

At the other end of the counter, there's the basket of turtle eggs. Maybe we're not too late. Behind Enrique, there's a small partially opaque tent setup that has a fridge inside it, and a prep table. I can see two people moving around in there.

I stalk over to Enrique. "Somebody got killed over this – and you're still doing it."

Enrique fumbles the tamale he's holding, and it slides across the counter and falls onto the sand, leaving him holding a crumpled banana leaf. He's still wearing the sweater Sonya made for him. I'm wearing mine too, so we seem to be the mildly ugly sweater club. Only – Enrique looks none too happy to see me. "What are you doing here?"

"Confronting a murderer," I say.

Enrique's hand drops to his side, and a puzzled expression crosses his face. "Murderer? What makes you think that?"

"Because your sunglasses were at the scene where Fabin died." I sound less certain as I keep speaking. And several of the people seated at the closest picnic table are obviously listening. "And Kimmy told us that you were with him, buying endangered sea turtle eggs from who knows who, probably with Fabin's money – which had to be the wad of cash that got hidden in my shop. And then you came back alone, after you did whatever you did to Mateo."

"I bought those turtle eggs *from* Mateo. He was fine when we left. In fact, Mateo locked the shop door behind Fabin and me." Enrique picks up the basket of turtle eggs and gestures towards the tent. "I can show you."

I look at Logan, who nods. "Might as well at least hear him out."

We follow Enrique into the tent, where there are lots of sharp objects he could use as weapons. I hope Logan's keeping a close eye on him. The two prep cooks don't even look up from their work as we enter.

I point at Enrique's MacBook, which is sitting on a table off to the side. I tell Logan, "That has to be to the computer I found the receipt for. Enrique really wanted the receipt back. We just need to figure out what information on the computer implicates him."

Enrique steps between me and the MacBook, then takes a look at Logan and thinks better of it and steps aside. "Implicates me of what?"

"Of killing Mateo, because he was threatening to rat out your little pop-up parties to the game warden," I say. "And Fabin because he knew about this dinner, and would have put two and two together after Mateo came up missing. Because there's no way Mateo was part of this. He'd have been horrified you were serving endangered sea turtle eggs for dinner. Endangered. Which is just monstrous."

"What?" Logan looks startled. It's the first time I've felt like I have more information than he does, and as horrible as the information is, that's a nice feeling. "I thought you got those people together out there so you could sell the eggs to the highest bidder. Why would anyone eat a sea turtle?"

Enrique shrugs and puts the basket of eggs on the table next to his computer. "It's not completely unheard of. In some cultures, turtle eggs are the ultimate aphrodisiac."

One of the prep cooks grimaces and makes a disgusted noise before saying something obviously derogatory in French.

I give Enrique a dirty look. I pull at the sleeve of his sweater. It may be an ugly color, but it was made with love, and he doesn't deserve it. "And here I thought you were a nice guy."

"It's not like that," he says. "Did you ever see the movie *The Freshman*?"

I shake my head. "Nope."

"Really? Matthew Broderick vehicle. 1990. Also had Marlon Brando?" He shakes his hands out in front of him. "Never mind. It doesn't matter. The point is, in the movie they were *pretending* to have this dinner club with exotic animals on the menu. They weren't going to actually let anyone eat them." He makes his way over to the fridge, where he takes out a giant egg and holds it out to me. There's a whole box of them. "Ostrich eggs, green food coloring and soy sauce. That's what we were planning to serve Fabin and his friends. There's no way they were going to know what real sea turtle eggs taste like, and ostrich eggs taste weird anyway. Even without Fabin, too many people knew about this dinner for me to cancel. Unhappy customers are the ones who complain to the police."

"But what about the turtle eggs Kimmy saw in your place?" I ask. "That you aren't even trying to hide in that basket."

Enrique doesn't even look embarrassed. "These are all tracker eggs." He grabs a knife and takes an egg from the basket. I gasp. Enrique cuts into it the egg, revealing some wires and some microchips and a silver packet inside a flexible shell. "Mateo got these from his new girlfriend, the one that works with sea animals." He must mean Haruka. "He told her he had a plan for catching a turtle poacher, and she has this huge soft spot for animals, you know? Anyway, we showed them to Fabin and told him they were real ridley eggs, and he gave Mateo a wad of cash for them, so that I could take them back to the house. If Fabin was the kind of jerk who would want to eat endangered animals, we figured, he deserved to pay eighty thousand dollars for an ostrich omelet. But Mateo was still alive when I left with the bag."

"Why didn't Fabin leave with you?" I ask.

"Fabin got it into his head that he wanted a souvenir from the Strand. It sounded like he was about to go off and steal one of the turtle sculptures right off the sidewalk, so I got out of there. I have no idea how he planned to get home with it without a car, but he told me he would see me later. Only he never showed, and I found out the next morning he was dead." Enrique's face looks earnest. I'm pretty sure that Enrique is guilty of something he could go to jail for. But I'm equally sure it's not murder. Enrique says, "You should look for the real poacher. Maybe he figured out what Mateo was doing and didn't want anyone horning in on his turf."

"What are you talking about?" Logan asks.

Enrique says, "Word had gotten out about our little pop-up dinner, and it spread farther than I had planned. A guy showed up here offering to sell me some more sea turtle eggs. Real ones. I didn't want to get involved with that, so I told him we were set. So he left."

"Can you describe the guy?"

"I can do you one better. I have one of those camera doorbells. My plan lets me archive the footage. It may take me a minute to find it, though. If you guys want, grab a couple of the appetizer plates while you're waiting."

"You don't have to ask me twice," Logan says. He exits the tent.

I'm not sure whether accepting food makes us party to an illegal event, so I don't follow.

"Why didn't you tell the police?" I ask Enrique.

Enrique gestures to the basket of fake turtle eggs, still on the table next to his laptop. "Do you think I wanted to wind up explaining all of this?"

My phone rings. I step off to the side to answer it, while Enrique starts reviewing footage.

It's Autumn. "Hey, I think I'm going to bail. People are starting to head home."

"I'm sorry I couldn't get back before the end of the party." I look back at Enrique. I can't believe I left, and this turned out to be a dead end. "I'm not off to a flying start as matron of honor, am I?"

"I'll give you a break, considering the extenuating circumstances," Autumn says. "Look, this turned into an amazing party. After you left, Carmen put on some salsa music, and Drake showed me he really knows how to dance. You should see his mamma on the dance floor, too. She and Miles were really cutting it up!"

"You've never danced with Drake before?" I ask.

"There's a lot of things I haven't done with him before." Autumn's tone gets serious. "I know you've had your reservations. But I think there's something to be said for getting to know him better along the way. We discussed the important things – how we feel about kids and jobs and all that. Everything else is just details."

I glance at Logan, who is heading back into the tent, carrying an appetizer plate with him. I haven't discussed any of those kinds of things with him. Then again, I haven't even been on a date with Logan. I'm not sure grilling him on his personal preferences would be appropriate.

"How's the search going for Mateo?" Autumn asks.

"Not great."

Enrique says, "Here's the guy."

In the video still that Enrique has pulled up, the guy on the doorstep is wearing a hat and has his face angled away from the camera, purposefully obscuring his identity. But I recognize the character on the t-shirt, from the shirt Nelson had been wearing on the beach the other day. Nelson must be a big fan of whatever anime Green Hair Guy comes from, for him to have two tee-shirts featuring the same character. And we haven't seen anyone else in all of this mess who is into cartoons, of any sort. Which means that has to be him in the video. Nelson is almost certainly a poacher. No wonder he was pushing to keep the turtle nests intact on the beach.

"What?" Autumn asks.

"Huh?" I reply.

"You just gasped."

I tell her what we just figured out.

Enrique waves a hand at me and says, "But one other thing. He kept saying we – like there was someone else involved."

"Felicity, you've got to try this." Logan hands me the appetizer plate and a fork.

Everyone in the tent is looking at me, so I break off a piece of the tamale and take a bite, juggling my phone still on the call with Autumn to do so. The tamale is filled with chicken and green chilies, with a good hit of cilantro. There's also some whole corn in here, and a bit of cheese. The flavors are balanced perfectly, and the texture of the whole thing is like velvet. The fried plantain is sweet, with a crunchy crust that contrasts the tamale. I tell Enrique, "You should open a real restaurant. It would be packed."

"I'd never finish school," Enrique says. "Even if I can avoid getting framed for this murder."

"Relax," Logan says. "We believe you didn't do it."

But who did? I think back to what Mrs. Guidry had said, about how there had been a girl with the killer, when Fabin was shot. "If Nelson is the one in charge of the endangered animal trafficking ring – could the girl be Haruka? It would be sad that Mateo's girlfriend might have helped kidnap him?"

"You're assuming Mateo is still alive. It's possible his girlfriend might have killed him," Autumn says, startling me. I'd half forgotten she's still on the phone. "Though I thought you said she didn't seem like the type. What about that girlfriend of Fabin's?"

"Kimmy has an alibi for the murder. How does your mystery writer brain work around that?"

Autumn makes a *hmmmmm* noise. "That's tricky, but it is possible. You just have to find a time frame inside the whole possible time of death, where you can disappear for a bit without anyone questioning where you were."

That tickles something at the back of my brain. "Oh," I say. But my idea sounds too stupid to say out loud.

"Oh, what?" Autumn asks.

"It's just – Tuesday night Wallace excused himself from dinner in the middle of our date. It seemed rather sudden and kind of weird. When I asked hm about it, he got evasive. And Mrs. Guidry said she ran into him leaving the pharmacy that got robbed later that night. But that was Tuesday. The murder was Monday. So it's probably not connected. Right?"

"It might be," Autumn says. "Have you asked him if he has an alibi for Monday?"

"Well, no." I look at Logan. "Is there any way to trace where Wallace was on Monday? We know he was in town. Maybe he was hanging out with his sister."

"On it," Logan says. He starts typing something into his phone. I don't know who he's texting, but he seems to have a lot of friends, who have access to a lot of databases.

It's ridiculous, of course. It's going to come back that Wallace is a perfectly respectable guy. And that I was just trying to figure out how to push him away, because I kinda like him, and I don't want to. Not when I have even the possibility of Logan. Which I'm not ready to do anything about, because I hate change, and I just want to distract myself from the memory of Kevin. Which means that there is absolutely no reason for me to take this case off in completely the wrong direction.

Enrique bumps the table and one of the fake turtle eggs rolls off onto the floor.

I tap my finger against my lips, thinking. "You know . . . Mateo was smart enough to hide the cash. Maybe he was smart enough to keep one of those tracker eggs."

Logan takes out his phone as he says, "Nelson always keeps one of them in his car. Something about how they're the next best thing to a Poké Ball." Which is some kind of device, from an anime. Even I know that much. Logan adds, "If we can't find Mateo, maybe we can at least find Nelson and question him."

I tell Autumn, "I need to let you go." Then I ask Logan, "How do we access the GPS for these things?"

"I'm already on it."

Enrique takes the box of ostrich eggs out of the fridge and then gets out a giant bowl. He says, "You two are on a whole other level."

I take the copy of *The Invisible Man* out of my purse. "If there's nothing incriminating on your computer, then why are you so desperate to get this receipt back?"

Enrique makes a gesture like it's obvious. "For my taxes. I need all the legit business expenses I can get."

"Your credit company could have printed you out another one," Logan says.

Enrique shakes his head. "I paid cash."

Logan looks at Enrique funny, then shakes away whatever he is tempted to say. Finally, he says, "Even if you're not really using illegal ingredients, those popups are still violating a couple of ordinances."

"Which is why I'm not stupid enough to record any of the details on my computer. I report it all as catering – from both the supply and the income end – so no, I'm not going down for tax evasion." Enrique is starting to look pretty pleased with himself as he takes the book out of my hand and puts it on the table. "This really is one of my favorites. I like the irony. Griffin burns down the boarding house to hide his experiments, and then gets caught up having to try to steal chemicals to reverse the process, when he otherwise would have already had them at home."

I look down at the cover of the book. "Kind of like whoever kidnapped Mateo might have to break into a pharmacy to try and get his prescriptions." I grab Logan's arm. "I knew it. He's still alive."

"And you know this why?"

"Because whoever broke into the pharmacy on Tuesday night didn't take anything. Because that particular pharmacy probably didn't have what Mateo had been prescribed." A memory of Wallace picking up the prescription bottle off the table pops into my head. But could Patsy's brother really be a bad guy? It just doesn't make sense.

There a commotion outside the tent. All of Enrique's diners look like they're leaving – in a hurry. Probably because

Detective Beckman is headed this way, with a uniformed officer for backup. The two approach the tent.

Detective Beckman says, "May we step inside?"

Enrique sounds flustered. "Hey, Officer. What's this about?"

Detective Beckman holds up a tablet, with the screen up for the article Ash had done on the secret popups. "I think we should talk for a minute about where you're sourcing your ingredients."

"I promise you, they're all legit." Enrique turns towards Logan and me. "Tell her, guys. Please."

Logan gives an exaggerated shrug, like he's not going to say anything to help. Enrique's face goes pinched, even though he can't possibly know Logan still sometimes works with the police. Logan laughs and says, "He told us he uses legit ingredients. And he seems to keep meticulous receipts. Plus, he just gave us some information you might find useful."

## Chapter Twenty-Three
### *Still Thursday*

Once Logan is back behind the wheel of his Mustang, he says, "I've got a couple of different locations popping up for the master tracking of these eggs. The closest one is in the parking lot across from the beach, near where we marked that turtle nest the other day."

"That doesn't feel like a coincidence," I say. "Let's check it out."

Logan drives with purpose, and it doesn't take long for us to get there. "That's Nelson's car, all right," Logan says.

The stickers all over the bumper with pictures of a dozen different anime characters gives it away. Or the Canadian plates. The car is a white Mitsubishi that could use a wash. I still have a hard time believing that dorky Japan-obsessed Nelson has jumped to the top of the list of possibilities for the Mysterious Z, leader of a ring of animal traffickers – and to the top of the list of suspects in Fabin's murder.

"But what would he be doing out here, right now?" I ask.

"I have no idea. He's obviously not the person I thought I knew. We have no idea if he's dangerous. He could be anywhere in this general area." Logan gestures to the other side of the street, where there's a kite shop and a gas station, and farther down, a couple of restaurants. Behind that, there are a number of houses. "How far do you think he could have gone on foot?"

"I don't know." I grab my phone and pull up a map of the area. What if he is our murderer – and now someone else is in danger?

"Sorry," Logan says. "I meant for that to be rhetorical. Stay here, while I check out the car."

"Okay." I watch as Logan peeks into the windows of the car, and then pops the trunk. A black car that is parked across the street pulls out and heads in the other direction. It looks a little like the car that tried to run me down. But I can't see the license plate. It has to be coincidence. There are a ton of black cars on the island. How would someone have even figured out that we were coming out here?

I convince myself that I'm just being jumpy.

Still, when Logan slams the trunk shut, I get out of the car and go stand next to him.

"Nelson just left his car here?" I ask.

"I guess," Logan says. "Something about this just doesn't feel right."

He scans the area. I make my way over to the footbridge, and look out at the beach. Several small dark spots are moving on the sand. "Hey, what's that?"

Logan follows my gaze. "Ah, man. You've got to come and see."

We make our way down to the beach, and as we get closer, I realize what I'm looking at: tiny sea turtles using their oversized flippers to cross the sand. There are dozens of them, silhouetted in the bright moonlight, all making their way to the surf. The motion is jerky and uneven, but there's something captivating about it. Logan stops a good ten feet away, not wanting to disturb them. He says softly, "Newly hatched sea turtles are more likely to emerge from the nest at night. A lot of their natural predators are asleep." He takes out his phone and sends a quick text. "I just need to report that they're hatching. I don't know what to do if any of them need help getting out of the eggs."

The first turtle makes it to the water, just as a wave approaches. It hits the little turtle, pushing it back and under, and the turtle starts swimming like mad.

Logan's hand reaches out for mine, and he intertwines our fingers. I remember what he said about these turtles symbolizing hope for him, and redemption. I look up at him, and I can see in his face how much this still means to him. And he's sharing this moment with me.

I can't remember that last time I've been this happy.

I know we can't stay here to watch it all. We're looking for Mateo, who may still be in trouble. And for Nelson, who probably *is* trouble. But I want to linger for a few more minutes. Logan seems content to stay, too, his hand in mine. He squeezes my palm, and I return the pressure.

We're slowly moving from the friend zone, into the realm of possibilities, just like those turtles going from the safety of the nest, to the dark, unknown ocean.

A motorcycle whizzes by along the road behind us, and I glance instinctively towards the noise. But I'm distracted by something closer to us than the road. There's a large dark shape nestled among the yellow flowers of the evening primrose at the edge of the sand. A chill bounces down my spine.

I haven't even said anything, but Logan notices the change in the pressure of my hand against his.

"You okay," he asks.

"Not if that's what I think it is." I point towards the dark shape, which looks like the outline of someone lying still in the plants. "Or should I say who."

Logan drops my hand. "I shouldn't have brought you down here without checking it out."

Still, he doesn't stop me as I activate the flashlight on my phone, and start walking towards the dark shape. As we get closer, it's definitely a person. My flashlight illuminates Nelson's face. His eyes are closed, as though in sleep. But the dark stain surrounding the hole in his tee-shirt would suggest otherwise. "So I guess he wasn't the Mysterious Z after all."

Which means Fabin's killer is still out there. Fabin's – and now Nelson's.

Logan leans down and examines the body. "This just happened, probably minutes before we got here. The stupid jerk must have gotten involved with something bigger than he realized."

"Logan," I say. "A black car drove away, right when you were looking inside Nelson's Mitsubishi. I'm guessing I watched the killer drive off into the night."

"I'm glad you're the one who's going to have to explain that to Arlo. That should be a fun conversation to listen to." Logan sounds like he's teasing, despite the fact that we're leaning over the dead body of someone he considered a friend. That gives me pause. Is Logan really what I need in my life? As much as I like him as a person, and as much as I find him attractive, we really are so different. How have I managed to push that aside so thoroughly? If I had any sense, I would take Wallace up on his offer of a second date. He's a bit dorky, but he imports furniture for a living – despite my wild imaginings earlier. He doesn't carry a gun. He's a safer choice.

I feel a little disloyal thinking that, after letting Logan take my hand in his, already knowing all the things about his history. And I still like Logan – a lot. I remind myself that I don't have to make any decisions right now. After all, there are more important things going on. People are dying.

I look down. Nelson's face looks so vulnerable, like he couldn't believe what was happening in the moments before he died. There's an unzipped bag near him, and inside the bag there's money. I tell Logan, "I'll bet Nelson was still trying to sell the turtle eggs. He just picked the wrong buyer."

"Or the wrong partner," Logan points out.

"Like the Mysterious Z? Whoever that actually is." I look back at all those tiny turtles, making their way to the water. "But why leave the eggs?"

Logan shrugs. "Maybe Z is more into selling live animals. Turtle eggs have to be kept in a certain temperature range, and ideally, you'd prepare Styrofoam containers with sand to keep from jostling them too much. On average, we're talking a hundred eggs to a clutch. Maybe there wasn't time to prepare everything properly. Or maybe Z went across the street to the grocery store to grab a dozen foam coolers, and is planning on coming back."

I shudder. We really don't have time to waste here. Walking a little way away from the body, I pull out my phone and call Arlo. "I'm sorry to have to call you again. But I've been having a really bad week."

"Why?" he asks. "Did you find another dead body again?"

"This isn't something to laugh about," I say.

"Wait. Crud, Lis, did you really find a body?"

"Yes, and this one was someone I know." I look back over at the wall, where Nelson is lying helpless in death. I explain what happened, and tell Arlo where to find us.

Before he hangs up, Arlo says, "I'm sorry for making a joke. That was inappropriate."

"Don't worry about it." Arlo's apology just reinforces how subtly inappropriate Logan's initial reaction had seemed.

Arlo says, "Stick with Logan. Please. We'll be there as soon as we can."

I promise him I will, and then I really do hang up the phone. And then I call Haruka. Because if Nelson had a partner in all of this, it seems likely to be her. Autumn was right. I need to check Haruka's alibi.

Haruka answers with a bright, "Moshi moshi."

I ask her, "Where are you right now?"

"I'm at dinner, with a couple of friends. We're eating Thai. Want to join?"

"No, I can't." I don't want to tell her that I was fishing for her alibi. But I still have to ask. "Just curious. Where were you Monday night?"

Some of the cheerfulness goes out of her voice. She's figured out why I'm asking. "I had these same friends over, and we were watching a movie. Mateo had said he would be at work until late, and not to wait up for him to call."

"You didn't think that was odd?" I've never once asked Mateo to stay late. He's already got another job and so much responsibility. "Especially after he asked you for those tracking eggs?"

"Maybe a little," Haruka admits. "I was worried. What he hoped to do was-" It takes her a moment to think of the word. "Dangerous. They are bad people."

So Haruka never did know the truth about Mateo and Enrique's scheme to rip off Fabin with the fake eggs.

"We haven't given up hope of finding him," I assure her. After I hang up with her, I tell Logan, "Haruka has an alibi. But there's one other person I need to call. Someone who might be upset enough over Fabin's murder to hurt someone she thought killed him."

"Cheyanne is not a murderer," Logan insists.

"I wasn't talking about Fake Leslie." I redial a number I'd recently called. When Kimmy finally picks up, I ask, "How's the movie?"

"Still going on. I just ducked out to take your call. I caught the seven o'clock showing."

"Sorry. I just had a quick question. How long were you at the spa?"

"About an hour. They did a facial and threaded my eyebrows too. You should check it out. They do a great job at Pearly Shells."

The spa's not terribly far from here, where Nelson was killed. The timing would have been really tight, but in theory, she could have had time to kill him after her spa appointment and still get to the theater in time to get a ticket stub that puts her in the clear. But she couldn't have been the one behind the wheel of the black car. But say the black car was just a coincidence . . .

I ask her a few more questions, then hang up and let her get back to her show. I don't think she killed Nelson. I tell Logan, "Kimmy's at the movies."

"Which means she's not near the other tracking egg we need to go check out," Logan says. "I doubt she did that-" He jerks a thumb in the direction of the body. "-to Nelson. Besides, she wouldn't have left the money. This feels like a dead end. We can't stay here to wait for the cops."

I tell him, "We have to. We shouldn't move evidence, and now there's a bag of money just waiting to tempt anyone who walks by."

"Fine," Logan looks frustrated. "But let's at least wait in the car. This spot feels too exposed."

As we're walking back, I ask, "So why would Z have left all that cash, anyway?"

"It's probably fake. Or underneath the top bills, it's cut up magazines." Logan shrugs. "Or it's real, and the killer saw us coming and took off without remembering to pick up the bag."

We go back up to the car, and Logan pops the trunk. He has a huge, overstuffed backpack sitting there. He leans forward and opens it, and it's bursting with emergency supplies. I heartily approve. I too have a fully prepared go bag in case of evacuation notices – only mine's in my closet. Because my life has never been full of on-the-fly emergencies before. Even in South America, I'd never gotten myself in trouble.

Logan takes out a pair of binoculars. They look high-tech.

"You always carry night vision binoculars?" I ask him.

He holds the binoculars out for me to take and examine. "I have an identical bag in each of my planes. It's better to be prepared than not, especially if you're going to be in the air. Though most of this stuff hasn't been out of the bag since I retired from private security."

I peer through the binoculars down at the baby sea turtles. The whole view is tinted green, but it's a surprisingly clear look at the little ones on the move. I watch for a minute, then I hand the binoculars back to Logan. "Those are cool."

Logan tosses me a packet of trail mix out of his backpack. "In case you're hungry."

I shake the packet. "This hasn't been in your pack for four years, has it?"

"Nah. I trade out the food every six months."

I glance down. Mateo's messenger bag is still in the trunk. "I thought Arlo would have taken that."

"He was okay with me sending him scans of the pages. I told him I wasn't sure I was done looking at those notes."

"He seems to have a lot less problems with you butting into his case than he did when I was trying to solve Emma's murder." I pick up the messenger bag and take out the binder.

"That's because a – I'm not a suspect. And b – I used to be a cop." He puts the binoculars to his eyes, scanning the area around us, checking that the crime scene on the beach is still undisturbed. "But we're not impeding his investigation, so there's not a lot he can do about it, anyway."

Plus, Logan still has connections that could give Arlo a lot of headaches.

I take the binder out. I'm not sure Logan would want me to turn on the car's interior light, so I use my phone's flashlight to read by. There' a lot of information here. I'd skimmed it, but it won't hurt to look over it some more while we're waiting. I flip through, past the pages of data I can't understand. There's a section here of information Mateo had compiled since coming to Galveston.

Now that I know Donnie's Doughnuts was the site of the document forging, the DD notations make more sense. Donnie told us that he'd been paid to create false documents to get someone into the country illegally, and that Mateo had questioned him about it. If it was connected to the animal trafficking Mateo had been investigating, then those papers weren't for random people. Those diamonds were meant to pay to get whoever Mateo had been chasing into the country. There are no names attached to these people – presumably Mateo knew their names so well he didn't bother writing them down. On a different page, there are notes about several of the illegal shipments he'd tracked down that show them having originated in Peru. Which makes sense. The beans that wound up taking a ride through my sorter had come from Peru, which means that likely one part of this group of "importers" is located there. Which means those papers were likely used to get either Fabin's killer, or one of Fabin's killer's associates into the country.

It also explains why Mateo had been so curious about what might have happened to me in Peru, back when Mrs. Guidry had asked about my trip. I gasp. Is it possible he took the job at my shop because he had thought I might be involved in all of this somehow? Because of where I'd chosen to source my cacao beans?

Logan gets into the car. I tell him what I just figured out.

"But we have no reason to believe any of the suspects are here illegally," he says.

I give him the binder, still open to the relevant page. "I don't know what it means. But I knew those diamonds had to be connected to this somehow. Me having imported those beans and Donnie needing to retrieve the bags can't be a coincidence."

"It can, actually," Logan says. "Things don't always wrap up neatly."

"What if the bad guys chose to come here *because* I ordered those beans? Because it meant easy access through the port?" The thought makes me feel awful – even though I didn't do anything wrong.

We're still trying to brainstorm what the connection between all of this might be when a couple of uniformed cops arrive on the scene. We get out of the car. They talk to Logan briefly, then head down to the beach and start securing the area around Nelson's body. Arlo shows up soon after. He's wearing a tee-shirt and jeans, driving his personal car. He was off duty when I called him. He jogs over to us. "Are you two okay?"

"Yeah," Logan says. "We found Nelson over here. Single gunshot wound to the chest, probably point-blank range."

Arlo takes one look at the body. "Thank you, Commander Obvious."

Arlo may have decided that he and I can be friends, but he still has some sort of professional rivalry with Logan.

"Well, I can tell you his name is Nelson Daye, and he's 28, Canadian, here on a work visa as a marine biology researcher, obsessed with Japanese anime, and was allergic to tree nuts. But he used to tell people he was also allergic to peanuts and pineapple, just because he didn't like eating them."

"You're waiting for me to go, 'How could you tell all that from the body?' aren't you?" Arlo gestures with his phone, which he has been using to take notes. "How did you know this guy?"

Logan says, "I sometimes worked with him and his brother when I volunteered searching for sea turtles about to nest."

"So what happened?"

I say, "We found out there were these fake sea turtle eggs with trackers in them, and one of them was in Nelson's car. So we came down here, because we thought Nelson might be the murderer."

Arlo's eyes are wide. "I can see this is going to take a good minute to explain. Start over, at the beginning."

So I do. I'm just explaining to Arlo about the black car and what it might mean when Logan's phone rings. He steps away to answer it.

Arlo asks, "So what's that about?"

I gesture in Logan's general direction. "You know. Logan's always getting calls."

Only, I saw the seriousness on Logan's face. I'm afraid he is getting the news he was looking for about Wallace. And when he returns, his frown tells me that whatever news he got, it wasn't good.

Logan cuts a glance at Arlo, then looks at me, like he's trying to tell me something nonverbally.

Arlo catches the look. "Spill it, Hanlon."

Logan looks down at the pavement, before looking up and making eye contact with Arlo. "Felicity had a hunch about Wallace. So I had a friend look into his activity on the day Fabin Obodozie died. He used a credit card at a shop on the Strand, not ten minutes before the earliest possible time of death."

Arlo squints at Logan, the light of the streetlight casting harsh shadows on his face. "So? He hasn't been back in town long. It makes sense that he would want to do a little shopping. Why does that have an ominous frown on your face?"

Logan takes a long time pacing out his words before he speaks. I get a look at the information up on the screen of his phone. And it seems to verify my worst fears.

I ask Arlo. "Do you know exactly what kind of imports Wallace is into?"

Arlo blinks at me. "Furniture, I think."

"I think he's into something more unique than that," I say. I gesture at Logan to show Arlo the phone screen. "He said he works out of New York, but he signed off on some shipments here at the local port, including a transfer of rugs from Indonesia. We're pretty sure that Fabin was trying to buy a Sumatran tiger. I mean, it could be coincidence-"

"You're darn right it's coincidence," Arlo says. "There's no way Patsy's brother is some criminal mastermind. He's nice enough, but he's the kind of guy who wants to barbecue and watch hockey. Just because he likes to travel-" Arlo's jaw snaps shut, and I can see he's weighing the possibilities.

Logan flips his phone's display over to another tab. It has data involving coordinates that I can't really decipher. It looks a lot like the data on some of the pages in Mateo's journal. Logan says, "This is the data on where all the active decoy eggs the turtle patrol has placed this summer currently are. Only – one of them is showing its location as being at the port. Which is a convenient coincidence."

"I'll believe it when I see it." Arlo crosses his arms. "Because what you're giving me is extremely thin circumstantial evidence."

"Then you're coming with us?" I ask. He's the one who keeps telling me to stop investigating things. To leave it to the professionals – like him. I never imagined he'd ask me to let him tag along.

"That depends. Where are you going?"

"To the port," I say. "We think Mateo may have had one of these tracker eggs on him when he disappeared."

Arlo shrugs. "It's a public place. I'm off duty. How's Hanlon's driving?"

"He's an extremely safe driver," I say.

Arlo looks skeptical. But he makes sure the guys down on the beach are good to go to process the scene. And then he gets into the back seat of Logan's car, directly behind me. As we're about to pull out, Fisk, the CSI guy, pulls up behind us and parks. He waves, then heads down to the beach.

As he pulls out onto the road, Logan says, "Felicity, you need to be prepared for us to find Mateo's body. If that egg really does mark his location, this isn't promising."

I nod. Though I'm not sure there's any way I could be prepared for that.

When we arrive, I can tell Logan wants to tell me to stay in the car. But before he can, I open the door and hop out. The whole area is well-lit, even at night, though everything is tinted slightly orange.

Logan flips the data on his phone over to a different view, which shows us the GPS signal graphically, overlaid on a real-world map. I guess we have to be close to the target for this view to be accurate. "It's over that way."

Logan points towards an area at the edge of the docks, where cocklebur-studded grass leads past the last of the shipping containers to a row of low bushes. And then there's nothing to break the landscape as it fades out into darkness. Oh no. Logan's right. If Mateo's out there – this won't be good.

We head towards the bushes, and I'm terrified about what we're going to discover on the other side. But when we get there and push the bushes apart, there's nothing but dirt and dead leaves. A startled cat hisses at us from farther down the foliage, and then dashes away.

"Lis," Arlo says. "You don't even know for sure if Mateo had one of those decoys. Let alone the one that seems to have disappeared out here."

But I have a horrible feeling. And Logan's already turned around, identifying the obvious solution to this puzzle. Arlo turns to follow Logan's gaze.

We stand there, staring at the row of shipping containers. Fear and adrenaline are coursing through my system. I'm terrified that we're finally about to figure out what happened to my missing shop assistant.

Arlo says, "It's been days. If Mateo is in one of those, chances are he ran out of air a long time ago. Cargo containers are meant to be air and watertight, so the cargo doesn't get damaged in transport."

I shake my head. "You don't try to steal meds to keep someone alive, just to suffocate them."

Logan says, "You might if they gave you whatever you needed, and you didn't have a reason to keep them alive anymore. And we're not even sure if they found the medications Mateo needs." He doesn't say, *if Wallace found*. He's trying to be diplomatic.

I turn away, not wanting to face the obvious: we're far too late. We're standing near some tall unmowed grass. I notice a dent in it. I lean forward and retrieve the decoy turtle egg. "He must have assumed they would search him once they got him inside the container." I swallow against the tenseness of this moment. "If that's even what happened. They might have killed him and thrown him in the Gulf."

"Or he might not even have been here," Arlo says gently.

"Well, we won't know unless we look," Logan says. And then Arlo and I stand there and watch as he starts picking the locks securing the containers, then looking inside for Mateo.

I get tired of holding the tracker egg, so I put it in my purse.

Arlo puts a comforting hand on my back. Which feels natural, a friendly, innocent gesture. Though I'm not sure Patsy would agree. Still, it is too much of a comfort for me to move away.

In the fourth container Logan assaults with the crowbar, we see light leaking out of the door. We all move forward. There's a battery-powered lamp on the floor in the middle of the container. Near the back corner, there is a pile of blankets on the floor, and there's Mateo, lying still, despite the racket we're making out here. Is he dead after all?

I rush inside. It's shallow, but Mateo is breathing. Some of the tension goes out of my shoulders. I sit down next to him and shake his shoulder gently. At first he doesn't wake. But then he opens his eyes, looking more alert than I expected.

He creaks out something that kind of sounds like, "Felicity."

He's obviously dehydrated. And without his meds, his illness has taken a toll. I fumble in my purse for the pill bottles. "He needs water."

"I have some in my car," Logan says.

"Hey what's this?" Arlo asks. He steps deeper into the cargo container to examine a large object in the shadows.

"Just furniture," Mateo croaks.

"I think this stuff is teak," Arlo says. He sounds accusatory. Like we're the ones who put it here, when Wallace was talking to everyone about buying Java furniture from Indonesia. And I know what he has to be thinking: if Patsy's the one living here in Galveston, is it reasonable to believe that she doesn't know what her brother is up to?

I'm not about to touch that one. Instead, I tell Mateo, "I should have brought a bowl of your mom's soup. She said it always makes you feel better."

Mateo says, "You talked to my mom?"

"Yes," I tell him. "She said she misses you. And your Dad kept your room, hoping you'd come visit."

"I'd like that," Mateo says. "If I make it out of here. I realized that life's too short for holding grudges." He looks up at the light holes, his only access to the outside world for what must have been days. "Way too short."

"I know how you feel." I'd had a moment like that, too, when I'd been come close to being killed – and it had changed the way I thought about my life.

Logan returns with his backpack. He unzips it and hands me a bottle of water. "Here."

I help Mateo sit up. He drinks greedily out of the water bottle.

"Wait." I open the medicine bottles, shaking one of each pill into my palm.

Mateo's eyes go wide, as he holds out his hand. He takes the pills, then finishes off the water. "Where did you get those?"

"Your apartment. I did have to go by and check on Clive."

"Come on." Logan holds out a hand to Mateo. "We have to get out of here. Can you walk."

"Not sure." Mateo tries to get up, but he's so shaky he winds up sitting down.

"Arlo come help me," Logan says.

Arlo comes over and helps Logan get Mateo to his feet. The two of them support Mateo's weight so he can sort of walk out of here.

Only, before we can get out the door, someone slams it shut. I hear the snap of a fresh lock clicking into place. Which leaves me as bewildered as I am terrified. How would someone even have known we'd be coming out here?

"Hey!" Logan shifts Mateo's weight over to Arlo and runs over towards the door. He kicks it hard, but it doesn't budge.

"Don't panic," Arlo says. "We may be able to reason with our captors." He takes out his cell phone. "Or at least stall long enough to call for help." Arlo's frown deepens as he looks at his phone screen. "No signal."

"Did you think there would be?" Logan asks. "We're inside a metal box."

Arlo's generous lips tighten into a thin line. "I'm sorry. It's my first time being captured by bad guys."

Air holes have been roughly punched into the metal roof of the container and are letting in light. So while we're trapped, at least we're not going to asphyxiate.

Just as I'm finding some solace in that fact, the light dims as a thick piece of blue-tinted plexiglass slides into place, stopping up the holes. Correction. We *are* going to asphyxiate. That glass must have been Wallace's plan for eliminating Mateo all along – once he got the information he wanted, he could just wait for Mateo to die, and then ship him off to who knows where, with the other containers.

I look at all three of these guys, trying not to panic about this hopeless-looking situation. They're smart, and they have the combined skill set to handle any situation. "So how do we escape a shipping container?"

"We don't," Mateo says. "There's no mechanism for opening a container like this from the inside. We're stuck here until we run out of air and die. I'm sorry. All of you, I really am. It was one thing for me to die as a result of my ill-planned investigation. But I'm sick at heart about taking all of you with me."

"So that's it?" I squeak. "We're just giving up?"

I look around at the container's walls. They suddenly feel a lot closer together. How much air can we even have in here split four ways? This isn't the way I expected to die. At least when I'd been threatened in my shop, I'd had a chance to fight back. Here, fighting would just use up all the air. I move back, leaning against the wall.

"You think you've got problems?" Arlo says to the room in general. "I was considering proposing to the woman I love. And now, I'm going to die before I can find out if she was the mystery girl helping out a coldblooded murderer."

"I'm sure she knows you love her," I tell him. "And I'm sure she didn't have anything to do with this. She loves you. There's no way she would have let someone lock you in here to die."

"You don't know that for sure." He turns to Mateo. "Was Patsy involved? She wasn't, right?"

Mateo says, "Who's Patsy?"

"Wallace's sister." Arlo waves in a dismissive gesture. "Never mind. Forget it."

"We need to stop crying over ourselves, and do our best to control the situation." Logan starts digging in his go bag, and he pulls out a small torch and a set of welder's glasses.

"You really do believe in staying prepared," I say.

"You can't use that in here," Arlo protests. "You'll suck out all the oxygen."

Logan gestures up at the sealed-off air holes. "You have a choice. Sit here and wait for the oxygen to run out. Or take the chance that I can cut a hole big enough to let in oxygen before the oxygen in here is gone. You know as well as I do that no one will rescue us. And our captors aren't likely to change their minds and let us out."

Arlo doesn't reply. After waiting to make sure that there aren't any other objections, Logan moves over to the back wall, where our captors are least likely to notice us trying to escape. He puts on the glasses and uses a disposable lighter to put flame to the torch.

"Had a little falling out with your friends?" Arlo asks Mateo, as he helps Mateo make it back to the pile of blankets and sit down again.

"What?" Mateo squints at him.

Arlo gestures around. "This must have been a far cry from what you were expecting when you set Fabin up. From what I've been able to figure, you and your associates used a promise to sell Fabin an illegally imported tiger as a ruse to get him to the island. Only something went wrong. Did your tiger not show up? Because I haven't been able to find it."

"That's not what happened." Mateo sounds offended. "I'm not associated with these people. They only have money where their hearts should be."

Arlo nods like he's considering this. "Still. I don't get it. Fabin was worth a ton of money alive. Why didn't they at least try to ransom him?"

Mateo shakes his head. "They weren't trying to kidnap him. Wallace wanted me."

Arlo looks like Mateo just slapped him. "You're certain Wallace Nash is involved in this."

"It's a long story. I first met Caitlin Clement in the rainforest. She was in the middle of everything bad that happened to me there. When I found out that she'd relocated to Texas, I followed. I thought she was the ringleader, and I wanted to blow the lid off of her operation. It makes me sick – the idea of kidnapping endangered animals for profit." Mateo stops talking because he's wheezing a little. He's still really sick. "I found out there was someone else in charge, but the trail kept growing cold, and the leads just disappeared before I got to him. I had no idea Wallace even existed at that point. I wanted to go on a little fishing expedition for the turtle poachers, and I wound up catching more than I'd bargained for when Wallace showed up. I have a friend who's a chef, and I convinced him to do this pop-up dinner."

"We already know about that," I say. "We had a long talk with Enrique."

Mateo waves his hand in a circle. "Then you know. Wallace found out about the pop-up and did a little research into who was supplying the turtle eggs for the event. It didn't take long for him to track me down. He didn't believe, after everything that had happened between me and Caitlin in Brazil, that I'd start endangering animals myself. By the time he got to the shop that night, he already knew I'd been taking notes on his operation, trying to shut it down."

I ask, "So then what happened? Did they kill Fabin because he was a loose end?"

Mateo gestures helplessly. "You'd think that, right? But Wallace thought Fabin had left in the car with Enrique. Instead, Fabin stepped out from behind a sculpture and tried to stop Wallace from taking me. He made a grab for the gun – and

Wallace shot him. Fabin might have been a jerk, but he had a hero streak in him."

So I was right about who the killer is. But what about the sidekick? "Was Caitlin the girl who was with Wallace when Wallace shot Fabin?"

"I don't know. I'm not even sure if she's part of the same operation. It was dark, and she'd been waiting in the car. Whoever the girl was, she stepped out and covered my face with a rag soaked in knock-out stuff. Wallace kept me from moving, while she held it there long enough for me to get sleepy."

Which doesn't match up exactly with what Mrs. Guidry said she saw – but it is possible it could have seemed like the girl was coming out of the shop, when she'd just gotten out of the car instead.

So we still don't know who the girl was. And that has to be eating Arlo inside out. Is Patsy part of this or not? Or is the girl Haruka or even Kimmy? Either one could have faked an alibi. Or is the girl someone else entirely?

"Assuming your story is true – which I doubt – there are still a lot of unanswered questions," Arlo says. "Number one is why are you still alive? But also, why do you seem to know everyone involved in all of this? And why would Fabin, who was known for being selfish, protect you?"

I've been wondering those same things myself.

Mateo says, "Wallace wants my notes. I told him I had enough information to implicate him. But I knew that as soon as I turned the documents over, he'd kill me. As for why Fabin tried to save me – I don't know. It's a weird thing to think about me being alive while he's not. He was even younger than I am."

"Yes!" Logan says, making me jump.

"Did you make us a way out?" I look over at him.

He points to a hole in the wall the size of a golf ball. "Not yet. But I did manage to make an air hole. One more, and I'll start on the exit."

This is going to take a long time. The air quality in here is already getting bad because of the torch, and I can feel cold in my lungs, like they're going to close up. I pull out my inhaler and take a puff, hopefully enough to forestall an asthma attack. I haven't had to do this since I'd finished my treatments. Somehow, it feels like a personal failure to have to do so now.

We pass the time chatting, about places we've been, and places we'd like to travel. Mateo, the youngest person in the container, holds the record for the most countries visited. Surprisingly, Arlo has been to Paris and Berlin – and the Grand Caymans. He's taken up diving sometime in the last fourteen years. He and Logan start planning a dive trip for next month. As though there's no doubt they're going to be alive to take it.

Finally, Logan's torch flickers off. "It's out of fuel." He kicks at the metal he's been cutting, bending it outwards. But the hole is only so big, and the bend only goes so far. Frowning, Logan leans forward looking out and up. He grumbles something I can't quite make out, then comes back inside and says, "There's another container behind this one."

Arlo and I go over to look at the hole. The circumference isn't very large, and the other container is quite close. Arlo edges up to it, and tries to squeeze out, but the space isn't quite big enough for him to make it between the two containers. He takes out his phone and holds it up as far as he can, trying to get a signal in the few inches of open air he can manage to reach.

"Well?" Logan says.

Arlo squeezes back inside. "Still no signal. There's probably not a cell tower in this direction." He turns to look at me, and I can't read the expression on his face.

Logan is looking at me, too. I don't like it.

"You're the only one of us who can fit through the gap," Logan says. "All you have to do is get outside and make a phone call. Then stay out of sight."

"That sounds reasonable," I say, though it actually sounds terrifying. This feels so much more like Logan's world than mine.

A world he's tried to leave behind. And somehow, even though I'm just a chocolate maker, in this room full of competent action guys, I'm the only one who can save us.

Arlo says, "Be careful of the raw edges, Lis." I notice that one of the sleeves of his shirt has been slit by the metal – and the skin underneath is cut. I have an urge to stop and treat it. He's already in enough pain.

But somehow, that wouldn't be appropriate in front of Logan. And I don't have that much time anyway.

Logan puts a hand on each of my shoulders and says, "You have to make it through this, Fee. You need to get home to give that parsley to Knightley. You're his whole world, remember? If you don't go home tonight, the bunny sure isn't going to understand."

There's a lot inside what he's saying, once I get past the fact that he's just given me a pet name for the first time. He doesn't want me to feel guilty if I make it out of this – and he doesn't. And I want back into my safe little world, where that possibility isn't even an option.

# Chapter Twenty-Five
## *Still Thursday*

As I squeeze through the hole, careful to press against the bent edge of the metal to avoid the freshly cut ones, I wonder if Logan was almost saying he loved me. But I may be reading far too much into his concern – and that one brief kiss.

As soon as I'm outside of the container, and my phone signal magically reappears, I call Miles. Surely he will be able to get us help. But the phone just rings. I leave him a voicemail, telling him things have gone wrong down at the port, and he should send help as soon as possible. But I don't know who he left with when the party ended, or if he stayed to clean up, so who knows how long it will take him to get the message.

I need to call 911. Only – I can see the black car with the damaged bumper. I might finally find out who was driving it, and then I can give the dispatchers more information when I make the call. I creep forward, away from the shipping container. I haven't gone far when the cold barrel of a gun touches my neck.

"Felicity, what are you doing here?" The voice in my ear has a distinct New York accent. It's Caitlin from the turtle patrol. The one I had discounted, because she was just a volunteer, and didn't seem to know anything about what was going on.

The Caitlin I didn't think could possibly be the same one Mateo had known in South America. But obviously is. She had been the first to suggest to me that this might have more to do with Mateo than Fabin – which had had the ring of truth about it, and made me trust her. But then she'd tried to lead suspicion off into another direction.

She must have had her hair pulled up under her hat that day we'd seen her on the Seawall. With the sunglasses and the baggy clothes, I wouldn't have guessed it was her at all. I'd thought the driver had been a guy. Caitlin seemed to specialize in changing her appearance. She's got a full face of makeup now, and a cute purple top.

There's a quaver in my voice, brought on by the proximity of the cold steel to vital parts of my brain. "I was looking for some friends of mine. They said they were coming down here, and Logan's car is here, but I can't find them. Given the gun, I assume they're inside one of those metal boxes."

Caitlin shifts the gun away from my neck, but keeps it trained on me as she moves around in front of me. She's buying this, so obviously she didn't get a clear look at us as we went into the container. She may not have any idea who's in there – who she's willing to asphyxiate. "Alarms started going off that the shipping containers were being tampered with. I had to get down here in a hurry. Though I'm sure if my boss realized you were here, he would have come himself."

"Good thing Wallace has you on hand to do all his dirty work for him. Did you kill Fabin too? Or just Nelson?"

"I didn't kill either of them," Caitlin says. She doesn't seem surprised I figured out Wallace was the ringleader.

"Then what was your car doing there where Nelson was killed?"

"I was just the driver. Wallace told Nelson he was a buyer, interested in sea turtles, and said he wanted to see the nest. Nelson was naïve enough to go alone."

The fact that she's telling me all this so easily sends chills through me. She really doesn't expect that I'm going to live through the night.

Since she's talking, I might as well satisfy my curiosity. "I don't get it. Why did Nelson have to die?"

Caitlin rolls her eyes. "Nelson told me he was close to finding where Mateo was keeping his notes, and in the course of looking into Mateo's life, he'd found out some things – things that had given him ideas. Which is why he had decided to try to sell the sea turtle eggs in the first place – once he realized how much money might be in it. Nelson was threatening to cut into Wallace's business – while at the same time sounding like he might be planning to blackmail us."

I wince. "You don't know he was planning all that. I was nearly killed once, because someone mistakenly thought I was trying to blackmail them."

Caitlin still doesn't look impressed – or sympathetic.

"Phone," she says, holding out a hand for my cell. I hand it to her, and she pockets it.

I'm in serious trouble here. I need to get my phone back, or find some other way to call for help.

My knees are still wobbling, and my heartbeat won't slow back to normal. But I need try to get more information so that if I do find an opening to escape, I can tell someone what's really going on. But I need to do this carefully. Some of my closest friends are trapped in that shipping container behind us – and who knows what happens to them if Caitlin realizes there's a hole letting in good air. "If y'all were willing to get rid of a loose end as insignificant as Nelson, why haven't you killed me yet?"

Not that I want to give her any encouragement.

She looks at me like I'm stupid. "Wallace really does like you. He keeps talking about how much you two have in common, and where he should take you on your next date. When you die tonight, it has to be him pulling the trigger. I'm not going to do it, and have him resent me for it."

Which means I'm safe-ish, for the moment. Which is comforting, I guess.

I take a stab at figuring out something that hasn't made much sense so far. "Those false papers Donnie made. They must have been for getting you back into the country, with a different name. Mateo's notes mentioned a woman that he met down in Brazil – which shares a border with Peru. We all assumed that whoever the papers were for was coming into the country illegally. But you were coming in with a new name and a clean record, so you could get easy access to the sea turtles you wanted to smuggle."

Caitlin says, "Donnie is actually lucky that the police made off with the diamonds. I was planning to go pick them up from Donnie's place, once he'd recovered them. A quick accident for Donnie – and Wallace never would have needed to know." The simplicity with which she says this chills me to the core.

"But if you went through all this to smuggle the turtle eggs, why did they hatch tonight on the beach?"

"Everything was under scrutiny, after Fabin got shot. We couldn't take the chance – raid one nest, but blow our entire operation. Nelson's death was supposed to look like a suicide. But he didn't cooperate."

So in a way, Fabin had actually saved the baby turtles.

Trying to draw out the conversation, I ask, "Were you the woman who was there the night Fabin died? Or was it someone else?"

Caitlin just smiles enigmatically. "Does it matter? After Wallace gets done with you, you won't be able to tell anyone what happened."

"It matters to Arlo. Even if we all die tonight, he's still going to want to know if his girlfriend is one of the ones who got him killed."

Caitlin starts to say something, but then the expression on her face changes. She tells someone coming up behind me, "She's all yours."

Wallace clamps a hand down on my shoulder. "For Patsy's sake, I was hoping you weren't going to wind up being part of this. It didn't seem like you had any information, that night I ransacked your office."

"But Donnie was the one who broke in," I insist. "We chased him and everything."

Wallace rolls his eyes. "You assume that only one guy can break into a place at a time? I figured it would be easy to toss the place while you were waiting for me at the restaurant. I didn't expect a whole room of people. I decided to go ahead, since the party was so loud no one was likely to hear me. But I couldn't find the information Mateo had on me. Which meant I couldn't kill him yet."

"But you realized he would be in trouble if he didn't get his meds. So you broke into the pharmacy. Only – they didn't have what you were looking for. That's why nothing was taken"

Wallace grunts assent. "I just had to hope I could get him to talk before his disease killed him. Which he refused to do."

"Mateo's dead?" I ask, trying to sound shocked, like I really believe it. Like I wasn't just talking to him ten minutes ago.

"Probably, by now," Wallace says.

Wallace and Caitlin have a discussion, right in front of me, about what they ought to do with me now. Caitlin suggests, "Just kill her now and dump her in the Gulf. Or put her body in the cargo container, to get shipped with the others."

Her words send shivers spidering across my skin. There's no way I can escape from both of them.

Instead, Wallace says, "You always look at things so dramatically, Caitlin." Wallace takes my hand in his. "Come on. Let's go talk. My temporary office here is basically across the street from the port."

"I haven't even searched her," Caitlin protests.

Wallace says, "Mrs. Koerber doesn't believe in guns. Arlo was quite upset about that, since she keeps poking her nose into dangerous situations." Wallace looks down at me as we walk, Caitlin following along behind with the gun still handy. "Caitlin's right. You're a liability, and I really should kill you. But you're Patsy's friend, and I've developed a serious crush on you. So it's a good thing I don't have to rush any decisions that would be – irrevocable."

Caitlin mutters something.

Wallace looks back at her, sharply. "What was that?"

"I said you're just putting off the inevitable. Even if she does seem compliant, she'll be lying."

She's talking about me like I'm not even there again. But I don't dare answer. What would I say that wouldn't sound like an obvious lie?

Wallace says, "I cannot overstate the importance that my sister does not find out what I actually do for a living."

"Patsy doesn't know?" I ask.

"Of course not! Do you think she'd be dating a policeman if she knew her brother was a criminal?"

"I believe you," I say. Which isn't a lie. But will Arlo believe it? Will it even matter?

We cross the street and walk down the sidewalk to a row of industrial buildings. One of them has been chopped up into office space. It doesn't make sense. Why would Wallace have set up an office, if he wasn't going to be here very long?

"I thought you were staying with Patsy," I say, as Wallace tugs on my hand, leading me towards a glass door. The inside of the place looks deserted.

"I am. But our special guest wouldn't be welcome." Wallace unlocks the door with his free hand. I have no idea what he's talking about.

Wallace leads me into a small room, where there's a couple of folding chairs and a refrigerator. There's a door on the far side of the room, leading deeper into the building. "Have a seat." He gestures to one of the chairs.

I sit, holding my purse on my lap.

"I'll be right out here if you need me," Caitlin says, closing the door behind her.

Wallace goes over to the fridge and takes out two diet sodas. Normally, I don't drink soda, but I'm not about to refuse any sign of civility.

"Thanks." I open the can and take a deep sip, manage not to grimace at the taste of artificial sweetener.

Wallace sits in the other chair. "What am I supposed to do here, Felicity?"

He's asking me to give him an out, so he doesn't have to shoot me in the head. I would love to give him one. Though I suspect, that even if I somehow convince Wallace to go against his better judgement, Caitlin's not going to let me leave here alive. She'll just kill me in a way where Wallace won't be able to be sure it was her.

"I promise I won't say anything to anyone," I tell Wallace. "Please. Just let Arlo out of the shipping container, and Patsy can have her perfect little life back."

Wallace freezes. "Arlo's one of the people Caitlin trapped?"

I'm not supposed to know that. Panic jolts through me. "I just assumed. He was with Logan, and I saw Logan's car."

Wallace looks even more upset. "Arlo *and* Logan? Those aren't the type of people who can just casually disappear." He stands up from his chair, looming over me, a gun suddenly in his hand. It's probably the same one he used to kill Fabin and Nelson. "I'm sorry. I don't have time for you. I have to figure out a plausible story to fix this."

I still have the pepper spray in my purse. I start moving my hand towards the open-topped front pocket.

Wallace leans in to run his hand across my cheek, a gentle way of saying goodbye. My skin crawls, and my heart is thudding with terror, but I have to stay focused. I grab the pepper spray and spray him point blank, right in the eyes.

He lets out an outraged noise and fires a bullet into the floor near my feet.

I shove the chair back and scramble for the door at the other side of the room. I don't know where it goes, but there's no window in this room, and I'm not about to go past Caitlin to get back the way I came. My knees are all wobbly from the fear, so I'm about as elegant as an injured gazelle. But I make it to the door, just as Caitlin bursts into the room from the other side.

I open the door and slam it shut behind me, moving away from it quickly, in case Caitlin decides to shoot through it. My lungs feel like they're closing up again, probably from the near-asthma-attack earlier, combined with adrenaline and fear.

This room is half-full of crates. There's a noise from behind one of them, an inquisitive, *mmmmmnnnrrrp*? And then a half-grown tiger walks out to see who I am. Of course. Wallace's special guest. This tiger had been intended for Fabin. Arlo had assumed that the tiger had been a figment, just a lure to get Fabin to the island. But it seems Wallace had had every intent of doing business with the kid. Who knows if he even realized that Fabin was his client, that night on the sidewalk when he shot him?

The tiger yawns, showing off an amazing display of teeth. It doesn't look all that upset. I try to remember what the animal control guy said. Don't make eye contact. But don't turn your back.

I need to get to that window, pronto. Which means climbing a couple of these crates. I try to look big, yet not aggressive as I half turn to get up on the shortest crate. The tiger walks over and sniffs at my shoe.

When I jump from that crate to the next one, the tiger jumps up onto the crate I just left. It seems to think this is a game. Fine. I'm okay with that. I jump to the third crate, and try to keep myself facing out as I open the window. The tiger again jumps to the crate I'm on, just as Caitlin opens the door. Her clothes look rumpled, like maybe Wallace had grabbed at her, trying to get help post pepper-spray.

I start climbing through the window.

The tiger is between me and Caitlin. It turns towards her and starts loping across the room. Her aim moves away from me, as she has to decide whether to shoot the merchandise or try to play with it to calm it down. I don't hear a gunshot, so I'm sure the tiger is going to be fine.

As my feet hit the pavement, a line of police cars come speeding up the street. I race across the parking lot and wave them down. Detective Beckman gets out. I explain what's going on, though I have to take my inhaler out midway through and take another puff. Afterwards, I ask, "How did you find me?"

"We got a call from Miles," she says. "We were on our way to the shipping containers you described when you flagged us down. You should probably come with me to help let your friends out. I'd prefer to keep you away from this building for the time being." She moves over and leans her head into the window of one of the other cars. I get the idea that they're going to capture the bad guys I had half subdued.

It doesn't take long to get back to where Logan parked his car, and then to get the shipping container open. But the whole time I keep thinking about Wallace, and how he had seemed like the safe choice, compared to Logan. If tonight has taught me anything, it isn't that there aren't any safe choices. And if something feels even vaguely wrong, I should trust my instincts.

When the guys come out, Logan walks over to me and says, "I knew you had it in you."

He gives me a quick hug, which could just be from sheer relief.

When I move away from Logan, I see Arlo staring back at the shipping crates. Arlo looks bereft. I move over to him, and I tell him, "Patsy didn't know."

But who knows what the fallout will be when she finds out?

# Epilogue
## *Several Days Later*

I'm back in my world, safe and comfortable at my chocolate shop. I'm doing a presentation about my trip to Peru. Mrs. Guidry is front and center. She keeps applauding every time I'm in one of the pictures. About a quarter of my audience today are people she referred to the event. I guess there's an upside for having an incredible gossip for a neighbor. They tell everyone the good things too.

Logan breezes into the shop. All of the chairs are full, so he makes his way over to the coffee station, grabs a cup of coffee and leans up against the wall, where he watches the rest of the presentation with interest.

Then he steps up and says a few words about how excited he is to be joining the business, how much he's already learned about chocolate already. His humility and charm get a laugh and some applause, especially from the ladies in the audience. I get the feeling him being here – even occasionally – will bring in a whole different crowd of customers.

And since he'd been the one to handle shipping for the gift baskets, he's already had a good hand in helping us keep our biggest client.

He's been busy for the past couple of days, with back-to-back charter flights, so he hasn't gotten to see what I've been working on in the kitchen. Once the audience members have made their purchases and headed for the door, Logan steps over to the center bin display, and picks up one of the new bars. I'm proud of what I've been able to produce. It's 70% dark, with a light touch of sea salt and small nibs incorporated throughout.

The image on the wrapper is Clive, one arm wrapped around a stylized reef outcropping.

Logan raises an eyebrow at me. "I thought all we produced was two ingredient chocolate, except for the truffles and cookies and stuff."

"True." I bring him a sample of the chocolate, so he doesn't have to open the bar. Those wrappers are expensive to print. "But I felt like honoring Clive, and that touch of salt reminds me of the ocean. This is a limited-edition bar, made with the Porcelana beans Mateo brought me."

"Must be a special chocolate." Logan pops the chocolate chunk into his mouth. A look of happiness crosses his face. "This is nice. Somehow, it does remind me of the ocean. I'm sure Clive is proud of you."

"Very funny," I say.

Logan flips the chocolate bar back over and examines the art. "If I'm really going to get into this chocolate making thing, maybe I should work towards developing a bar myself. One where I can put the Kemp's ridley on the wrapper."

"Maybe you should. What would you put in it?"

Logan thinks about it for a while. Finally he says. "I don't know. I guess I've got a long way to go before that happens."

"I guess so."

"I like your world," he tells me. "It's a lot more fun than the circles I used to hang out in. I also like that you're letting me be a part of it."

I'm not quite sure what to say to that. He still carries a gun. And he hasn't tried to kiss me again since that night at the port. How much about him has really changed? How much about us?

Before I can respond, Mateo walks in. He's wearing the sweater Sonya made for him. Mateo is still ill from his ordeal – and his chronic problems will never go away – but he's going home to his family for a while, to heal in a way that I hope will be more than physical.

Mateo says, "I wanted to say thank you again before I leave."

"We're all just glad you're safe," I tell him.

"You tell your father it was never about him," Logan says. He gives Mateo a hug, clapping the younger man on the back before letting go. "He'll understand, I promise."

"I know," Mateo says. "You've been there."

I don't know what happened exactly in that shipping container after I crawled out of it – but the three guys came out as friends. Logan and Arlo really are going on a dive trip together – though their competitive banter hasn't disappeared.

Mateo asks me, "Do you want Clive? I've decided not to donate him to anyone. I don't know how strangers will treat him. And Haruka won't be here to keep him either."

"Why not?" Had she gotten kicked off the research team? Or what is left of it, anyway? I was afraid there would be consequences to her problems with the data – despite the fact that it really was Nelson's fault – and Nelson is dead. Surely they'd cut her some slack after that.

"Haruka's going to Spain with me. My family has agreed to host her for a week or two, until she can find a place. She's going to be doing some research along the Spanish coastline, before she goes back to Japan. I think she deserves a fresh start, don't you?"

Logan and I both nod. One thing where we match: we both believe in giving people second chances.

Logan says, "Arlo's meeting me here. Maybe he knows someone who can properly take care of an octopus. It has to be someone willing to put in some serious time. They're not casual pets."

I hope Arlo is doing better. Patsy keeps claiming she had no idea what Wallace was up to – but things are still strained between her and Arlo because Arlo arrested her brother. I have a great deal of sympathy for them both. They're such a good match. I hope they find a way to work through this.

Caitlin's been arrested too – but nobody is bothered by that.

"Arlo knows people who keep aquariums?" Mateo asks.

"Arlo just knows people," I say. "He's always been very outgoing."

"You sure you don't want Clive?" Mateo asks.

I point to the giant sign with the picture of Knightley up on the wall. "I have a rabbit and home, and with Clive's tendency to go walkabout and eat anything that looks defenseless, I'd be afraid of Knightley getting hurt."

"Maybe you could keep Clive at the shop."

That's an interesting idea – but I think I have a better one. "Why don't you ask Miles? He can use someone in his life to look after."

"I might just do that." Mateo reaches into his messenger bag and draws out a book. It's his copy of *The Invisible Man*. He says, "Enrique wanted you to have this. He would have brought it himself, but he's keeping a low profile right now."

I take the book and flip through it. "You finished notating it."

Mateo gestures towards the book with both hands. "Enrique said it gave you inspiration for finding me. It might be worth something, given the notoriety surrounding everything that happened."

"Probably," I say, "But I won't sell it." This slim little paperback has earned a space in the display case, alongside the *Emma* volumes.

Kimmy comes in. She says she's about to leave town, too. She joins the group of us standing there, and she briefly squeezes my hand. "I want to thank you. You made sure that Fabin's death wasn't for nothing. I'm glad to see that tiger safe and sound where it belongs in the zoo."

"Fabin was trying to buy it for you," I remind her.

She nods. She's wearing the outrageously expensive pink and white diamond earrings that she'd had on in the picture in the photo album. "But if he'd given it to me, I'd have donated it to the zoo. Fabin had a huge house, and he had hired a guy to take care of his pets. But I don't have time for that. And I already have two cats. Who knows if a tiger might up and decide to eat my little calico furbabies?"

I guess I can kind of understand her reasoning.

Logan said, "I heard that Fabin left you all his exotic pets in his will."

Kimmy laughs. "Yeah. And I plan to make sure they wind up in a facility that can take care of them." But her laugh never gets anywhere near her eyes. Because she's still grieving.

"Wait," I say. I go and get one of the chocolate bars from my Sympathy and Condolences line. Bruce the dog's soulful eyes have an expression perfect for what I'm feeling right now. I grab a Sharpie and write on it, "Always remember, he really did love you."

"What's this?" Kimmy says as she reads the message.

I tell her, "You know that thumb drive you gave me? I looked at some of what was on it. And part of what he said on there is that he would sacrifice anything to keep you safe."

She clutches the chocolate bar to her chest. "That means a lot."

She's going to be fine, financially. And I hope that, whatever else comes out of all of this, she's learned a bit more about what love really is. And what she really wants.

I think I've learned a bit about that too. I'm happy that Logan's part of my company now, and that Miles is becoming part of the regular crew. I call Carmen over and take a selfie of all of us, with me, her and Logan in the center if the picture. It'll be perfect to show off who we are on the web site. Greetings and Felicitations is becoming a real part of the community, and I'm glad it's becoming about something bigger than just me.

# AUTHOR NOTES

The portrayal of how sea turtles are handled in this book is entirely fictional – but the endangered Kemp's ridley is very real, as are the Turtles Around Town sculptures on Galveston Island. A lot of work each year goes into scouting for nesting turtles of a number of varieties, relocating eggs to a monitored colony on a safer island, and rescuing cold-stunned turtles which have found themselves in trouble after sudden temperature drops. If you spot a sea turtle, or think you have found a sea turtle nest, the best thing to do is call the local Parks and Wildlife Department and report it. They will be able to get you in touch with the appropriate agency to handle the situation.

Parts of this narrative were inspired by a trip to the Sea Turtle Rescue Center outside Acapulco, the year I started doing lectures aboard cruise ships. On the tour, they explained about turtle imprinting, and we got to see some hatchlings awaiting release. (Not Kemp's ridleys, alas.) Those tiny turtles stuck in my brain for a good decade and a half, showing up in the first book in this series as the logo for Logan's business. And then recently, I read an article about how the fake tracker eggs I used here as a plot device were inspired by a scene in The Wire, where the characters put a device inside a golf ball. I realized the turtles needed a plot of their own.

## ACKNOWLEDGEMENTS

Special thanks to Jael Rattigan of French Broad Chocolates in South Carolina, who consulted on this manuscript. And to Sander Wolf of DallasChocolate.org, who put me in touch with so many experts in the chocolate field.

I'd also like to thank Dr. Donna Shaver of The Division of Sea Turtle Science and Recovery at Padre Island National Seashore for sharing her knowledge of sea turtles.

I have to thank Jake, as usual, for reading the manuscript umpteen times, being my biggest fan and cheerleader, and doing all the formatting things to make this thing happen. He always keeps me going, even when things are stressful.

And thanks to my agent, Jennie, for her input on this series, and her encouragement to keep moving forward.

And for this series especially, I'd like to thank both my family and Jake's (especially my mom and dad, who always use the good sausage to make breakfast sandwiches to fuel our day-trips across the ferry to Galveston – now that we live in Dallas having them close to the Island has helped us have a "home base" when we've gone to film book trailers and background videos). The Cajun side of both our families comes through in Felicity's family in the books – and now in Mrs. Guidry, her fictional neighbor who runs a Cajun café. This has given me an excuse to reach out to family members for recipes, such as for Cajun-style crab cakes, that are going on the Bean to Bar Bonuses section of my website.

Thanks to James and Rachel Knowles for continuing to sharing their knowledge of bunny behavior (as well as videos of their ADORABLE bunny – Yuki pics will always make my day).

And to Mika for being our Japanese language instructor for the past five years. Your patience is incredible. Especially when it comes to me and short-form verbs.

I'd also like to thank Cassie, Monica and Tessa, who are my support network in general. I don't know how I would have gotten through this year of social isolation without you three.

Thank you all, dear readers, for spending time in Felicity's world. I hope you enjoyed getting to know her. Her third adventure will be available for you soon.

# Did Felicity's story make you hungry?

Visit the Bean to Bar Mysteries Bonus Recipes page on Amber's website to find out how to make some of the food mentioned in the book.

AMBER ROYER writes the CHOCOVERSE comic telenovela-style foodie-inspired space opera series (available from Angry Robot Books and Golden Tip Press). She is also co-author of the cookbook There are Herbs in My Chocolate, which combines culinary herbs and chocolate in over 60 sweet and savory recipes, and had a long-running column for Dave's Garden, where she covered gardening and crafting. She blogs about creative writing technique and all things chocolate related over at www.amberroyer.com. She also teaches creative writing in person in North Texas for both UT Arlington Continuing Education and Writing Workshops Dallas. If you are very nice to her, she might make you cupcakes.

www.amberroyer.com Instagram: amberroyerauthor